A GIRL
CALLED
SIDNEY

Gibson House Press
Flossmoor, Illinois 60422
GibsonHousePress.com

ISBN-13: 978-0-9861541-2-6 (paper)

LCCN: 2017930899

Cover design by Christian Fuenfhausen. Text design and
composition by Karen Sheets de Gracia in the Palatino Linotype
and Strangelove Next typefaces.

Printed in the United States of America
21 20 19 18 17   1 2 3 4 5

♾ This paper meets the requirements of ANSI/NISO Z39.48-1992
(Permanence of Paper)

A GIRL CALLED SIDNEY

THE COLDEST PLACE

COURTNEY YASMINEH

GIBSON
HOUSE
PRESS

CHICAGO

PROLOGUE

When it's
February in
Minnesota, and
you're as far north as you can go and
still be in America, you're in the coldest
place on the continent. Not a comforting
thought as I woke at six in the darkness to
be sure I made it to the bus. If I missed
the school bus, I was scared that I might
get so cold that I wouldn't be able to
make it back to the cabin. I could get
so cold I'd freeze to death on the trail,
frozen solid before anyone came out from
town to look for me.

That morning, Grandpa's old thermome-
ter bottomed out at forty below zero Fahrenheit. I
knew it had to be even colder than that, because the red
line of mercury was already near the bottom at two that
morning, when I got out of bed to be sure the one spigot
of well water I had still going in the kitchen wasn't freezing. I opened the cabinet doors under the sink to let as
much heat as possible get to the pipe and I lit a match

and started up the old gas oven too. I stoked the wood stove in the main room and went back to bed wearing a big wool cardigan that I found in Grandpa's closet over my one-piece, red wool long underwear.

At six, I rolled out from under the pile of wool blankets on my bed and went to the kitchen where it was warm. I splashed water on my face, hoisted myself up and peed in the kitchen sink because the toilet had long since frozen and it was too cold to bare my rear end outside. I told myself I'd wait to poop until I got to school so I didn't have to deal with my other option which at this point in the winter was to do the job in an old tin wash pan, fling it as far as I could out into the woods, and then rinse the pan with dish soap.

I went back to my room and put my jeans and wool sweater on over my long underwear. Since the deep cold had set in after Christmas, I had given up on removing my long underwear ever, at all. The wood stove wasn't a match for the bitter cold creeping in through the summer cabin's thin knotty pine walls. Back in the kitchen I poured some Cheerios and milk in a bowl. After I ate, I stood by the open door of the kitchen oven and wrestled with white tube socks, then snowflake-patterned, wool cross-country ski socks that came up over the knees of my jeans. My outerwear was a red down vest and a blue down coat. I had a fur trapper hat with earflaps and leather chopper's mitts. I tied on my heavy suede hiking boots with the red laces. Before I left for the bus, I carried in a few armloads of wood from the covered back porch and made sure the wood stove was as stoked as I could get it.

I headed out at 6:45 in the dark. I threw my backpack over my shoulder and walked out the driveway, which was now a solid two-foot layer of ice and snow packed down by the wheels of the old pickup truck that had to stay plugged in with a block heater under the carport so it would start in an emergency. Half a mile down the peninsula was where the road plow officially turned around in the winter. This was the first year it ventured farther down the point, and only after I asked if they could plow down all the way to my grandpa's old place because I'd be staying out there for the winter trying to finish high school, trying to hide out from my family's craziness, trying to make a whole new life, trying not to freeze to death, trying not to give in to despair.

I arrived at the familiar spot where the old, wheezing, yellow bus turned around and made the fifteen-mile trek back into town after picking up the ten kids from the reservation and maybe ten more who lived around the lake. The only footsteps in the snow were mine. The only eyes that would see me waiting were those of a squirrel or a deer or maybe an owl. But in this cold, at forty below, no living creature had journeyed out but me.

My eyes stung from the cold at this temperature so I closed them and stood listening and praying, "Please God, let the bus get here soon."

After a few minutes, squinting against the cold, I saw the headlights of the old bus. I heard the roar of the grumbling old engine. Through the crystalline silence I could already make out the thump of the bus driver's favorite sound track to this winter in the North Country.

As the bus tires crunched the snow that was so frozen and packed down it looked and sounded like styrofoam, and the accordion doors cranked open with a clatter, my face was struck by the heat blasting and the blaring eight-track sound system. I was greeted as I had been every morning since this adventure began with a rock album by a guy called Meat Loaf, singing, "I Can See Paradise by the Dashboard Light." We heard *Bat Out of Hell* in its entirety almost every bus ride. The driver with his Elvis Presley mutton-chop side burns and slicked back, dyed black hair beamed, "Hey Sidney! Welcome aboard! Impressive showing! Are you sure you aren't part Eskimo?"

I laughed halfheartedly as I stood in the heat for a moment, pulling the ice chunks off my frozen-shut eyelashes so I could see my way to take a seat with my fellow scholars.

In the winter of 1978, as Meat Loaf was howling out his rock opera tribute to adolescence and all the North Country kids sat dozing in their seats at seven in the morning on an old rickety bus in the middle of the great continent of North America, with just a few scraps of sheet metal between us and the brutal winter air, I stood for a moment before taking my seat and said out loud, "What the hell am I doing here?"

THE DECISION

When I was seventeen, I followed a crazy gut instinct that set my family's demise in motion. We lived in suburban Chicago in the '70s. My parents had been fighting because my mom was super paranoid about money and she didn't want to let my dad remortgage our house so that he could save his seat on the stock exchange. The stock market had seen some major upheavals that had my dad on the verge of bankruptcy. I honestly think my mom should have chosen to be happy instead of right and everything would have just worked itself out. She could have gone along with my dad's plan. Instead, my dad was beside himself, drinking and threatening violence toward her and myself.

He had always been a cruel guy and was very hard on my one sibling, my older brother, Preston. My brother was a sensitive artist type but also a good athlete and my dad had played college football so he was always riding my brother's ass to be better at the game. But my dad also prided himself on being a philosophy major who put himself through law school so he bothered Preston about academics too.

My mom was his beautiful hothouse flower and he had loved only her and had sex only with her his entire life, so when she wouldn't go along with his refinancing idea, when he was utterly desperate and took to driving a cab to keep things afloat, he lost it.

I was the one witness to my parents' strife because my brother graduated from high school, went backpacking in Europe, got a job at a vineyard in Nice and didn't return for a couple of years. He sent about three postcards in all that time. After that he went to a liberal arts college where he wrote papers in French.

I was the only referee left in the house and I didn't like it. I hated my parents. I had no respect for them. Worse yet, I could see that neither of them cared about me. They were wrapped up in themselves. I walked around the house feeling like they didn't know who I was at all.

When I asked either one of them for one thing every month, the check to pay my flute teacher, neither of them would oblige. My payment was always very late and my teacher always had to ask me multiple times. Worse, they didn't like to drive to her house and back for the lessons. I usually walked to the teacher's house on the other side of town, several miles away. After my lessons I would lie to my instructor and say I was just going to walk to the corner to wait for them. She probably knew there were problems in my family, and maybe even guessed that I walked all the way home most nights.

My flute teacher wanted me to have a metronome for practicing. She wanted me to buy a certain kind that was more advanced, an electronic gadget. It cost about a hundred dollars but she said it was worth it because it was so precise. I knew there was absolutely no way my parents would take me to a music store, much less pay for the metronome. I made a few attempts, explaining to each of them how important this was. Every lesson, my teacher would inquire and I'd say that we didn't get the metronome yet but we were going to do so the following weekend. One day she asked and I said, "Yep, we got it."

She started writing elaborate notes on my flute music sheets with the numbers and setting instructions for each piece. I was horrified with shame. I was caught in the stupid lie. Then one lesson she stopped me part way through a difficult new piece and asked, "Have you been using your metronome with this piece?"

"Of course," I answered.

"Well, it really shows. Your time is so much more consistent than it used to be. Good work. See, I told you it'd make a big difference."

Lying to people sucked. Living with my parents sucked. I slept with my door locked because they would wake me up even on school nights to have me referee their bullshit. One night, they picked my lock with my mother's hairpin, came in my room, turned on the extra-bright overhead light like it was an interrogation and my mother started, "Sidney, please, your father is threatening me! You have to help me!"

"This isn't my problem. I have school in the morning. Get out of my room."

My mother was wearing her Pucci nightgown which was cut to the navel and very sheer. Even if I did not want to, I could see every detail of her perfectly slim body. My dad was only in his long, Izod polo nightshirt with nothing else on, so if he really got revved up and started waving his arms, as he was doing, I could see the family jewels which I really didn't want to either. "Dad, come on, go back in your room. I don't want to see this."

"You don't want to see this! You better want to see this! Your mother is trying to ruin me! She's cutting off our only chance to save my business. She's turning to other men. She's whoring herself! Do you know this Sidney? Get up! This is your mother we're talking about!" he shouted back.

He had my mother's thin arm in his grip and her bare shoulders looked fragile. She whimpered, "Please Sidney, do something. He's hurting me. Please, Sidney."

I got up out of my bed and rushed toward them. My dad let go of her arm and ran back to their room. My mother was sobbing into her hands. I stood there in the doorway to my bedroom. The overhead hallway light was too bright and I was squinting. My body ached from being woken up in the dead of night. My dad came bounding back with my mother's purse. He was telling her he would take her purse and she couldn't go anywhere or do anything until the papers got signed. She turned wild with desperation. I couldn't bear to see her tortured like this. I lurched at my father, "Give her the purse! Give it to her!"

I tried to grab the purse away. Then I started hitting him with my fists. I hated him so much right then, I felt like I could kill him with my bare hands. He tried to grab me by my short choppy hair but lost his grip. I remembered the self-defense class at school and lifted my knee to his groin. I was sickened to feel his soft flesh collapsing against my thigh.

He doubled over and I thought I could grab the purse and give it to my mother. Instead he stood up taller, with a deep craziness in his eyes, like an angry bull, saying, "You think you can knee your father in the balls? You think that's okay? Does that make you feel good? Come on. Do it again. Can't take it? Come on, knee your father in the balls, come on."

His horrible red face pressed up to mine as he grabbed my arm. I rammed my knee into him again. It had no effect. I did it again. No effect. I tried to break away. We were all at the top of the stairs in the hallway. He shoved me away then and I tumbled down the stairs. I landed with my neck hard against the front door in the lower hall and looked up to see my parents, my father bellowing about getting his hunting gun out and killing my mother, my mother trying to grab the purse out of his still-clenched fist. "That's it Ingrid, I'm getting the gun. Is that what you want?"

I scrambled to my feet, opened the front door, and burst out into the pristine suburban night. I was barefoot and it was raining. The street was shining black and wet. The well-maintained houses were all quiet and dark. I was wearing my old flannel nightgown and underpants with rips in them. There was no wind, just the raindrops coming straight down. There was a smell of spring. I knew what I was going to do.

I was not going to just let this happen and watch my dad shoot my mother. I ran across the street to my friend Jenny's house. Her parents are Polish Catholic and have seven children. They seemed very stable and decent to me. I rang their doorbell and after many desperate attempts, the overweight father came bumbling to the door. He had a big construction business and did well financially. The house was newer, sort of like a mini medieval castle. They were not my favorite people and I probably wasn't their favorite neighborhood kid either. He opened the door only slightly. He was clearly not happy to see me. I frantically explained what my parents were doing over at our house, but he didn't really care and looked disgusted. "Sidney, I'm sorry, but I have to protect my family. Your father is a dangerous man. I don't trust him at all. I am not going to let you in here and have him come over here with his gun. I'll call the police, but you can't stay here."

I was shocked when my father was suddenly behind me. I was so embarrassed, so afraid. He started yelling at Mr. Wilson. "You stay out of this! This is my family. Sidney, get back home right now!"

"Stay out of this? You're a madman! You take your child and get off my property! You are not welcome here! You aren't going to come here and disturb my family!"

Mr. Wilson was holding the door tightly, bracing his weight against it. I could see he was afraid my dad was going to try to bust into his house. My dad suddenly turned and ran back across the street. He was wearing his slip-on penny loafers and his nightshirt. I watched him in despair and shame. What an idiot! Mr. Wilson assured me then that he would call the police. He told me I needed to go home and wait for the police to come. I told Mr. Wilson I was sorry about everything and burst into tears. As I put my hands up to wipe my eyes I heard the door slam right in front of me and I heard him bolt both the locks. "Whatever, Mr. Wilson. Thanks a lot."

I crossed the street slowly feeling the raindrops hit my face. The smell of spring was tender and innocent, bringing memories of worms and daffodils. The neighborhood was quiet and still. I looked at our house and wished my parents would stop all of this.

By the time I opened the front door, I saw that the upstairs hall light had been turned off. All I wanted was to go back to my room and shut my door and go to sleep. I locked the front door and climbed the stairs as quietly as possible. My brother's door was shut which meant my mom had holed up in there to punish my dad. The door to my parents' room was shut too, which I hoped meant that my dad had gone to sleep.

I crawled into my bed and felt the dampness on the shoulders of my nightgown but I didn't care; I just wanted to go to sleep. "Please God, make this all work out okay. Please don't let anything bad happen. I'm sorry for everything bad that I've done. Please God, forgive me. Please don't let Dad lose our house. Please don't let them get divorced."

I slept the rest of the night without interruption. Good old Jenny's dad probably never even called the police. Or maybe they drove by and we were all in bed. In the morning, when I came out of my room, dreading what I'd find, my dad had left for work. My mom was all dressed in a pale-grey, wool sweater dress and lace-up, tan suede boots when I came downstairs. She was wearing her big diamond ring, a gift from my dad, and an African gold coin on a gold wire encircling her neck making her look like an exotic goddess. She had on her thick, gold, hoop earrings that she didn't wear often. Her caramel hair was smoothed and grazing her shoulders.

We stood, mother and daughter, in my mother's kitchen with dark wood and colonial-style wallpaper. A sign on the wall from an old New England pub hung over us, like the letters HOLLYWOOD hung over the people in *The Great Gatsby*. It read: "Money's the root of all evil, it's treacherous, slippery and vile, but the baker, the banker, the preacher and I don't think that it's gone out of style."

I stood there looking at the sign. "Yeah, okay, I get it." I looked down at myself, my body, the way I was dressed. I would have been categorized as a tomboy, not by desire maybe as much as by necessity. I couldn't shop with my mother because she would insist on wildly impractical things that I could never wear to school or really anywhere. I would get so angry at her foolish ways and there would invariably be a scene in the dressing room at Saks Fifth Avenue or Lord & Taylor and I would emerge with my hopes of finding something nice to wear to school dashed again and my mother's condemnation of my taste newly inflamed. By now I had a closet full of my old clothes since kindergarten that my mother wouldn't get rid of because they were "so expensive and barely worn." Dressing myself was an exercise in frustration every time. There was the pale blue, angora sweater dress that was way too clingy for my busty figure even if she bought it for me when I was only twelve. Mom kept insisting I should wear it whenever I said I needed a new dress. "A new dress? You've hardly ever even worn that beautiful sweater dress I bought you. Oh, it doesn't fit now? Well, what have I been telling you about stuffing brownies in your mouth every time I turn around?"

I tried sneaking into her glorious walk-in closet with the designer items each under a plastic shoulder protector to keep the dust off. She would invariably discover that I'd been in there. "Don't you dare try on my things, you're too fat. You'll stretch them all out of shape."

I couldn't think about myself and my clothes issues now; I had to help my mom. I was planning to go to school, but she started talking to me about her situation and I realized that I wouldn't be able to leave until a decision was made and it was pretty obvious to me that I was going to have to bite the bullet.

"Sidney, your father is serious about these papers. He left this morning threatening to kill me if I didn't sign them. I think I should leave. I am not signing away our home. He wants the money for his business. Well, he's had plenty of chances. I gave him all I had when my mother died. I gave him money for law school. I don't have any more. This is our beautiful home. I am not going to let this happen. I don't know where to go. I was thinking I could go to the cabin but it'll be too early. There's probably still snow. And I don't know what you'll do then."

I thought about calling my friend Sophie on the kitchen phone once my mother went back upstairs to fuss over herself some more. My friend Sophie was the

Junior Miss of our suburban town and a senior with a car, which was huge for me because I had only just turned seventeen, and had no hope of getting my parents to help me learn to drive or let me borrow one of their matching Jaguars to take the driver's test. I had never even heard of being Junior Miss until I met Sophie. She was the most interesting girl I knew at our suburban public high school. She had a strange defiant streak but was also totally involved in the fabric of the high school and the town. She once told me that when she was crowned Junior Miss, she gave the pageant manager the finger behind his back, but only her friends who were at the side of the stage could see it. I thought that was very daring and made up for the fact that she was in pageants in the first place. For me, the best thing about Sophie was that she hated her mother like I hated mine. When I once went to Sophie's house for a sleepover birthday party, I saw that her mother was very cruel to her. The next morning, her shockingly thin mother was in the kitchen pushing waffles and bacon at all the girls including me. I watched as she set half of a grapefruit in front of Sophie and gave her the evil eye. She wanted her daughter to keep being the Junior Miss and that had a lot to do with being thin. The mother had said, "Eat up girls! None of you are beauty queens so it doesn't matter but Sophie has a big future ahead of her so she can't afford to eat like that."

Sophie's mom was right about her daughter, I thought. Sophie knew a lot of people, she knew a lot about our town, she knew the lay of the land and where the power was. I had none of those skills, and I admired Sophie.

I knew hardly anyone and my parents had practically no friends. My mother did not speak with any of the neighbors and they were all suspect in our house, suspect or looked down upon by both my mother and father. My dad would say, "Oh there's that fat ass Wilson. Look at him, driving that junker of a car. He's pathetic."

I was taken off to northern Minnesota every summer to fend for myself all day with no friends, no playmates, no activities. I had no understanding, no access, no context.

My mother didn't like my friendship with Sophie. She knew that Sophie had her number. She knew that Sophie didn't like the way I was treated. My mother was aware that through Sophie I was getting out beyond her tiny torture chamber of influence and I was seeing another way.

But as much as my mother wanted to dislike her, Sophie was very fashionable and beautiful. Sophie's parents were well connected. Sophie was the Junior Miss. My mother would be too impressed to treat Sophie badly. Sophie was perfect leverage for me. Plus Sophie really loved me and I knew it. And I loved her back.

Sophie's mother answered the phone. I didn't like to be polite and schmooze but I had to if I had any hope of talking to Sophie. "Hello, Mrs. Carlson, this is Sidney. May I speak with Sophie? Is she at home by chance this morning?"

I could hear her disgust through the phone. Mrs. Carlson thought I was no good. But she was honest, thank God, and she answered that Sophie was at home, finishing an important project for school.

My heart leapt to hear Sophie's funny bratty voice. "Hello? Miss Sidney? To what do I owe this honor?"

I felt myself smile and it felt like smiling was the most foreign thing in the world. "Hi Sophie. I have a big problem. My parents have totally gone crazy."

"Well, we saw that coming."

"I know. My dad says he's gonna shoot my mom with his hunting gun tonight if she doesn't sign some papers that he left on the kitchen table."

"Wow. Seriously? He said that? That's so intense. Are you okay?"

"Aside from the fact that my hands won't stop shaking and I can hardly hold the receiver, I'm fine. I want my mom to get on a Greyhound bus and go up to our cabin today. It's gonna be pretty cold up there this time of year, but at least she won't be dead."

"Okay, that sounds good. Do you want me to call the bus station and find out when buses leave for where . . . Duluth, Minnesota? Is that a real place? Is that where you go in the summers?"

"Yeah, well that's still way south of the cabin, but it's the right direction anyway."

"Okay, you stay by the phone. What's your mom doing? Will she go along with this?"

"She's upstairs primping or crying or vacuuming. Those are the only things she ever does. Yeah, she'll do whatever I tell her to do. She really doesn't have any choice and she keeps asking me what she should do, so this is it."

"Okay, I'll call you right back."

I got off the phone and took the pale-green carpeted stairs by twos. I banged on my mother's pale-green painted door. The color she reverently referred to as Celadon.

"Mom. I have a plan. Open the door."

This kind of approach often worked with her. She knew on some level, as I did, that I was the only sane one in the bunch, and when I got serious, I could think my way out of just about anything. She also knew that she could not say the same about herself.

I was not surprised when I heard some rustling around, which meant she'd been lying on her perfect-ly made bed with the custom-sewn French toile quilt-ed spread that matched the French toile wallpaper, all in the same sickening pale green. The bedspread had a silky sheen to it and made a noise like the rustling of a ball-gown skirt if anyone lay on top of it. Ridiculous.

The door opened and there she stood with her per-fect hair and her not-that-pretty-and-very-sad-almost-all-the-time face. I watched her look at her daughter and I grinned. I was wearing ripped jeans that I wore all last summer at the cabin with a heather grey turtleneck wool sweater that my brother brought back in his knap-sack from Europe but didn't take to college and is mine now. I had suede Minnetonka beaded moccasins on my bare feet. I saw her looking at my messy hair. My hair was cut short like a boy's. A young and Italian Vidal Sas-soon woman came to our house a while ago and cut my mom and dad's hair while they were all having wine in the kitchen. My dad knew her through someone at work downtown. My parents thought it was super cool to have her there and it probably cost them a lot. The woman had a short, sexy haircut straight from Milan. She was busty like me and I liked her Italian attitude. She asked me if I wanted a haircut too. At the time, my hair was long but cut in an awkward shag that I didn't like. I said sure, and she cut off all my hair right then on the patio and I didn't even have a mirror to see what was happening, just big locks of hair falling everywhere on to the cement floor. When she was finished I went inside to the powder room to look at the result. I liked it. I liked it a lot. It made me feel rebellious and cool. The next day, people at school said, "Why did you have to cut off all your hair?" as if I had a disease or something. Teachers complimented me on the new cut. I kept it short after that. Sometimes if we went into Chicago, people stopped me on the street and asked where I got my hair cut.

But times were changing fast, and I was standing at my mother's bedroom door with my expensive haircut growing out and my ripped jeans with the knees completely gone and I was saying, "Mom, you're going to have to go up to the cabin. It's April, it won't be that bad. I can call my friends up there and they can give you a ride and help you. Unless you are going to sign Dad's papers . . . "

"I can't sign those papers! He is trying to ruin us! He is going to lose this house, he is a madman! He is going to lose everything!"

I could see she had not had a change of heart. I believed her. My dad seemed reckless. He had already been through investigations by the SEC regarding insider trading. I didn't know what it all meant, but I knew it wasn't good. He hung around with some strange characters too. There was a guy who would come to our house. He said he used to be a priest. He was poorly dressed in a shabby suit and seemed to be unbathed all the time. He had become a stockbroker and was hanging out with my dad. They both had an air of desperation about them. They would sit at night in our kitchen after carpooling to the stock exchange for the day. They would read the sign over the kitchen table and drink red wine and laugh about how absurd and philosophical it all was. It seemed like they were fooling themselves about something. The idea for the papers was spun out of one of their late-night, wine-fueled conversations—a brilliant last-ditch effort to use the equity on our house to infuse cash into the business so they wouldn't have to give up their seats on the exchange. I could see that my mother didn't like Dad's friend, the ex-priest, any better than I did. And when the papers arrived on the kitchen table some weeks ago, she made her initial outrage clear. I thought my father would back down or my mother would give in. I didn't expect Armageddon.

"Okay, Mom. I am going to get Sophie to give us a ride to the bus station and you can just buy a ticket for Duluth. I can call Jay and see if he'd come down and get you."

My mother had her hands up over her face and she was crying again. Shit. I was so scared I was trembling on the inside. I couldn't picture how the situation with my dad could get any worse without him pulling the trigger next time. I thought about hiding the gun, but he'd go crazy if he found it missing.

The phone was ringing so I ran down to the kitchen to answer it. Sophie was saying, "Hi, I called the Greyhound station and there's a bus at four. She rides all night and gets there in the morning, but whatever, it's better than staying here and being dead in the morning. Right?"

"Yeah, right, I'll tell her. How much does it cost, do you know?"

"It was like a hundred dollars, I think."

"Okay, yeah. So when can you come?"

"I'll just come get you at like three, is that good?"

"Okay, thanks Sophie. Okay. See you then."

I ran back up the stairs and told Mom the plan. She was sniffling and slowly packing a small leather suitcase with her beautiful pieces of lingerie, each wrapped in tissue paper. She had some camel color wool pants and her elegant cowl neck sweaters in camel and cream laid out on the bed. Her long wool coat was out as well. I thought for a moment how impractical a cream-colored coat would be, but I didn't say anything for fear of worrying her or worse yet, making her mad at me.

I decided to go back to my room and wait. With the door closed, I thought about playing my guitar, but I had a strong fear that my dad might be coming home early to resume the fight and I thought I'd better be listening for the electric garage door to go up just in case.

I lay on my stomach on my bed and read the textbook for my English class. I hated missing school. Most school years I only missed one or two days the whole year. I loved the other kids and I loved the teachers. Everyone was fun, and funny things were always happening. Teachers liked me and I almost always had good grades. I had known some of the kids since kindergarten and I had fun rivalries with some of the smartest ones. We were always comparing grades. I usually felt great about my abilities in the classroom. I was in band and orchestra, playing the flute, and I loved that too. I was second chair out of maybe twenty flutists by my junior year. I always wanted to be first chair, but some other girl was always beating me out of it.

Sophie arrived at three. We got my quivering, sniffling mother into the car. I was struck by how thin and frail and frightened she was. Sophie was very thin too but strong and confident. My mother seemed like a small child that day. We drove her and her leather suitcase to the Greyhound station. She let out a whimper when we pulled up. "Oh, this place is horrible."

"No, it's not that bad Mom, look at those people over there, they look nice." There were many men who looked down on their luck standing around smoking. There were hobos, men unshaven and threadbare, and there were hippies with long hair and love beads, army coats and knapsacks. There were more conservative-looking older people over on a bench. My mother didn't look like anyone there. My mother looked like she belonged in her husband's Jaguar going for a Sunday drive. Once she got to the cabin she'd be okay, I told myself. She'd been going to that cabin all her life. She knew people there.

The cabin had been built by her parents when she was a little girl. My grandmother had delivered a stillborn son and after that my grandfather brought his wife and little daughter to northern Minnesota from Chicago to buy a summer cabin. My Scandinavian grandparents had been to the area on their honeymoon, because it reminded them of the birch forests of Sweden. A cabin was purchased and from then on, the three of them spent every summer— all summer—about fifty miles from the Canadian border on a sparsely inhabited and often treacherous big lake in the northern wilderness. My mother knew that place. She knew the locals. She would be in her beloved cabin where she seemed to have nothing but good memories.

The bus for Duluth pulled in to the loading area. My mother was sniffling in the front passenger seat of

Sophie's dad's old tan Buick. I was sitting in the back. Sophie's parents were very conservative and practical and it flitted through my mind that nothing like this would ever happen to Sophie because of her parents' values and temperament. "It's okay, Mom. It'll be fine. I'll make sure Jay gets there at the right time. The cabin will be nice. You can have a fire in the fireplace and Jay will help you get the truck started. You'll be fine. I'll come up when school's out and this will all be like it never happened."

My mother was nodding and dabbing her eyes with a tissue. "Okay. I better go. Thank you Sophie for all your help. What would we have done without you?"

I opened the door and got out of the car. We hardly ever hugged and she stood stiffly as I came toward her. She allowed me to hug her. Her white wool coat was soft and smelled of her perfumed elegance. I felt a deep pain in my heart and the fear in my throat was rising. The gravity of the situation rose around me, and for the first time I glimpsed what was about to happen.

"I love you, Mom."

"I love you, Sidney."

"I'll call you once I get there. I don't know where I'll be able to call from, but there will be a pay phone I can use."

"Okay, Mom."

My mother said goodbye to Sophie. I got in the front seat. Sophie leaned over and hugged me. "It's gonna be okay, Sid."

I watched my mother in her white coat, with her Halston bag and her tan leather suitcase, as she walked to the teller's window to buy her ticket. I watched as she fumbled for her money with slight and trembling fingers. I watched as she picked up her suitcase and walked to the back of the line of passengers waiting to board. Sophie and I sat in silence as we saw my mother walk down the aisle on the bus and carefully adjust her things and herself in a window seat about a third of the way back. She waved at us with her thin hand. She was wearing one of her pairs of kidskin gloves. We both waved back. Everyone boarded and the bus door closed. The driver eased his vehicle out of the loading space. He shifted into drive. They pulled out of the Greyhound parking lot and out onto the street. I kept watching my mother. She was still waving at us. I knew then that this was the exact moment that my childhood ended.

THE UNWINDING

That evening Sophie left our house and said she was worried about me being there when my father got home. I told her I was too but I had nowhere else to go. Plus there was our big old boxer Brandy, whom my mom always fed and took care of, and although he mostly slept and looked out the window all day, he needed me now and I couldn't desert him. Brandy had been my companion for long walks when I was younger, but I had almost forgotten about him in all the chaos. He had learned to avoid the shouting and the scuffles. He kept to himself in his dog bed behind the table in the kitchen near the heat vent that he loved. But Brandy and I were in this together now and I was newly grateful for his companionship. After Sophie drove away, Brandy and I sat in the darkening living room watching the street. I was never allowed in the living room and my mother would freak out if she saw "footprints in the new carpeting" which was also celadon green and a finely woven short shag that showed every mark. This first night without my mother in the house, Brandy and I sat on the silk brocade loveseat with the down cushion. Mom could tell if anybody used it and you'd get in trouble for that too. Brandy and I perched on it and I rubbed my bare toes in the carpet, making designs. Brandy's big neck was perfect to wrap my arms around and I sat with him and cried for my lost childhood.

The sun went down and I watched the lights come on in the houses on our street. My mom always turned on the outdoor lights, which included the lanterns on either side of the garage door, another lantern over the front door, and some spotlights that were hidden in the front landscaping and made the house look classy. I didn't have the heart to turn them on without my mom being there. Those lights meant a lot to her. I left them off out of respect in a way, I thought. I wondered if my dad would show up at all. Maybe he would know my mom was gone and he wouldn't come back at all. I didn't know what was going to happen. I went to my room with Brandy. I filled the porcelain drinking glass that sat on the sink in the bathroom my brother and I were supposed to use and brought it into my room in case Brandy or I got thirsty. I pushed my big brown wooden dresser up against the door. I knew this would make my dad mad if he tried to open the door, but I also knew it would be harder for him to come into my room and if he was really crazy, I'd have time to maybe get out through the window or something. I left my clothes on in case I needed to make a run for it, and I got in bed. Brandy needed

help up but he got on the bed too and we curled up together. I cried some more.

Around midnight I heard the garage door open. I
thought about what to do or not do. At the last minute, I
decided to push the dresser back to its place on the wall
because if my dad tried to come in, finding the dresser
there would make him so much madder.

Brandy stood up and thought about barking but I
whispered, "Shhhh . . . please don't bark. Just be quiet.
Let's both just be quiet. Go back to sleep. It's just Dad."

I heard him come into the house. My heart pounded. I promised myself no matter what he did to me, I
wouldn't tell where she'd gone. I heard him mount the
stairs. I hoped he'd leave me alone and just go to bed. He
was at my bedroom door.

"Sidney, unlock this door."

I didn't want to make him madder. I got up. Brandy
jumped off the bed. We opened my door and there stood
my father with his three-piece suit all rumpled, the vest
unbuttoned, his tie loosened and crooked, his eyes red.
He took off his horn-rimmed glasses he always wore and
started wiping them on his untucked shirttail.

He walked into my room, pushing past me and
Brandy. I couldn't remember when I'd ever seen him inside my bedroom and I was afraid, but I was angry too
and the anger was winning out. I could feel by his demeanor that he felt sorry for himself. I hated his weak-
ness after being a bully. I thought of all his perverted
undertones and his psychological twists in every argument designed to trip up my mother or my brother or
me. I steeled my heart against feeling pity for him.

I clenched my fists and I screamed in my brain, "You brought this on yourself. You brought this on all of us."

He looked around my room and I realized he was hoping she was hiding in there with me. Then he sat down on the edge of my bed which he had never done in my life and I could see he was breaking.

"She's gone, isn't she," he whispered in a sincere tone that I'd never heard out of him ever before.

"Yes."

My heart went out to him. I felt like putting my arm around him and consoling him and helping him to solve this and get it all back on track. I knew he loved her with all his heart. But this was the man who had done so many awful things. My mind raced through all the terrible memories of his brutality toward my brother—the many times I put my body between him and my older brother, because my brother wouldn't defend himself against his beloved father. I watched as my dad browbeat his son mentally and physically so many times. My brother loved our dad so much. I didn't. I couldn't. I had seen too much. This grown man, defeated, on the edge of my bed in the middle of the night was a stranger to me now. I couldn't put down my pride, my self-protection, my anger and righteous indignation and comfort him.

His shoulders shook. He was slumped over in a way I had never seen him. He was sobbing. I watched him and my heart was torn, my arms yearned to hug him.

Instead I steeled myself and spoke, "Dad, I have school in the morning. I have to go to bed."

He looked up at me suddenly as if seeing me for the first time.

"What? How can you just stand there watching your own father cry and not want to comfort me? What is wrong with you? You're a monster! You have no feelings for anyone but yourself."

He stood and stared at me. I thought he might hit me and my heart pounded in my chest but I stood still and said nothing. Then he walked to the hallway.

He turned around with his hand on the doorknob, "I won't do anything for you. You remember this when you want anything from me. You better get yourself a job because you are cut off."

Then he slammed the door.

MONEY AND WHEELS

I f the phone
rang in the kitch-
en, I dashed to answer
before my slumbering
father would hear it because I didn't want
him to get up and come out of his room. This
morning it was my mother on the phone as I
was always praying it would be. I missed
her. I was afraid. I was lonely and miserable. I was worried about her.

"Hi, Mom."

"Oh, Sidney, how are you doing
honey?"

I almost started crying because I wanted
somebody to care so badly.

"I'm okay. I'm fine. How's it going?"

"It's a beautiful morning up here. The weather is
warming up a little. The truck is finally working . . . Sidney,
I want you to know that we have a friend who is helping
us. I don't want you to be worried. We have a friend."

"What are you talking about, Mom? What friend?
Why are you talking like that?"

My mother had a creepy way of delivering cryptic lines that made me think she was the most evil person in the world. I had no idea who or what she was referring to. In one way, it was very comforting that she sounded so surprisingly well acclimated. In another, it was entirely unexpected and disconcerting. My love and hatred were in perfect balance. I listened halfheartedly as she kept saying the same crap. There was no talking to her about my situation or my plans. She said goodbye promising to call again soon. She really didn't even ask me what was happening with me.

May had come, and the school year was almost over. I couldn't get checks out of my dad any more so I just stopped going to my flute lessons. We didn't have answering machines or anything, so I didn't know whether my flute teacher tried to call me. I saw a handwritten bill for the last month's worth of lessons. My dad just kept throwing all the mail away. If I answered the phone and it wasn't for me Dad had instructed me to say he wasn't there and that I would be happy to take a message. I usually just hung up on anybody who asked for my dad. No one ever called asking for my mom. A few times I got disgusted if my dad was standing right there in front of me in the kitchen and I'd say, "Yes, he's right here" and attempt to pass him the receiver but he'd get so mad that I was afraid he'd hurt me so I usually just let him hiss at me—"take a message, I'm not here" and then I'd have to write some number down that I knew he was never going to call.

My dad was obviously struggling. He was driving a taxi at night and going to the stock exchange during the day, trying to make a miracle happen. I knew there was more to it that I didn't understand. The papers were gone from the kitchen table and no one was telling me anything.

One morning I came downstairs ready for school, and he was ironing his dress shirt in his sleeveless white undershirt and pin-striped trousers. He looked at me with tragically sad bloodshot eyes and I could barely look back. To see my father so defeated was heartbreaking and frightening. I felt so guilty. I had the terrible feeling that I had brought this all on us by sending my mother on the Greyhound bus.

"Don't look at me like that. Don't look at your father with pity in your eyes. What are you doing to help? Do you have a job? Have you picked up a dust cloth? Do you even know how to run the vacuum? Look at these shirts I'm wearing! They're threadbare! Do you think I want to dress this way? Look at my suits, they don't even fit me any more. My pants don't even stay up. I'm wasting away. What are you doing to help out around here? Sitting around at night jacking up the phone bill, whispering to your mother, your boyfriends, your spoiled gossipy girlfriends. Where's that little bitch Sophie these days? She doesn't want to come around now, does she? Fair-weather friend. Those people you surround yourself with, none of them care about you. You're a fake. You don't have anything. Have you told your teachers what's happening here? Are you telling people your mother has run off and left us?"

"No Dad, the people I talk to do care about me. I do have real friends. Sophie is a real friend. The teachers don't know me well enough for me to say anything to them."

I tried to defend myself. I tried to think of things to say to change the way my dad saw me. But he wasn't listening. He didn't care. He put on his dress shirt and before I knew it he headed out to the garage. The garage door opening. The car door. The car engine. The garage door closing.

Alone in the deserted kitchen, I tried to think about my dad and his family. Dad was Italian, raised in the city by an Italian father and a half-German mother who didn't speak to their families and were decidedly not Catholic, never went to church at all. They seemed to harbor strange secrets, and I knew only conflicting information. They lived near us for a while and then something happened between my father and his parents. After that his sister and her family, including their daughter, my cousin Cindy, my only close friend when I was little, and all the rest of them suddenly moved to Florida and never spoke to us again. I got the idea, maybe true, that my dad had lost some or all of their retirement money in the stock market and they couldn't forgive him. But then I heard that my grandparents had a pool at their new house in Florida, so they couldn't have been completely broke.

The last time I saw Cindy was in the autumn a few years ago. I walked home from elementary school right past the junior high where she was in the eighth grade. She was getting on the school bus when I spotted her. We were both wearing the purple, wool, fringe ponchos our grandmother had bought us the year before. We used to get cute matching outfits that I loved because she was older and so beautiful and I felt so happy being her little cousin. There she was climbing the stairs of the bus with her pretty long yellow blonde hair smooth down her back and I called to her. She looked very pained to see me, the poignancy of us seeing each other after so long and in the same clothes was not lost on her I imagine, and she stopped on the steps of the bus and turned after I called her name for a third time. I knew she had to hear me, other kids in line were looking at me.

"Sidney, I'm not supposed to talk to you . . . "

I said, "What? What are you talking about?"

She answered, "We're moving away. We're going with Grandma and Grandpa and we're all moving to Florida."

Then she disappeared onto the bus. My heart sank. I was so alone. I loved her so much. I felt invisible. I did not matter. I was alone. I walked home and thought about what had happened during the early years.

Cindy had an older brother just like I did. When I was nine, Preston spent a summer hanging around with Tommy who was a year or two older. We hadn't known these cousins much because they used to live further away in the city and now they had a new house near us in our same suburb. Preston thought Tommy was weird but I think he liked that Tommy was older and that's about it. One Saturday morning I was sitting in my little pale blue nightgown that I loved because it had a family of embroidered yellow ducks marching across a pale-green velvet ribbon over the chest. I had floral-print underpants underneath. I was nine years old. I was watching cartoons. Our parents had gone grocery shopping together because they were having people over for dinner. Preston never talked to me. He never even looked at me. Suddenly as I was curled up on the family room sofa watching cartoons on television I noticed Preston looking at me with a strange keen interest that I had never seen on his face.

"Hey little Sid, how you doing this morning?"

"What? I'm fine. What's the matter with you?"

"Hey, guess what Tommy told me. He said that Cindy's been playing a weird game with him at their house down in the basement. He said they've been painting her with sparkle paints and stuff and it's weird but it's really fun.

"What do you say we try it? There's this little game called Get that they play.

"Here, come here."

Preston sat down right next to me, right up against me.

"Tommy says you just take your hand and you just put it right here . . . see like this . . . I'll do it . . . isn't that nice . . . you just keep your hand right there and then I just move my finger like this . . . there see . . . good . . . Sid . . . good . . . that's right . . . just enjoy it . . . isn't that nice . . . it's nice right . . . I just put my hand on your panties so I can play Get with you . . . like this . . . mmmmmmm . . . that's right . . . you love it don't you . . . we can do this whenever you want . . . I'm gonna do it faster . . . yeah . . . good . . . just stay right there . . . just stay still . . . good Sid . . . good . . . oh . . . oh . . . yeah . . . oh . . . "

Then Preston abruptly got up and left the room and shut the family room door, which nobody ever did.

I just sat there. Then I started watching the cartoons again.

I didn't tell Cindy about this the next time I saw her. But Preston told Tommy. The next time Cindy's parents came to our house for dinner and brought their kids along, everyone stayed up late but I was youngest and I was tired so I went to bed in my room with my door shut. It was a Sunday night and I had school the next day. There was a tap on my door. I didn't answer because I was already asleep and I didn't want anyone to come in. Cindy's mom had driven her home so she could get to bed early too, so I knew it wasn't her and she was the only one I'd be happy to wake up for. So I didn't answer but I heard my door open. I thought it might be my mom checking on me, which would be extremely unlike her. I heard Tommy's voice whispering right by my ear. "Sidney, are you awake? Shhhhhhh . . . don't make a sound . . . Preston told me what you like to do . . . I'm gonna do that for you . . . shhhhhh . . . just close your eyes . . ."

I was so flattered that Tommy who was so old and cool would ever pay any attention to me that I stayed still and pretended to be asleep. I guess that what they did—putting their hands on my panties and moving their fingers back and forth—seemed pretty harmless and it felt great, giving me a feeling of overwhelming love for them. I knew nothing about anything sexual, and had no conscious interest in it. I didn't know whether this was something everyone did or no one did. My cousins seemed very conventional to me. Cindy was a very pretty, quiet, reserved young girl. Their parents, my aunt and uncle, owned a small office-supply company and went ballroom dancing. Their family seemed more normal than mine. If this was what their kids did, then it was probably okay. That's what I thought.

Preston approached me one more time to play the little game. I was in my bedroom and he came and sat on my bed right up close to me when I was in my nightgown getting ready for bed. This time, he really got into it and it lasted longer. I felt like I was going to cry. I felt this great overflowing love for my brother and I opened my mouth and said the words, quietly and sincerely, "I love you, Preston."

My brother awoke from his reverie as if lightning had struck him. He jumped up, knocking me from the bed where I was perched with my legs apart so he could get closer to me. I tumbled to the wood floor and watched him flee my room, slamming my door. We did not speak again.

I felt shame for the first time in my life. I felt that I was wrong to tell him I loved him. I felt I had ruined it. I also felt for the first time that what we were doing was wrong.

I started thinking about that feeling a lot after that, whether it was wrong or otherwise. I wanted that feeling. For whatever reason, I did not think it was right to do that to yourself. I think my parents had always told me not to touch myself there. I felt that I could try to get other boys to do it for me and I could be more careful not to say the wrong thing and scare them away. After that I looked at every boy as a potential conquest, as a potential partner. It was subconscious, I think, but it was real.

All these memories ran through my head when I was thinking of Dad. The legacy from his side of the family was definitely pretty dark. I made a concerted effort to put them all out of my mind.

I let Brandy out to go to the bathroom before I left for school and then headed out with my backpack. I could thankfully walk to my high school from our house. By the end of that year, many kids were driving to school. I knew that many were going to get their driver's licenses.

There was no way I was going to ask my dad to take me for the test. I had taken the in-school mandatory driver's ed class and barely passed with a D, the only bad grade in my academic career. The instructor was a former drill sergeant with a flat-top crew cut and a mean face. He would lean right up next to your right ear as you were coming down the entrance ramp onto the Dan Ryan Expressway and start shouting "Pick It Up! Pick It Up! Merge! Merge!"

The teacher's approach was in stark contrast to my mother's modeling of driving etiquette. On the rare occasion when she decided to brave the expressway, she would drive onto the ramp, start to accelerate and then get really scared and start saying, "Oh God, oh my God, Sidney, Sidney, hold my hand . . . "

I would give her my hand, which she would clutch mercilessly, crushing my bones until she maneuvered the car into a lane. I would want to say, "You should have both hands on the steering wheel," but I was too afraid of making her mad or having us crash, so I just closed my eyes and screamed on the inside. Despite the barely passing driver's-ed grade and bad modeling from my mom, I was determined to get a license and a car. The Jaguars had both mysteriously disappeared over the winter. My dad was driving a used car—a green hatchback Opel with a manual transmission that he complained was ruining his left knee from working the clutch.

I was thinking a lot about Dad saying I needed to help out. I wanted a job, but I had to get the license and the car first. There wasn't anything within walking distance of our house except the school. Sophie worked at an ice cream parlor across town and she said she could get me a job if I could get transportation worked out.

By some miracle, I was in my driveway with Brandy one morning, when Jenny came out with her mom. I hadn't talked to her in months. She got rides to school with her older siblings and never walked like I did.

"Hey Sidney, are you getting your license soon? We're going to take the driver's test."

"I don't know. I don't really have a way to get it right now, I guess."

Mrs. Wilson, who was not usually nice, suddenly said, "Come with us, Sidney."

"Well, I don't have any of the stuff ready," I was thinking of the check necessary to pay the fee, "and I haven't practiced since the driver's ed class. And I got a D."

Jenny was nice and laughed good-naturedly. "No girls ever get good grades from that guy. I got a C minus. Just come with us. My mom knows who the easy testers are."

Mrs. Wilson was nodding, "You can drive on the way over so you can see how our car works. Do you have the certification from the class? You need that, and your student ID."

I couldn't believe they were being so nice to me.

"Yeah, I have them. Okay, can you wait a minute and I'll bring Brandy in and get my stuff?"

"Sure Sidney, no rush. I can pay your fee and you can pay me back whenever."

I got my license that day. The Wilson family had given me a crucial gift. I knocked on my dad's door the next Saturday morning when he was sleeping in. He was blurry-eyed in my parents' big bed, the sheets all rumpled, the room disheveled, so unlike the way it was when my mother was there. My heart ached for the return of that order and beauty. Everything was dusty now. Everything was out of place.

"Dad, sorry. I wanted to tell you, I got my driver's license. Look, here it is."

"How did you do that?"

He sounded incredulous and I detected a note of surprise that I could be so resourceful.

"The Wilsons brought me."

I knew he hated the Wilsons, and this would make him hate them more than ever.

"Huh. You would go to them. Make your parents look bad. You are unbelievable."

"No Dad, Jenny was outside and Mrs. Wilson just invited me. It was totally spur-of-the-moment. I didn't plan it or anything."

"Who paid for it?"

Mrs. Wilson had paid for my license but I thought Dad would get mad so I lied, "I saved the money you and Mom gave me for my birthday and I had just enough."

"Huh."

I needed to get to the next part fast before this blew up, "Dad, I can get a job at the ice cream parlor where

Sophie works. They said they'd hire me right away but I need a car to go there. They said I can work every day after school and all day in the summer too."

"You want me to supply you with a car now? Are you kidding me?"

"Dad, please. I can't do anything without a car."

"Why haven't you left yet? Aren't you going to run off and join your mother? Aren't you just waiting for an escape? Why would I do anything for you now?"

"No Dad, I want to stay here. I want to get a job and help out. Isn't Preston coming home soon? He and I could share the car. Maybe he could get his license this summer too."

I don't remember how it arrived, but soon after, a car showed up in the garage and there were keys on the kitchen table where once the infamous "papers" had lain. The car was a Volare, which was not cool by anyone's standards, but I was thrilled. I think I remember throwing my arms around my dad's neck and kissing him on the cheek and thanking him with genuine gratitude. I am not sure if that moment ever happened. Maybe I didn't thank him at all. I hope I didn't complain about what a stupid car he got me.

With the car, the world opened up and I felt better about life. The ice cream parlor became my source of food and income. The manager was sleazy and kind of mean but I didn't care. He could make some of the girls cry if they made mistakes with the cash register or ate too much free food, but he was a pussycat in my eyes compared to what I had dealt with so far in my life, so he and I got along fine. I ate a lot of ice cream but I wasn't getting fat so I didn't care. I was so used to my mother telling me not to eat just about anything I wanted to, "Do you really think a brownie's a good idea, Sidney?" or "Doughnuts are poison" or "French-fried potatoes are just about the worst thing you can put into your body," that I was enjoying the freedom to eat a burger and fries and a strawberry shake all in one sitting for the first time in my life. There were a few girls from my school besides Sophie who worked at the ice cream parlor and it was fun to sit with them before and after work and order root beers at the counter. And then I got a paycheck on top of it! I worked as many hours as the manager would give me. The other girls were in more activities and had family obligations. I had nothing ever on my calendar and no boyfriend either, so I worked many hours and my paychecks were the envy of the other girls. Sophie helped me open my first bank account so I could cash my checks and I started transferring a portion of each check into savings. On top of this money, one weekend, some of us were hired to do the inventory at a warehouse that somebody's dad owned. Sophie did this with me. We counted boxes of screws and nuts and bolts all day and into the night for two days and we each got paid handsomely for our efforts. I deposited that check in its entirety so I definitely had some money. A car and an income made all the difference, for now anyway.

PRESTON

My brother Preston went through an intense football obsession from grade school through the fall of his junior year of high school. My dad had been a college football player and he pushed Preston really hard. Dad sent Preston to a special camp in Texas one summer where the kids train for real with the Dallas Cowboys. My dad knew a guy who played for the Cowboys who got Preston in. I met that guy a couple of times. He was gigantic, and he wore an immense fur coat because he thought Chicago was very cold, and I suppose because he wanted to look cool, which he did. He also wore a massive gold ring that he got for playing in the Super Bowl, which he let me look at up close. He seemed like a gladiator to me.

Preston was not a big guy at all. He was only five foot ten and fine-boned like our mother. Our dad was six foot one, big and scary, and had huge shoulders. Dad wanted Preston to be the quarterback of our high-school football team, which was known for being great. Preston wanted that too, and he did it.

There was a big game that changed everything forever. Our school was playing their biggest rival. Preston was the starting quarterback for the game. He was just beginning his junior year and was first-string quarterback. My mother had been saying that the coach was putting Preston under too much pressure. My dad said he could handle it. For the homecoming game, my parents got all dressed up in stylish sweaters and nice denim jeans and my mom wore her glamorous long shearling coat and high-heel boots. I wore my nice wool coat with fake shearling trim and a big cozy hood lined with the same fur. The coat came down to my calves just like my mom's did, and I wore my new brown Frye boots that came up almost to my knees. All that day our parents were talking about what they were going to wear and it felt like we were making a big public appearance. I knew that Preston was very worried and excited about this game and it seemed like an important occasion for all of us.

Preston headed over much earlier and I waited around while my parents got ready. I stood in the front hall all bundled up in my coat, ready to go, so I wouldn't get in trouble for slowing them down once they were ready to leave. We drove over in the four-door Jaguar, even though we could have just walked, but my mom was wearing high heels and my dad probably wanted people to see his car. The three of us looked pretty good I thought, as we entered the high-school outdoor stadium and climbed the stairs to get good seats up in the stands. Mom and Dad didn't know any of the other parents, and I was too young to know many of the kids who were there. My dad set a wool stadium blanket down over the bleacher bench and my mom sat down with him. I squished in next to her in the crowded stands. My mother watched with interest as they crowned the new homecoming king and queen. The queen from the previous year was there and she seemed grown up and was very beautiful, wearing high boots and a big fur coat. The marching band played, which always interested me because I was studying the flute. Then the game started and I just sat watching people mostly.

Near the end of the second quarter, things were not going well for our home team. It seemed to me that my parents were concerned with Preston's performance. My mother was worried and my father looked angry. Suddenly, everyone on our side started booing and shouting. I couldn't tell what had gone wrong. I was trying to ask my dad but the crowd around us was so loud I couldn't talk to him. Then in the next play something bad happened again and our side started shouting to have Preston replaced. All around us in the stands people were angrily shouting to have my brother taken out of the game. My face burned red. I tried to see my brother's face on the field but I couldn't get a glimpse of him in the jumble of players in the middle of the field.

After that, all I remember is Preston being called off just before a new play was to start, and people clapping as he jogged slowly toward the benches with his head down. Those minutes of watching Preston with his shoulders slumped over and his head down, with my mother's overly dramatic laments in my ear and me worrying what my dad was going to do to Preston for this, were excruciating for me. I watched in aching terrible pain for my brother. I watched as a friend of Preston's who was older and bigger was sent out to replace him and people around us cheered and called out that boy's name. My heart ached for my brother. I thought about how he lay in bed in the middle of the night and would shout out the plays in his sleep. I used to tease him about it in the morning. "And Duncan is going out for the long pass . . . no . . . he's running! He's running for the touchdown!"

My mom and dad were upset. They spoke to each other in complete shock and as if this was a very shameful thing that was happening, as if these people were against our family, as if it was a rejection of our family by the entire community. That's the way my parents acted and that's the way it felt to me. My parents stood and gathered our wool blankets from the bleachers and said, "Come on Sidney, we're leaving."

I followed them, but it seemed wrong to walk down the bleachers right then, before the game was finished, just after their son had been called off to the bench. I saw people's heads turn and I thought they were looking at my parents. I followed slowly behind thinking that this felt worse than if we had stayed. We stood huddled together at the base of the bleachers as the game roared on around us, my mother talking to my father, saying it wasn't right what the coach had done by putting Preston in so soon, blaming my dad for getting Preston's expectations so high about football in the first place. We walked to my dad's car in the big brightly lit parking lot with the roar of the game behind us and Preston somewhere down in the bowels of the high school football machine. I was worrying about him. How would he leave? How would he get home? This was a big celebration night and kids would be going out in groups after the game. But what would Preston do?

My parents and I drove the few short blocks back to our house and I ran up to my room and locked the door. I heard my parents arguing about my brother and football and the coach and the people at the game.

A while later I heard Preston come in the house. I don't know whether he walked home or if someone gave him a ride. He went in his room and locked his door. I listened, holding my breath for a very long time. There was only silence in the house. I went to bed with a heavy heart.

After that game, Preston quit football. My dad was mad. There were many fights, my father yelling, Preston earnestly defending himself, our stupid mother, crying helplessly. I heard Preston say that the coach and some other boys he knew from football passed him in the hallway and the coach called out, "There goes the quitter."

One night when the football season was still going, soon after Preston had quit, Seymour Hoffman and his wife invited my parents over for dinner in their screened-in porch. It was nice because they kept a fire going in the big brick fireplace, making the porch very cozy in the late autumn. The Hoffmans lived in our neighborhood even before my parents bought a house. Our old third-floor walk-up apartment was across the alley behind their house. They had a son who was Preston's age whom we had known since my brother and I were little kids. My parents wanted Preston to come along because their son would be there too. I knew I had to go, it wouldn't have occurred to me to do anything else. Preston was in his room refusing to come out and when he did, he looked disheveled and miserable and my dad yelled at him to spruce up and "get a decent shirt on." We drove over together with my brother slumped in the back seat next to me like a beaten dog. My heart broke to look at him.

We arrived there and everything was just as it used to be when we were younger. Seymour and his wife were glad to see us. Their son came down from his room and he and Preston exchanged awkward but friendly greetings. The screened-in porch was at the back of the property attached to an old stone garage so we carried the salad and the dishes out through their nicely tended garden to the porch. The porch had a stone wall at the back and a built-in fireplace. The fire was going and there was a grate with cooking barbecued chicken and baked potatoes. I was excited that we'd be having a nice dinner. My mom looked beautiful in a cream cable-knit sweater and slim jeans with lace-up boots. She was wearing her heavy gold hoop earrings, her gold bangle bracelet, and her wide gold band wedding ring that had one very large rectangular diamond. She had an ability to look very regal in her casual attire, which I admired and loved. I think Manhattans were made for the adults. My mother said she'd sip that one drink the whole night and still never finish it. Seymour's wife, Mrs. Hoffman, said she'd be ready for another pretty quickly so Seymour should keep 'em coming.

The food was good and the grownups were in high spirits as we ate. The boys were allowed to drink beer.

I got the feeling that the boys were drinking beer faster than the parents were aware, but I don't think anyone cared. I was just watching the fire and enjoying the cozy porch. The boys were gone for a while, I thought they were inside watching television. The parents were drinking some more. My mother was starting to get agitated. Her voice was wary as she started saying, "Oh honey, do you really need another one?" with each of my dad's drinks or freshly opened cans of beer.

I knew it was getting late. The colder night air was starting to win out over the warmth of the fire and I was wishing I had a warmer coat. I put my hood up on my pale blue windbreaker jacket and tied the strings tight. I got out of my little metal folding lawn chair and crossed to the back corner away from the screen door and sat down on the stone edge of the fireplace. I stuffed my hands in my pockets and leaned back as close as I dared to the fire.

I was getting very sleepy and no one was talking to me so I wasn't really paying attention until I saw that the boys had returned to the porch for more beer. They were looking kind of wobbly and my dad picked up on that and started accusing my brother of stealing extra beers. Seymour's son Sam tried to defend Preston. "I offered him the beers, Mr. Duncan, it's my fault."

My dad got madder. "Shut up, Sam. This is between me and my son. Preston, do you think you're an adult? Do you want to drink like a man?"

"No Dad, I'm sorry Dad."

"No Dad? No what? You think you aren't a grown man? But you want to sneak beer like a little coward, and drink it anyway?"

"No Dad, I'm really sorry Dad."

I was worried that Preston couldn't take this right now. This was too much for him. I knew it. Our dad should shut up and leave him alone. Mom started in with, "What? Have the boys been drinking all this time? Oh my god . . . we need to go home . . . our family needs to go home. This isn't right. How did this happen?"

My mom stood up and started cleaning up dishes and glasses. She was talking to Mrs. Hoffman who seemed pretty out of it, encouraging her to start bringing things back to the house. "Let's get the dishes going. I don't want to leave you with a mess." Mrs. Hoffman was mumbling, passing a careless hand over the direction of the wooden table covered with serving platters and plates and glasses, beer cans, liquor bottles. "We can clean it up in the morning, this is nothing."

But my mother was insisting, gathering more plates in her arms and beseeching Mrs. Hoffman to join her. Eventually the two women left the porch with their arms full and Mrs. Hoffman stumbled along behind my mother up the path to the kitchen door. They disappeared inside. I thought I'd get up and clear dishes and go in too, hoping it would be warmer in the house. But that's when Dad and Preston started up again, worse than before, and there was no way I would be able to squeeze past them to get out the porch door. I sat on my perch by the fire and hoped things wouldn't get bad. But Dad was livid and he lurched toward Preston.

"God damn it Seymour, my son needs disciplining. He is spineless. He's a sneak and a coward. Do you know what he did Seymour? Do you know the shame he's brought on us?"

Mr. Hoffman said, "Hey, come on Don, calm down, there's no reason to get into this."

"Get into this? It needs to be talked about. Am I supposed to pretend it didn't happen? Walk on eggshells around my own son?"

"Dad, stop it. Everybody knows what happened."

"Oh are you talking now? Preston Duncan, the family coward? The quitter? The sniveling little cripple who couldn't take the pressure. You couldn't handle it could you? You choked!"

"Jesus, Don! Take it easy. It's over. Come on."

But my dad couldn't stop, wouldn't stop, "Is this how I brought you up? What, do you take after your fearful whimpering mother is that who you are? You fucking little pathetic worm! Come here. I'll teach you not to steal beer from your father's friends. What the fuck is wrong with you?"

He lurched, he grabbed, my brother let out a yelp. In one fell swoop my brother was on the stone floor of the porch, my father was shouting, "You aren't my son! You're a fucking worthless piece of shit on the fucking ground! Look at you! You're an emotional cripple, you're weak, you are weak and sickening!"

My dad started to kick my brother's crumpled form, my brother winced as my dad kicked him in the stomach. I wanted to stop him but I was afraid to, he was so out of control. I was trying to get Mr. Hoffman to do something.

"What's wrong with you? Get up and do something!" I shouted at him. He sat shaking his head, "This is between a father and a son and there's not a thing anybody . . . "

He was drunk and cowardly and I could see in his eyes he was lying and afraid to intervene.

I yelled, "You know this is wrong! You aren't doing anything!"

My dad busted out of the porch, smacking the screen door so hard it slapped against the back wall and stomped toward the house yelling my mother's name, "Ingrid! Ingrid, goddammit let's go! Let's get out of this shit hole! These people are all going nowhere! My son can stay here and fucking rot for all I care! Get in the car!" I went straight to my room when we got home and I locked my door and got into bed and tried to sleep, but all night I wondered if Preston was okay.

Preston didn't leave his room much the rest of that semester. He yelled at anyone who tried to talk to him. Mom would make me knock on his door to get him out of bed for school. If by chance his door was unlocked and I poked my head in to wake him up, he would grab one of the many books lying about in his covers and whip it as hard as he could at me. If I was lucky I'd close the door before it hit me. If I saw him coming out of our shared bathroom I was struck by his drastic change in appearance. His face had broken out into bright-red acne. Both cheeks were covered in a rash that seemed to be multiplying by the day. He looked much thinner and terribly sad. Our dad took it upon himself more than once to berate Preston for not washing his face enough. I knew that wasn't the problem because Preston took a shower every time he went out and he had different skin products on the counter that he seemed to be constantly applying. One night my dad came home with some horrible loofah thing, brought my brother into our bathroom and with the door open, and as my mother and I stood there horrified, he "taught his son how to scrub this disgusting fungus off his face." The blood ran down Preston's neck as our dad held him with one hand by the neck and brutally scrubbed his sores with the other. That night I threw my body in the middle of the scene and started screaming for Dad to stop but he knocked me aside so I turned to our mother who put her hands over her face and went into her room and closed the door.

Preston started reading philosophy books and studying French and German saying he wanted to read the philosophers in their original texts. Our dad had been a philosophy major in college and used to talk philosophy and literature with Preston. I was not involved in these conversations even as they swirled around me. Sometimes if the family sat down together for dinner, usually on a weekend night, our dad would open a bottle of red wine, which often turned into a second bottle, and then he'd talk about authors like Hemingway and Fitzgerald and philosophers like Sartre and Nietzsche. Every once in a while, I would recognize the subject matter as something I had studied in school and would try to join in. Our mother never tried to participate, she just cooked and served dinner and did the dishes. But I wanted to engage in the intellectual discussions. So I would try to add something I felt had been overlooked like a fact about an author's life that I had maybe studied for a class report.

My father would invariably turn his scrutiny on me and with great sarcasm and amused displeasure, say something like, "Are you part of this? Are you talking? Did anyone address you?"

To which I would gamely answer, "No Dad, but I just thought you guys should know that . . . "

He would cut me off with something like, "Have you read the works of Aristotle? Plato? No, I didn't think so. Did you read the *Wall Street Journal* this morning? Did you read *Barron's? The New York Times?* Do you have any idea what's happening in the world? No. How old are you now, ten?"

"I'm thirteen, Dad."

"Thirteen. Thirteen years old. I'm sorry, but thirteen does not deserve an audience. Let me know when you grow up. Thirteen doesn't cut it."

Preston got involved with a very unusual girl around this time. They were in the same advanced philosophy class at the high school. She had dark eyes with dark circles around them and long wavy black hair that she said her parents said would never be cut. Her family was Jewish, of a very liberal mindset, very Bohemian and intellectual. The girl played the flute, as did I, so I talked to her about that whenever I saw her, but she was much more keenly devoted to the flute and had a more fitting demeanor for a flute player than I thought I did, so I always deferred to her in conversation. She was four years older than me, but beyond our age difference, she seemed to be from an entirely different time. Her clothes were handmade and exotic. She sometimes had stars painted on her face. The girlfriend's family allegedly grew marijuana in their yard and had live chickens—both daring acts in our community at that time.

One Saturday night my brother and the girl showed up very late at our house. Awoken by the sounds of arguing, I came down the carpeted steps so I could see what was happening. There stood my brother with black stars on one cheek, wearing a long caftan of rough woven cloth.

Our mother was looking at Dad, "This is terrible, he can't walk around like this. They're on some kind of drugs. I'm telling you they're on something!"

"Mom, these caftans are very common for the men to wear in Morocco."

"You aren't in Morocco. Preston what has happened to you? Are you taking drugs with this girl?"

Dad was saying, "Get upstairs and take that ridiculous thing off and scrub that shit off your face. And you need to go home to your parents, little girl, and let them see who their daughter is."

Preston was swaying, his eyes red and squinting, but he got a sudden burst of clarity and announced, "No. She's not leaving. She's staying with me."

With that our parents let out a simultaneous roar, "What?! No she is not."

My dad started scuffling with the two of them, grabbing the girl by the arm saying, "You are getting out of my house! You will never set foot in this house again!"

The girl screamed, "Preston! He's hurting me!"

My brother grabbed Dad's arm, "Dad, come on, she's okay. Come on Dad take it easy."

The girl escaped out the front door and was on the porch and Dad was yelling at Preston, "Look at you. You look like a clown. You look like a loser. You want to be with this girl so bad? This filthy slut of a girl? Are you fucking this? You are, aren't you! You're only sixteen years old! You want this? Then you aren't my son! I don't want you here! Get out! Go over and fuck at her parents' house and see what they think of you two idiots! Get out and don't come back!"

"Dad, please, you don't understand. Dad!"

Preston went out onto the front porch and I heard him let out a sob. But I also heard the girl saying, "Preston, come on, let's go. Fuck them. Come on, Preston."

Preston did a surprising thing then. He left that night with her and didn't come back. He lived with the girl at her parents' house, for the rest of his junior year. I never saw him. He never came to the house. He came in to get things from his room maybe once or twice early on, but after that, I never saw him.

The next thing I heard was that he would be graduating from high school a year early. Then I heard he was coming back to our house to get ready to leave for Europe. I can only guess at all of this. I know he broke up with the girl but not because he didn't love her—he told me he did. Much later, he told me that the mother let him get eggs from the chicken coop and he made himself fresh eggs and it was the best breakfast in the world. Also, I remember him saying that the parents were very kind to each other and to their daughter, and to him as well. He made it sound like it was a very foreign thing for people to be so kind and contented. I thought it sounded so different from our home life that I could barely imagine it. He might have stayed there forever, but there must have been a pull to get out on his own. Preston wanted to know the world. He loved languages and was reading more material in French. The girl spoke to Preston in French. He seemed to have a strong desire for a larger world experience.

Preston somehow made amends with our father. I

don't think our mother was ever really mad at him, she was always just sad and upset and hurt and confused and wrapped up in her own emotions. Dad paid for a plane ticket to Europe—one way—for his son as a graduation present. Our mom was against the whole thing. She said my dad was pumping crazy romantic ideas into Preston's head about Europe and about traveling and being a writer like Ernest Hemingway. Nobody listened to her.

Before he left, Preston was only home for a short time. His skin was smooth again with a few red scars. He was very thin now, not all pumped up from lifting weights and drinking protein shakes for football. He had a cool new bohemian sense of style. He had an incredible pair of Levi's blue jeans that were pale blue from years of wear. You couldn't buy jeans that were that perfectly faded like a summer sky. His girlfriend's mom sewed patches on the jeans because she knew how much Preston liked them. The effect of all the torn holes and threads and patches was a true work of art.

He knew how much I liked them; one day before he left for Europe he came into my bedroom with them, "Hey little sis, little Sid the sis, you want these don't you?"

"What? Yeah! I love those!"

"Well guess what, your old brother is gonna give them to you as a little token of his affection."

He came over and kissed me on the forehead, which I don't know if anyone had ever done in my whole life.

"I'm sorry I haven't been around. I bet it's been pretty hard on you having to deal with them on your own."

"Well, they mostly just ignore me."

"I know. I see that now. I'm sorry you've had it so

shitty. You don't deserve this. You're smart and you're pretty and you're a really good person."

I started to feel like I was going to cry so I just said, "No I'm not. Shut up. Give me the pants and get out of my room."

Preston started laughing, "That's my kid sister! Tough as nails! That's gonna see you through, kid. You're gonna be okay, I know it. Well, let me know if they fit. I'll be leaving tomorrow and you and Brandy are the only ones I'll miss. Actually, the weird thing is, I'm gonna miss those lousy parents of ours too."

The jeans fit me great, and my big brother left the next day. He was in Europe for many months, almost a year. He sent a few postcards, addressed to our whole family. He called collect once from London when his wallet was stolen and spoke only with our father who wired him the money to proceed and helped him get new identification papers. Otherwise all we knew was that he had found work clearing rocks for a vineyard at the base of the Pyrenees Mountains near Nice in France. He lived in a hut with an old man who had spent his life working on the vineyard as a laborer, clearing new land, planting and caring for new vines. Preston later told us that the old man read philosophy and literature at night. The old man drank red wine every night and so did Preston. If Preston's pronunciation was not right, the old man would throw something at Preston's head, a book or the leather cap the man wore. Preston said it was the best studies he ever had. He learned wines, he learned the French language, the great French writers Zola, Proust, Genet, Sartre.

Our mother became very ill with pneumonia during his absence. Much was said about it being a bad case of double pneumonia in both lungs, and a surgeon pronounced that one lung should be partially removed. I heard all of this in roundabout ways, never directed toward me, snippets of phone conversations and discussions between my parents. My mother was thinner than ever, very weak and wrapped up in her illness. I started scrounging around for food because she wasn't making dinners any more. Somehow a plan was made that instead of undergoing lung surgery, my mother would travel to Florida to convalesce at the winter home of an older couple who were my grandparents' friends.

My father went shopping at Bonwit Teller's downtown and came home with a vacation wardrobe for my mother. There was a white pants suit and a wraparound, designer one-piece bathing suit, and a few other matching pieces.

My father drove her to O'Hare airport one Saturday morning and she was gone. While my mother was in Florida, my great-aunt Evelyn, my mother's only living relative, came to stay with my father and me. She had scoliosis and was always in pain. She lived alone and had never married or had children. I knew that Aunt Evelyn loved Preston very much, and she thought my parents should not have sent him off alone to Europe when he was only seventeen. She talked about him a lot. That was fine with me. I missed him and I wondered about him too. When I was little she liked me a lot and brought me wonderful little dolls and wonderful treats from the bakery near her house. But when she came to stay this time she didn't like me at all. I was thirteen and she couldn't relate to anything about me. She hated that I insisted on wearing the jeans and moccasins I had from our northern Minnesota summers all year round, and especially to school. She hated that I did my homework in my room with my door closed, but it was a habit I didn't want to change. She didn't like to cook and I didn't know how to cook, so we didn't eat well at all. She was always tired and angry because of her scoliosis, but also because she had some crazy ideas that kept her up at night. She would call me down at two in the morning, on a school night, to hysterically say that the refrigerator was about to blow up and that she didn't want to wake my dad but that I should take a look at it.

The first time this happened, I stood in the kitchen with her, both of us in long nightgowns and slippers, she with a lovely quilted robe my mother had given her for Christmas the year before. We stood facing the fridge, waiting for the noise she said indicated that the blowup was imminent.

Then it happened and she said, "There, what's that?! You see? Something's wrong with it! We shouldn't be standing this close to it!"

But I said, "Aunt Evie, it's the ice maker. That's how the ice maker always sounds."

"No, it can't be that. Don't tell me it's just that. This is serious and you haven't even looked into it. You won't even open the door and check to see what's really happening. Nothing that's working properly makes a noise like that."

The new refrigerator always made that noise. I was sure it was nothing but that. "Aunt Evie, I'm sorry, but I have school tomorrow and I'm going back to bed."

"What? You're going to leave me alone with this? Do you want me to wake up your father?"

"No. I think you should go back upstairs and go to bed."

I turned my back on her and climbed the stairs to my room. Aunt Evie had Preston's room in his absence, and I wanted her to go back and shut her door and go to sleep. That's how a person survived in this house, not by getting all worked up about everything. But instead of going back to Preston's room, she tapped on my locked door, and whispered for me to come out and check the refrigerator again. I ignored her and tried to squelch the anger that was welling up inside me. I wanted to scream at her. I wanted people to stop knocking on my bedroom door. I wanted them to stop picking my feeble little lock with a hairpin. I wanted them to leave me alone.

The next morning, I came down dressed for school, very tired and not in a happy mood. There was Aunt Evie, sleeping at the kitchen table, across from the refrigerator, situated so she was facing it, and under her head and folded arms on the table was the huge Chicago city phone book turned to the emergency fire department page.

I prayed every night that my mother would come home. When she finally returned she was listless and self-pitying. Her beauty and air of sophistication were enhanced by her exaggerated weight loss and I was struck by what an exotic creature she had become. When she arrived from Florida, my father picked her up at the airport and brought her home. I was in the kitchen when she walked in. My father was all worried, "Sidney? Sidney, here, help your mother. Ingrid, would you like to sit down? Sidney, help your mother pull out a chair."

Pull out a chair? I thought she was supposed to be better. She was wearing her white turban with her shiny auburn hair tucked behind her ears and hanging straight to her collarbone. I had never seen anyone wear a turban before. It was by Halston, made of a heavy stretch fabric and pulled on like a cap. The turban complemented the white pantsuit and the bathing suit my dad had bought her. Suntanned, she had perfectly painted toes and was wearing light-tan suede sandals, and her gold coin necklace. She wore no shirt under the white jacket, and it fell perfectly against her impossibly thin body. I looked at her in wonder. I really didn't know that people could look so exotically perfect. After a long while, she noticed me looking at her and, now sitting in a kitchen chair, looking like she did not belong there at all, stretched out a thin tanned hand and said, "Come here Sidney dear and give your mother a kiss."

I didn't—and did—want to. I approached her slowly and tried to hug her but she didn't let me, she just turned her cheek toward me and closed her eyes. I kissed her cheek and went up to my room.

Aunt Evie stayed another day or two, helping my mother get acclimated. One afternoon she told my mother that the big brick house on the corner was housing some kind of nighttime drug-trafficking operation. I knew the house was owned by a prominent doctor and his family.

When I shared this with Aunt Evie, she turned to my mother and said, "You see? Just as I suspected. That's how they're getting the drugs."

"Aunt Evie, cars go in and out at night because the doctor is on call. It's just one car and it doesn't go in and out constantly. My room faces their house. Nothing weird is going on over there."

Aunt Evie turned to my mother, "You see what I mean about her? This is how she talked to me the entire time you were gone."

"Mom, Aunt Evie woke me up in the middle of the night a million times telling me the refrigerator was blowing up. I told her it was the ice maker."

"She wouldn't even answer her door when I knocked. She has no respect for anyone. She doesn't listen to anyone."

"How am I supposed to have respect for a bunch of crazy talk about stuff that isn't happening? Forget it! If it isn't real somebody gets to say so!"

My mother was getting upset and who knew what might happen. She might faint, or have to go to bed for the rest of the day. She lifted her shockingly thin wrist to her smooth forehead, ready to make a pronouncement: "Sidney, please . . . "

I did not want to hear one of her invalid speeches.

"Never mind. I'm sorry. I have to do my homework. I'll be up in my room."

After all that, I knew Aunt Evie would never like me again.

Preston returned in May. My dad drove to the airport while Aunt Evie, my mom and I got everything ready for his homecoming dinner. We hadn't seen him in over a year. Aunt Evie made a relish tray and cut little red radishes so they looked like little red and white flowers. I didn't like anything on the relish tray but appreciated that it looked so fancy. My mom was making a beef roast and mashed potatoes, Preston's favorite. Aunt Evie was also overseeing my peeling of the chilled shrimp, making sure I left the tails on for the shrimp cocktail that I was to arrange on small white plates shaped like shells. I was happy Preston was coming and that everyone was cooking together. I was happy that my mom seemed much healthier. She was still very thin, but she was doing more and she seemed happier. We heard the garage door opening and Brandy got up and barked as if he knew somebody special was coming.

The door to the garage opened and there stood my brother, so different. His hair was longer, sun-bleached. His face was wind-burned and tanned like he had spent many hours outdoors. His expression was changed, more serious, thoughtful, older. He was wearing faded jeans and a cotton button-down collared shirt, one I remembered always liking, but which was faded and worn soft like a favorite T-shirt. His eyes were a bit dazed I thought, and I couldn't tell if he was glad to be home or not. He hugged Aunt Evie first, whom he had always loved, and she wiped away tears as he let her go.

Mom gave him a big hug, "Oh Preston, you look good. You look strong like you've been working hard."

"Yeah, I was telling Dad I worked long hours in a field clearing rocks every day unless it rained hard."

Preston was talking in a strange way like he had a foreign accent.

Mom smiled, "Oh, listen to you! I can hear your French accent."

"Yes, well I speak French pretty damn well now. I told Dad I could maybe test out of at least French, maybe German too, for college. I was in Germany at first. I worked for a farmer and he had two wild daughters who were really fun and we had a great time but he didn't need help after the hay was brought in last year so that's when I went to France . . . "

Mom was getting worried about the roast in the oven and said, "Preston, we can hear all about it later. You can't sit down at the table like that. You need to go take a shower and change your clothes."

"No, I don't. I'm fine. I'm not showering every five minutes like you people do any more."

My mother immediately looked at Dad, "Don, please. He needs to shower. We've made a nice dinner. Please, Preston. You need to put on deodorant."

"They don't use deodorant in France, especially not in the countryside where I was."

"Alright well, that's fine for them, but we aren't going to live like that here."

The shower was taken and we all bustled around getting the dinner on the dining room table. It was a chilly rainy evening so Dad started a fire in the fireplace which didn't happen very often mostly because Mom didn't want to get the living room dirty.

From my seat at the dining room table I could see the fire and loved it. Our house felt like a home. My dad poured red wine into all the crystal wine glasses and even a small amount in mine. Preston came down clean and dressed in a heavy, olive-green wool sweater with suede patches on the elbows.

My mother kissed him on the cheek and remarked, "I love that sweater, what a great color on you now with that suntan Preston. You look so European and grown up!"

"Yeah, I forgot I had such nice clothes."

Dad made a toast: "To our young man returned home after a great adventure! May we hear stories for many nights to come and then it's off to college! To Preston!" And we all raised our glasses, "To Preston!"

Preston took a drink. He put his glass down and dropped his head. I was watching him carefully, realizing again that I did not know this changed young man who had been my brother. Really I probably had never known him. I didn't think anyone at the table knew him either. And so much had happened. Were they all pretending that they didn't remember anything bad that had happened? Or did they just want to make it all go away?

Preston was crying. Mom noticed and said, "Preston, are you okay?"

Dad jumped in. "He's fine Ingrid. Leave him alone. He's fine. Preston, come on. Your mother made you this beautiful dinner. You're not going to spoil it now when you just got here?"

Aunt Evie jumped in, "Don, the boy is upset. Something must have upset him."

Mom stood up to refill her sterling silver gravy boat, "I knew he shouldn't have gone. I knew this was too much for a young boy out there alone all that time, who knows what went on . . . "

I looked at my brother again, his head bent, and I noticed a scar above his left eye, a reddish line that ran along his eyebrow and then trailed off to his temple before it disappeared. I wondered what it was from and I knew there was a lot we didn't know about him. He was only eighteen. I knew he was a very sensitive person. I knew that a lot of things hurt him.

I remembered then how on my twelfth birthday our parents did something very out of the ordinary and took us to see Cat Stevens play a big-arena show.

I loved his music and the show was a real life-changer for me. But one of the most moving things was when Cat Stevens sang "Father and Son," one of his most famous numbers, about his frustrations trying to get his aging father to understand him. I was mesmerized by this lone man at the front of the stage in this packed arena singing a song that made every person freeze and not make a sound. At first, as Cat Stevens sang, I didn't notice my brother crying. He was next to me, and when I put my hand on his shoulder I could feel his body wracked with sobs. I started to cry too and he put his arm around me and we let the words Cat Stevens was singing envelope us and speak for us. We were silent all the way home that night.

As I was lost in thought, Aunt Evie was single-handedly saving the homecoming dinner by asking Preston sincere and enthusiastic questions about all the places he'd been and things he'd seen. Later, after we had each eaten a piece of our mom's homemade apple pie, Dad brought out more red wine and he and Preston began to talk in more serious tones about what had happened to him over his long absence. He told the story of the scar while mom was distracted doing the dishes so she wouldn't get too worked up.

"Early on before I took the ferry across from England to France, there was a guy in one of the bars in London who didn't like Americans, or didn't like me, probably both. He kept hassling me until I told him to back off which is when he knocked his glass bottle on the edge of the bar to make a weapon and started yelling, "Come on, come on!" like he was a crazy pirate which he may have been. I was pissed off and told him to leave me alone and pick on somebody his own size because he was pretty heavy, and out of nowhere he jabbed at my face. The bottle was so sharp! It jumped out and cut into my skin so easily. It was like a thing he knew would work."

Mom was back in the dining room holding her dish cloth, her apron with the ironed white ruffles tied around her waist over a sleeveless pale-pink wool dress. "Preston, are you telling the truth? Let me look at the scar," and she lifted her hand to his face and looked closely at the red line, "How did it heal? It looks like it was a very deep cut."

"Well, that's the best part. The bartender saw this guy go after me and now my forehead is bleeding down into my eye."

Aunt Evie, my mother and I all gasped.

Preston excitedly continued, "So he just grabs me by the shoulders and lifts me up 'cause he sees I'm about to faint, and he has me lie down on top of the bar so he can see better. He gets a needle and thread out and he pours me a shot of whiskey. And then he sewed it up with a couple of stitches!"

Preston got the response he wanted from all of us then. Dad was impressed and Aunt Evie and Mom were horrified. I was impressed too. Preston's face was beaming. This was a good night. When it was over, I went to sleep on the carpeted hallway upstairs in my pink flowered sleeping bag because Aunt Evie was staying overnight in my room. Since she didn't drive, Dad would take her back into the city the next day. We were all under one roof, we had good food in our stomachs, and we all loved each other. We really did.

THE CABIN

P reston did test out of French and German and was accepted into a good liberal arts college in Minnesota he wanted to attend especially because it was closer to the cabin our grandfather had always kept north of Duluth near the Canadian border. He had the summer to prepare and then he'd be off to college in the fall. My school got out for the summer and the whole family got in the car like we did every year and headed north. Brandy sat in the back seat of the Jaguar in between Preston and me. We were squeezed in and Brandy drooled on us constantly, but we were excited so we didn't care. Preston curled up and slept most of the way. I usually got carsick on long rides, so we had to pull over a couple times. When I did, Preston woke up to make jokes while I stood knee-deep in wild flowers along the old highway, doubled over. "Sister Sid always barfs right around Janesville. Good job Sid, you made it all the way to Spooner this year."

My parents liked to make this drive. They had similar tastes in music and the drive gave them a chance to listen to whole albums together. They played Beatles tapes in the car's cassette player: "I've Just Seen a Face," the Righteous Brothers: "You've Lost That Lovin' Feeling," the Supremes: "Baby Love," Creedence Clearwater Revival: "Lookin' Out My Back Door."

Our parents sang along and I did too. I liked to riff a harmony part even when there wasn't one on the recording. They listened to folk singers like Simon and Garfunkel and The Kingston Trio too and I liked it all equally. Sometimes my family would say I was a good singer. Sometimes they'd say I was singing so loud that they couldn't hear the tape and they'd make me stop. I knew all the words and could just keep singing along straight through every tape my dad had.

Twelve or thirteen hours in the car is a long time, but we were all so happy to be returning to the beautiful Northwoods that there was no arguing or trouble. On the final stretch down the winding gravel road that lead to Grandpa's old place we rolled down the windows and my mom exclaimed, "Smell that air! It smells like pine! Look at how green everything is! And the lake is up! It must have rained a lot this spring. Look at all the flowers! Isn't it beautiful . . . "

The narrow road was lined with the first blooms of summer, yellow buttercups, white wild daisies with yellow centers, wild phlox in white and pink, Queen Anne's lace.

When Dad eased the car into the old driveway in front of Grandpa's cabin, there was only a faint path of car tires in the grass, which was as high as my knees. We opened all four doors and spilled out. Brandy went crazy with the tall cool grass up to his chin and started darting around back and forth running farther down toward the water each time and back up to the car. He was not a swimmer and the shoreline was rocky, so he stayed away from the water.

My mother fished the old skeleton keys out of her handbag. Grandpa Pederson had been dead for at least five years. He died up at the cabin at the age of 86. In his final years, he stayed all winter. The story I heard was that the natives found him face down in the snow, not far from the cabin door. He may have just had a heart attack. Preston told me Grandpa killed himself on purpose by going out and freezing to death in a snow bank but that didn't make sense to me at all and I told Preston that was stupid. Preston added that Grandpa was an alcoholic and that he got really drunk and then went outside to die. I never believed that either.

My mother had been an only child so now the cabin was ours. We hadn't been there since last August, so the place looked pretty deserted. There were some huge branches lying around in the high grass. The cabin was white with a red roof, "just like in Sweden" my grandfather used to say. And the birches were white "just like the birch forests of Sweden" he would say. Painted red shutters lined each window and each shutter had a pine tree cut out in its center. We all stood examining and admiring the old place. There were branches on the roof too but it was quickly agreed that there was no damage anywhere.

My dad took the keys and fussed and swore until he got the main door open. Everything was orderly and cool and quiet inside. I didn't like to see the cabin with newspaper taped to all the windows and sheets on all the furniture. I helped my mother and we quickly got the windows uncovered and opened to let in the warm fragrant air and the sound of the lapping waves on the rocks below.

Oh God, what a beautiful world it was there! My grandmother had died much earlier but her touches were everywhere. Mom would often refer to things as "my mother's soup tureen," or "my mother's embroidery." My mom was not the kind of parent who made the extra effort to give their children a sense of shared history by saying, "your grandmother's soup tureen," or "your grandfather's tool chest." We always had the feeling that we were guests in her shrine to her parents' memory, to her own wonderful childhood as the precious only child of two people who were very much in love. We were not real players in the game, just spectators as my mother lived out her childhood summer life with her parents.

I was there alone with her for weeks on end throughout my childhood. My dad would take Preston with him and they'd go back to civilization. Preston would have summer school or football camp. Sometimes he would go down to the floor of the stock exchange with my dad in the summers and be a gofer. I heard them talk, but I had no idea what the stock exchange was like and no clue what a gofer would do. I was left to fend for myself all day every day in a beautiful but completely primitive wilderness. Other kids would come for a week or two and stay with relatives or at the resort down the road.

The families that came for just a short time all acted manic, riding on the water, in the water, through the water, in every possible vessel and contraption known to mankind.

The hyper-positive dads in the vacation families would invariably stop by our dock in their speed boat with their kids and water toys spilling out on all sides and try to get me to join them. "Sidney! Hey, Sid! Come on out and join us! Can we pick you up? You want to ski? You want to go tubing?" To me their invitations all sounded like, "do you want to ride around like a bouncing idiot on our inner tube?" and my answer was always a resolute "No thanks."

I hated it when they tried to get me to join them. I would be sitting on the dock in the only bikini I had, a sweatshirt of my brother's over it. My flute and guitar were often laid out on a big quilt covering the wooden boards. I'd have my notebook, and some songbooks, and an issue of *Seventeen* magazine my mother would have bought me the last time we "went into town." I had my day mapped out with practicing, journal writing, songwriting, studying the construction of a famous artist's song. When it got really warm in the mid afternoon I'd swim and work on my stuff some more. I had no goals. I had no dreams. I did not envision myself becoming anything except maybe more fashionable when I went back to school in the fall. I never thought about status clothes like my mother's. I thought about cutting my hair short again and maybe wearing a piece of leather tied around my neck with a few beads on it. I thought about wearing my hooded sweatshirt that was way too small, but pushing up the sleeves and wearing it super tight because it hit right at the top of my jeans and made my curvy figure look pretty nice. I would think of new style ideas during the day and then try them out at night when I would sometimes be allowed to walk down to the resort lodge and play ping pong with the vacationing kids. Many nights my mother didn't let me go because she said I shouldn't make myself into a fixture down there especially since we didn't rent a cabin there. When I was allowed to go she would give me a few quarters which I could ponder the best use of on my walk to the lodge down the gravel road. The local kids from the towns near the lake were around all summer like I was but I didn't run into them very often. Even though I was up there all season long, they didn't entirely trust or understand me probably because I was delivered in a Jaguar from the city of Chicago and went back at the end of the summer never to be heard from again until the following year.

At the cabin, from just after Memorial Day to just before Labor Day I was a girl without a society. My queen was a cruel and unapologetic ruler. I was her Cinderella. I folded clothes, washed windows, swept bugs off screens, spiders out of corners, pumped water from the red iron pump on the porch. I assisted in the kitchen in every conceivable way. I vacuumed the white wool rug in the main room whenever she made me. I carried a big aluminum canoe down the crooked stone steps whenever I wanted to get on the water and carried it back up to the grass each time to be sure it didn't blow away in a storm. But I had endless hours to myself as well. I often begged my mother to come canoeing so I could show her all the wonderful little secret treasures of the shoreline that I had discovered. She maybe ventured out with me in the canoe twice a summer. Usually she got upset and we had to turn back. Mostly I went alone. I liked to go early in the morning and paddle right up to the lake's middle. If it was very still, the sun would come up and shoot its rays in a fine spray of diamonds that would come up right to the edge of the canoe. I liked to go in the mid-afternoon when it was hot enough, even that far north, for me to be wearing just a T-shirt and bikini. I'd paddle to a small island that we could see from our dock slowly around to the far side where the resort people couldn't see me so I could get out of the canoe and drag it by its rope like a pet horse. I'd walk in the cold water in the few places where the bottom wasn't rocky but beautiful fine sand. I'd watch mother ducks with their babies. Mergansers, mallards, wood ducks, all with their own personalities and preferences. I'd watch loons with babies riding on their backs, and painted turtles sunning themselves on floating logs. Most of this was very easy to observe on the far side of the little island. In the early evenings there was the sunset, majestic in its color and splendor, reaching across the big sky over the lake. If I canoed then, I liked to watch the heron getting in his last lone fish of the day. I loved the heron the most maybe because he was silent and serious and alone. As was I.

If I was feeling bitter, I would remember the mid-summer night when I was eleven, at the cabin—only my mother and I. The cabin next door, a short walk by road or through the woods, was full of kids. There were several girls, all cousins, around my age. The parents knew my mother from childhood. These were second and third generation cabin people just like us. Most of the summer I walked the path past that cabin and it was closed, ghostly quiet. But it was alive that week with shouts of laughter morning until night. Canoeing, fishing, boating, swimming, skiing, hiking.

Everyone at that cabin knew me. They tried to include me to an annoying degree sometimes, but this night I especially wanted to be part of their boisterous big family life because they were having a bonfire and they had invited me to bring my guitar and be a part of the evening. One of the dads was a decent guitar player and singer and he had mentioned to me several times that we could play songs around the fire. I put on my best top, a floral-print, long-sleeved, button-up shirt, and dark denim flare jeans. I pulled on my Frye boots. Assessing my getup in the mirror over the pink dresser in my room I looked pretty cool and the mosquitoes wouldn't be able to get at me.

My mom and I were supposed to eat with them at the cookout, after which there would be the bonfire. I was hungry and excited for all the good food.

"Mom, come on, they said five o'clock. Let's go, come on."

"Oh Sidney, I don't think we should just show up and bother them. It's their family. We aren't part of that."

"What? What are you talking about? They invited us! We're supposed to be there already. They are probably wondering what's taking us so long."

"I doubt it. They're having a wonderful time together. They don't need us there. I think we should just stay home."

"What? Mom, no, please, please don't change your mind. They invited us. I'm supposed to bring my guitar and everything."

"Well, that's just them trying to be nice to you. And you can't resist a chance to show off can you? All the more reason we should stay home where we belong. I can make us some tuna salad sandwiches."

"Oh my God Mom, I'm going. I'm going right now. I am invited and you can stay home if you want but I'm not missing this. Goodbye. I'm going. I hope you change your mind. If you don't show up, I'll tell them you weren't feeling very well."

I took the path along the water with my guitar over my shoulder like a hobo with a bag on a stick. As soon as I emerged from the dense foliage the kids all started squealing with delight, "Sidney! You made it!"

The guitar-playing dad greeted me with, "Hey Sid. We were hoping you'd show up soon. We've got lots of good stuff going on that grill and we're gonna need help eating it all. Where's that hermit mother of yours? Isn't she going to make an appearance?"

"I don't know. She says she's not sure if she's up to it tonight."

"Okay, well she's kinda like that. Always has been. You know, I've known your mother since we were little kids up here. An only child is an only child. I'm sure glad you brought that gee-tar. You get better every time I come up here. I bet you're way better than me by now. You're gonna show me up tonight around the fire aren't ya?"

"Well, I don't know, but I do have some new songs."
"Can't wait to hear 'em Sid. Good for you."

I ate with all the crazy fun cousins laughing and joking around at a picnic table set up right by the water's edge. We had hot dogs and cheeseburgers and corn on the cob. I had one of everything. The kids were all excited to make s'mores around the fire afterwards. My mother said s'mores were too unhealthy and messy so I never got to have them.

The bonfire was roaring by the time we finished eating. We burned our paper plates in the fire. The moms had the stuff for the s'mores set out and there were lots of long sticks for roasting marshmallows. I stood with my face getting hot from the fire, shoulder to shoulder with all the other kids. The girls my age were so nice and cute and funny. I was so glad to be a part of their family. Even though I only saw them all once a year for a week or two, I had known them all my life and I felt like they understood me and liked me for who I was. I felt like I belonged. I loved them.

We were stuffing graham crackers and melting chocolate and oozing marshmallow into our happy mouths when my mother came walking silently down from the road.

I heard one of the women greet her and my heart skipped a beat. I looked up and through the twilight I read that face that I knew so well. I watched as they offered her something to eat, something to drink. Someone offered her a beer and I thought, "Oh boy, you guys really don't get her, do you?"

She only accepted a little Dixie cup of the children's lemonade. I knew she was holding herself apart in her head, observing their behavior, their choices, their language, their clothes, and deeming herself superior in every way. I couldn't tell whether they understood what she was really like or whether they just thought she was shy. They were being very nice to her.

Everyone gathered around the fire and the dad with the guitar told me to get mine—I had left it propped against a tree. He sat down next to me on one of the fat low logs set up as stools around the fire pit. I started to play my guitar and he said, "Here Sidney, I'll tune it up for you. Do you know how to tune it?"

"Yeah, I have a pitch pipe for it," I answered.

"Good for you. Okay, let's hear you girl!"

I started in quietly, just kind of playing background music for all the laughing chattering group around the fire. I was determined to not let my mother's face ruin my night. I didn't even look in her direction. I knew instinctively that she would hate that I was playing my music for these people.

I started singing a song that was very popular at the time called "Country Roads" by John Denver. Everybody probably knew the words to that song and sure enough, everyone around the fire, young and old, stopped talking and started humming or singing along. I was glad I had worked as hard as I had on that one. I had the guitar part down and knew all the words. The guitar dad started playing along with a nice picking part that made my performance sound even better. He knew how to sing harmony and he joined in on the chorus and we sounded as great as anything I'd ever done with music so far.

We just kept going after that. He'd start a song and I'd know the words and we'd be off and running. I was so happy I even forgot about my mom. There was a break in the action and I went to use the family's outhouse. When I came out, the girls my age were all gathered in a circle with their moms excitedly scheming.

One of them grabbed my hand. "Sidney, our moms say you can stay overnight! We can all sleep out in the yard in the big tent! Just the girls! The dads are getting the tent out! Ask your mom! Ask your mom!"

I loved the idea of sleeping in a tent. This was something I never got to do and the idea of an all-girls slumber party was really magical to me.

I was so excited I ran over to where my mom was talking to the other moms. "Mom! Did you hear about the big plan?"

My mother turned toward me and the other moms looked at my face and I could immediately tell. They had already broken the idea to her on my behalf and she wasn't buying it.

"Sidney, we need to get going. This is their vacation time and they want to be together. They don't need another child to be responsible for tonight. No, we can go home and sleep in our own beds and get out of their way . . ."

"Mom, they want me to stay."

The girls were all around me now. "Please Mrs. Duncan, let Sidney stay! We want her to! Please!"

"Sidney, get your guitar. It's dark now and we should be getting home."

"Mom, please. I never get to do anything like this."

Now she was hissing, "Sidney, don't you dare embarrass me like this. We are going home."

I pushed past my fear of her. "No Mom, I'm staying. This is a really special night and I am not going to miss out on it."

My mother knew that everyone was aware of what we were saying.

"Sidney, so help me, you get your guitar right now and don't you say another word or you won't be allowed out of the cabin for a week."

"Mom. No. This isn't fair. No."

"Sidney, so help me God . . . "

I snapped. "I Hate You. I'm Not Going Home With You. You go home and be miserable. I'm not coming."

And then she grabbed me by my hair at the back of my head and marched me with her hand tearing at my scalp up the path. I was crying.

"Mom, wait, please, my guitar."

"Go get it."

I ran back down, sobbing, grabbed my guitar. I tried to thank them, but I was so ashamed. I was so broken-hearted. I was so afraid of her. I hated her so much. We walked back to our cabin along the road with my mother's flashlight to guide us. She didn't say anything. I was sniffling. I was thinking about the tent and the girls and the fun we would have had. I was thinking of all the cousins giggling and telling stories with flashlights and sleeping bags in the tent. I felt so tortured to be missing out on one of the rarest of rare chances for me to feel included, to feel like I belonged, to feel like I was part of something. We got to the cabin and once we were inside she started yelling at me.

"Don't you ever think you will ever embarrass and humiliate me like that ever again! Do you think I would ever, ever have told my mother I hated her? You stood there, you little brat, you stood there in front of everyone and said 'I hate you.' Well, you will never do anything like that again. You get in your room and you don't come out. How many days do they have left up here?"

"Six."

"Okay, well that's how long you're grounded. You won't see them again. You won't see anyone. You'll have plenty of time to think about what a terrible girl you are."

The girls came to my bedroom window over the coming days bringing me little treats and telling me stories and secrets about their time at the lake, whispering and tiptoeing around our cabin so my evil mother wouldn't catch them and send them away. The morning they left, my mother let me out. I ran down the road to see if their car was still there but the drive was empty, the cabin closed up with newspapers taped up over the windows.

But that was when I was eleven and now I was fourteen. Preston was staying the whole summer so it wouldn't be just me and the evil queen. With it being Preston's last summer before college, my mother wanted to get as much out of him as she could. She decided he should repaint the cabin—it was white, and she wanted it to stay white, so it was a foolproof project. He was to use a big steel brush and get rid of any loose peeling paint, and paint one side at a time. The cabin was small and only one level so he was pretty cheerful about it. I was happy to have him around.

The summer started with fine weather in June. My mother said it would rain a lot near the end of the month, before the fourth of July, so Preston had better get going with the paint project. Luckily, I didn't get asked at all. I was fourteen, I could have done my share. No one even suggested I help. Apparently painting was perceived as men's work in my family.

Preston and I were held to very different standards in all things. For the most part I was not encouraged to learn or to excel in anything at all and my efforts, as in my flute lessons and choir practices, were seen as annoyances. When it came to grades, Preston was held to very high standards. Once when he was in junior high, he did very poorly. The report card came home with handwritten grades from each of his teachers. All the grades were a C or below. There was at least one D. When Dad came home that night our mother made Preston put the report card on the kitchen table for him to see. Dad took one look at it and lurched at Preston, grabbed him by his shirt and started screaming into his face, "What the hell is this? What are you, retarded? Are you unable to learn? Are you lazy? What the hell did you do all semester? Do you sit up there playing with that little pud of yours? Are you playing with yourself instead of studying? I ought to kick your ass right out of this house for this!"

I always earned good grades and teachers usually said how much they liked me. I was often singled out for higher-level small groups and activities. In sixth grade, I was invited to be in a special test group for gifted children called the Learning Inquiry Lab. The parents were to attend a presentation on the individual classroom projects their sons or daughters were working on. Mine was an oil painting of the lake in the summer as seen from our cabin window. My parents came, my father in his three-piece suit, acting very uncomfortable and constantly whispering to my mother, "Let's get going. We've been here long enough" loudly enough for me and the others to hear him. My mother seemed to view the event as an honor and smiled when she inspected my painting. They were supposed to walk around the small classroom and observe each kid's project. People were making different kinds of things. I thought it was very interesting and exciting and loved being a part of it. I thought we were all brilliant as did our strangely eccentric teacher who didn't teach anything else at the school and was referred to as Doctor. She wore her dark hair in a bun and had an elegant stance and a ballerina's long neck. We probably didn't understand the full weight of her background or personality. I got the feeling that my parents could not understand how incredible an honor this was for me to be a part of this group with a brilliant woman as our guide and instructor. They left that night in what seemed to me a mutual shrug, "Huh, that Sidney. Well, that was interesting. Kind of a weird deal. And what an odd woman the teacher was."

The scraping and painting were in full swing all summer. Preston would sleep in very late and then start drinking a lot of coffee and smoking cigarettes, which he had started doing in Europe. He would put on a white T-shirt and an old white canvas boating hat that belonged to Grandpa. He wore torn jeans with plenty of air holes to stay cool and his rubber flip-flop sandals. He stood on one of the porches, smoking, thinking, drinking coffee. Brandy would cry at the screen door to sleep in the sun on the porch at Preston's feet. Brandy didn't like the woods that much and he didn't want to go down on the scary wooden dock since he didn't like to swim, so he enjoyed having Preston up around the cabin all summer. One morning I let Brandy out to see Preston and decided to stay out there and talk. Preston started talking philosophy. I knew very little of the names and the perspectives he was throwing out. When he started ranting in French I had to interrupt and say, "I can't understand you!"

"Sister Sid, you got to get an education! What the hell are you learning? I thought you said you take French at school."

"I take French. I don't speak French. I don't understand anything you say. You speak way too fast for me. And you're probably using words I've never even heard of."

"No excuse. Get one of my books out and read it. Read it out loud. Do it."

"I'm not reading in French, forget it."

"How about in English then? You probably don't know half of those words either. Get a book off the shelf in there from the ones I brought. Pick one and start reading it out loud to me. It'll be fun. I'll help you."

I went inside the cabin and I saw that Preston had added a small stack of new paperbacks to Grandpa's tall double bookcase groaning already with impressive old collections like the entire works of Mark Twain. Preston's books all had foreign titles and shiny paperback covers. I picked one called *L'Assomoir* by Emile Zola because the cover showed a painting of a beautiful and very young girl.

I reappeared on the porch and Preston looked happy.

"Zola, bon choix!"

The book was a translation in English, but Preston was right, it was still difficult for me at fourteen. I read out loud as the little girl went through her terrible troubles, and Preston painted and we had many happy hours that way.

At night Preston went down to the one-room guest-house by the water and wrote his own stories at his small black metal typewriter.

He would put on his big wool sweater and black wool beret and write well into the night, all the windows open to the sounds of the water, moths flapping madly to get through the screens to the lamplight. Sometimes I went down to see him. He'd step outside and light a cig-arette and tell me strange tales of Europe. Our mother read a book or flipped through fashion and home-deco-rating magazines. She also knitted a pretty cream-colored hat, scarf and mitten set for herself, although a cou-ple times she had me try them on and said I could wear them. She also worked on some very intricate argyle socks for Preston and my dad and taught me how to use the bobbins of different colored yarns and how to read the pattern book and count the stitches. We didn't have a television at the cabin and we were all proud of that.

Although I had much to keep me busy—my musical instruments, journal for writing down song and poetry ideas, and my sketchpad and colored pencils, along with forays out in the canoe, I still had many hours with noth-ing to do. I often walked the roadside with Brandy with a small basket in case I came upon good raspberries.

My grandmother's straw hat hung in the cabin's liv-ing room and I liked wearing it. My mother didn't like it herself so she didn't care that I wore it. I had made a halter-top out of two red bandanas I found in a dress-er drawer. I borrowed the idea from an article in *Seven-teen* magazine that showed how to take a piece of white rope and two bandanas and with just a bit of sewing, make a really cute summer top to wear with jean shorts.

Surprisingly we had everything I needed and I fashioned mine just the way the model's looked. It tied with the rope at my neck so it came up high and the two bandanas met in front so it didn't show any cleavage; it was all just gathered fabric in front. But my stomach showed which was nice because I was in good shape and a bit suntanned. I loved not having to wear a bra with it. I wore my high-waisted denim shorts and paired them with my tan leather sandals with thick cork soles that showed off my long legs. I wore this outfit whenever I went raspberry hunting with Brandy and I felt great, like a Northwoods version of a pin-up girl, or maybe even a movie star.

One day I was out with Brandy, picking berries on the side of the gravel road. Out of nowhere against the blinding afternoon sun, a cute boy peddled right up on a bicycle and stopped just inches from me. I had never seen him before.

He was smiling and had sunburns on his cheeks and nose. His hair was sandy blonde and tousled in the way that was truly beautiful because it was so natural. I immediately thought, "This is a wood nymph or a leprechaun. This is not a real person. Or a centaur maybe . . . " But he was my size, a few inches taller, and wearing a T-shirt and jeans like a regular kid. He seemed to be my age.

He said hi and I said hello and I felt my face breaking into a wide genuine smile. Whoever he was, he was wonderful. Maybe he was an angel. We smiled perfectly mirrored smiles.

"My name is Jay. I think you know my cousins. They have the cabin next to yours."

Yes, I did know them. I'd known them all my life. But how had I never met this boy? He said he grew up in the nearby town and didn't come out here much but this summer he was helping his dad fix up their lake place, which was right down the road, to be his parents' new year-round home.

I introduced him to Brandy. "Ha!" he laughed, "I've never seen that kind of dog in real life. He looks so ferocious, but he's gentle, isn't he?" I noticed the lilt of his charming northern accent, much like a Canadian's. Brandy was licking his hand.

"Yes, he always scares delivery men when they come to our house in Chicago. They think he's a mean watchdog but he isn't a good watchdog at all. He wags his tail at everyone."

The boy was quiet. He was obviously thinking about something I said. "Chicago, huh? That's a long way from here. Do you miss your friends at home?"

"I don't know, not really. I don't usually have a lot of friends and I am used to being here every summer."

"Well, do you have many friends here?"

"Not really. I know a lot of kids but most of them only come up for like a week."

"Well, the good news is now you know me! I have to go see my cousin, but I will look for you again, okay?"

"Yes of course! I'm always around. Usually down on our dock."

"Okay, well now you have a new friend. Remember Jay, like blue jay. That's my favorite bird."

"Okay, I will remember. And my name is Sidney."

"I kind of already knew that."

"You did?"

"Well, there aren't many interesting people up here so word gets around . . . interesting and pretty."

I smiled. He did too. He said goodbye to Brandy and rode off. I thought about him the rest of the day and at night when I went to bed. I tried to remember his happy face. I hoped I'd see him again soon.

My days were magical as the summer progressed. I read to Preston. I played my instruments and wrote songs and stories and poems in my notebook. I took out the canoe and went wading and swimming. I walked Brandy and picked berries. And soon I looked forward to Jay stopping by as he often did. I found out he was two years older than me, that his dad was a carpenter, and that he had two older sisters and two older brothers. He was the baby and his whole family was crazy about him.

My mother liked him a lot too. Almost too much, I thought. And Preston did too. Everyone enjoyed his company, his lilting accent, his cheerful open personality. He kissed me on the cheek one day when we were sitting in the grass with Brandy, just talking and enjoying the warm sun. That was my first kiss from a boy and I thought it was perfect that it was so sudden and sweet and on my cheek. I loved it and took the thought of it with me everywhere.

DAD ARRIVES

The
cabin was
bright white by
August and Preston had a tall stack
of loose white paper covered with black
typewriter ink in the little guesthouse. I
had a journal full of my earnest efforts and
had written a song or two on my guitar
which I performed for my mother, who
said they were too depressing, and
for Preston who said I was very smart
and was going to amount to something
some day if I just kept going and didn't
listen to our stupid parents.

I was standing out on the back porch talking
with Preston one morning while he smoked and
drank coffee when I heard Jay's loon whistle approaching. Jay would cup his hands, blow between his thumbs
and flail his fingers to let the air out in a whistle that nicely
imitated a loon's call. I learned how to do it too. Jay would
whistle before he came onto our property. It was like a
warning to me that he was going to be coming down

the path from the road. It was like a courtesy at a time when we had no phones and his arrival was always unplanned and unanticipated. I heard his call and realized he'd be undoubtedly meeting my father for the first time.

Dad arrived the night before and slept much of the morning. I thought my dad had a very difficult transition coming from the big city of Chicago, from the floor of the stock exchange all day. Everything at the cabin was a very different experience. During the day it was about self-directed activities and sun and wind and waves and the hot dusty road. At night it was still, the moon bright over the water, and sometimes the cabin didn't cool down much, and you could hear the lapping of the waves and the calls of the loons. There was no white noise of air conditioning or traffic. There was no television to stare at from your bed late at night. When Dad did wake up, who knew what kind of mood he'd be in!

Jay appeared out of the woods on foot. He had taken the old deer path along the water along the point. Preston, Jay, and I began talking and joking.

Within minutes my mom came out onto the porch exclaiming, "Well, Jay! I didn't know you were here! I would've come out sooner!"

Mom was wearing one of her favorite nightgown and robe combos, ridiculously glamorous and mod, especially at the cabin. Made by one of her favorite designers, Emile Pucci, it was a slinky and somewhat transparent swirl of psychedelic pastels with a plunging neckline. It had a matching transparent robe that had one little fastener at the waist to hold it together. Her suntanned chest was all exposed and you could see the outline of her breasts.

Jay was polite and nice as always, "Hello Mrs. Duncan. It's a beautiful day! You should be outside enjoying it!"

"Oh yes it really is Jay, and you know what I said about calling me Ingrid."

I didn't like that my mother insisted he call her by her first name.

"Yep, Ingrid, got it. Well, you're missing the sunshine."

"Oh well, I am slow today, but I'm going to get dressed now and get going!"

Mom pranced through the living room to the bathroom and shut the door.

Good old Preston chimed in, "Yeah and quit walking around in your half naked nightgown Mom . . . too much information for our friend Jay here . . . too much information for anybody . . . "

Suddenly Dad was in the doorway, "Preston, don't talk to your mother that way. Why what is she wearing anyway?"

Preston smiled, "Dad, she came out to say hi in her slinky nightgown. She was being a not-ready-for-prime-time player."

Dad was silent for a moment, then asked Preston, "Where the hell's the coffee?"

Jay and I looked at each other and I felt that he could read the expression on my face. He and I had already had a few conversations about my family. I was surprised that each time we talked he was so clear and honest in his observations. I often thought about what he said to me about my mom, "Sidney, your mom is very competitive with you. It's not right. A mother should be proud of her beautiful, intelligent daughter but instead she tries to make you look bad to me and herself look good. It's wrong and it makes me feel so sorry for you to have a mother like that." I wondered what he'd have to say about my father.

Dad was back on the porch now with a steaming cup of coffee and he turned to Jay, "Who's this?"

He was staring at Jay, expecting him to answer.

Dad was already dressed for the day in a short-sleeved oxford dress shirt and Madras plaid Bermuda shorts, peering accusatorially at Jay over brown horn-rimmed glasses. He had a very close-cropped dark beard and was nearly bald. He was six foot two to Preston's five foot ten and Jay's five foot nine, and weighed over two hundred pounds when each of the boys were probably around a hundred and sixty. I looked at my father through Jay's eyes and guessed that my father looked pretty arrogant and vain. Everything he wore looked brand new and as my dad would say "classy."

Jay, in his faded blue T-shirt and his dirty jeans, smiled his impish but knowing grin as he addressed my father for the first time, "Hello, Mr. Duncan. I've been looking forward to meeting you. I heard you were coming up last night. My name is Jay and I'm a friend of your daughter's."

"A friend of my daughter's? You don't get to decide that. You don't announce that to me. I'll decide whether you're a friend of anybody's around here. Things are going to straighten up around here now that I'm back."

"Yes, I can see that sir."

Preston looked at me and I tried not to smile.

My mom was dressed and out of the bathroom. She was wearing one of her very short daytime dresses, yellow and white with white plastic buttons down the front and matching yellow shorts underneath. She had a few buttons unbuttoned so the shorts could show more. The outfit was very cute on her with her suntan. She had white Keds that she bleached if they ever got too dirty. She never wore much makeup, and especially at the cabin, it was just a little bit of mascara and some peachy lipstick. Her hair was shoulder-length and shiny brown. She had it pulled back in a low ponytail and her high forehead made her seem very elegant.

Mom hurried into the kitchen and came back out onto the porch offering Jay some of her homemade blueberry cake, setting a slice on a little china plate with a fork. Jay loved my mom's cooking. He loved anybody's home-cooking. He was that kind of kid. He immediately started eating.

I hadn't had breakfast yet so I went to the kitchen to get myself a piece too. I saw my mother looking me up and down in my cutoffs and tight T-shirt, "What are you doing? Oh, no, you're not eating cake for breakfast. You ought to be having something less fattening and more nutritious. I can make you some scrambled eggs."

My mom knew I loved her blueberry cake with fresh whole blueberries and cinnamon sugar crumble topping. She knew I loved it. She also knew I despised scrambled eggs. When I was little she used to make me sit at the table until I ate all the scrambled eggs she put on my plate. I hated them then too. She would make me sit into the afternoon. The eggs would be hard and cold. I would be crying. I hated the eggs and I hated her. I had no way of knowing that melting a piece of cheese over it would have made all the difference. If I had known, I could have suggested it. But she probably did know. She knew I loved cheese. Why didn't she ever offer to make them differently? No, just the same miserable, hard, salty, horrible, rubbery eggs every day and the same punitive struggle. Then when there were pancakes or waffles or blueberry cake she would make me feel bad for feeling happy about it.

"Here Sidney, bring Jay this glass of orange juice."

I was mad, "Mom, who said he wanted orange juice?"

"He loves this, and his parents don't buy nice fresh-squeezed juices like this . . . he told me that . . . you really don't know him very well do you? Come on now, bring this out to him and put a smile on your sour little face so he can see your good side and not just your grouchy old Sidney side."

"Bring it to him yourself if you think he wants it so badly."

"Sidney, don't you dare start talking to me like that or I will get your father in here and you can tell him how you've been talking to me."

I grabbed the glass of juice. When some of it spilled, she took it right back from me and pinched my upper arm with her other hand.

She hissed through her teeth, "You brat. If you don't watch it your little boyfriend is going to get sent home. You better get an attitude adjustment and put a smile on that long face."

I stayed inside and let my mom go out on the porch. I heard her being extra cheerful and energetic and flirtatious with her male audience. Two things she really got revved up over: putting down her female adversary, and enjoying her all male conquests. I stayed inside because I was so full of rage. I was a happy person. I didn't have a "long face." I was not grouchy or mean. I only acted like that around her and then she thought that's how I always was. When she went to my conferences at school, on the rare occasion she ever did, she would come home saying, "Well Sidney, they all think you're just the most wonderful girl in the world. I told them, 'I don't think we're talking about the same person!' I just laughed when they said how helpful and cheerful and talkative you are. You sure have them fooled."

I went into the bathroom and shut the door. I looked at my face in Grandpa's old shaving mirror. "What good does it do to hate your own mom like this?" I said out loud to myself. What good did it do to sit around and miss out on the fun? Nobody else cared that I was in here suffering under her stupid injustices, least of all her. I went back out. Everyone was laughing and talking. I was happy that everyone liked Jay and I was glad he was willing to stand around and talk with my family.

A couple more days passed with all four of us living in peace and then my parents said we'd be shutting off the water and getting ready to close up the cabin that night. We'd be leaving the next morning to take Preston to his new school which was about five or six hours away.

I felt much worse than I thought was possible about leaving Jay. Although we had only known each other for a few weeks this summer, I felt he had shown me in a new light. His compassion for my circumstances within my family was something I had never experienced. I knew my relationship with him was special. My mom knew it too. I kept thinking of a conversation I had with her about Jay.

One night a few weeks earlier, my mother was making me vacuum the living room rug before I could go out for a walk to the lodge with Jay. It was early evening, very warm, with the late summer sun streaming into the cabin front windows and the lake was sparkling and blue. Jay had arrived and I had just put the vacuum away.

My mother was standing in the living room with her hands on her hips saying, "What do you think you're doing Sidney? It still has leaves stuck in it. Look at this. You can't just wave the vacuum over it. It's not a magic wand."

She was catching Jay's eye and trying to be mocking and cute at the same time. "Come on Sidney. Get that vacuum out and do it right or I guess Jay will be going down to the lodge without you tonight."

"Mom, those leaves are just stuck in there. They don't come out. It's too thick of a carpet for a cabin. Who has a cream-colored shag carpet in a cabin? It doesn't make any sense."

"This is a fabulous piece and since when do you know anything about decorating. You're just going to have to get down there and pull the bits that aren't getting picked up with the vacuum by hand. You're going to have to do some real work for once."

I turned on the very loud and very large old metal vacuum so I couldn't hear her any more. She and Jay were in the kitchen talking and I was on my knees trying to get little bits of dried leaves untangled from the cream wool of my mother's large expensive designer rug. I kept at it until it looked pretty close to perfect. I turned off the vacuum and put it away in the front closet.

Jay and I headed out the door. On our walk Jay said to me, "I really hate to see your mother treat you like that. It isn't right."

I didn't like to think anyone would feel sorry for me so I brusquely answered, "It's no big deal. She's just like that sometimes. She's a neat freak."

When we got back to the cabin that night Jay only stayed a minute and then walked back to his cabin. My mother was reading in a chair in the living room. She stopped me before I went in to get ready for bed.

"Sidney, that Jay really thinks a lot of you. I think he's in love with you. I've caught him just staring at you a few times."

"I don't know about that but he is nice. I really think he's a good person."

"Well, you've got him wrapped around your finger."

"It's not like that Mom."

"He's a very special young man. I'm not sure what he sees in you or why he thinks so highly of you. It's really something! I just hope you appreciate how much he cares about you."

"He's nice. Yeah, I know. It's not that big of a deal."

"Really, not that big of a deal? Well, when you were finishing the vacuuming tonight he turned to me in the kitchen and said he didn't like to see you have to be on your knees doing that kind of work. I said 'Oh please, a little vacuuming isn't going to hurt her' and he said 'Yes, well what she is having to do is beyond that.' I mean, I never knew a boy to be so tenderhearted, so concerned."

"He is really nice I know. But also, it's not a very practical carpet. Goodnight."

"Goodnight? You aren't in charge of the decorating. My parents left this place for me so I would have something. I have tried to keep it nice and make improvements. Do you think I ever complained when I was asked to help? My mother was dead by the time I was eighteen. I would have given anything to have her here with me. I was just trying to tell you that I think Jay is a wonderful young man, really darling and special."

I thought of my mother's words over and over when I went to bed that night. I thought of them as I tried to get prepared to say goodbye to the cabin, the lake, and Jay.

On our last evening at the cabin Jay came to say goodbye. He and I stood together out on the kitchen porch looking over the lake. I was teary about leaving the cabin, leaving the woods, and leaving him. I was saying how Chicago was so different and how I couldn't just go out in the woods or get in a canoe and be free there.

My mom came out onto the porch. "Jay, have you ever been to Chicago?"

"No, I haven't. I've been down to The Cities a few times though."

"Oh well 'The Cities' of Minneapolis and St. Paul are nothing compared to Chicago. Chicago is truly world-class. These Minnesota cities are like farming communities. They have so little to offer.

"You know, I was thinking maybe you could ride down with us and spend a few days with us in Chicago. Preston will be dropped off after the first part of the drive and then it'll just be Sidney and Brandy in back so we'd have room. You could stay in Preston's room for the weekend and we can buy you a Greyhound bus ticket to come back up the following Monday. What do you think?"

I was astonished. I couldn't even imagine how she had come up with this. I wasn't even sure it made any sense or was a good idea at all. Take the wood nymph out of the woods? What would Jay look like next to the city kids back home? What would his T-shirts and his home-cut curls hanging over his eyes look like in the Chicago suburbs? I didn't know if I wanted to find out. How would his self-assured ways, his loon calls, his knowledge of trees and changes in the weather be altered by putting him in such a different environment? What would it be like to expose him further to the ugly inner workings of my parents' home life and their treatment of me? What would happen if they really got mad and he saw how they act then? I wasn't sure he should be exposed to any of this. On the other hand, maybe it would be great for me. I could take him around and show my city friends what a real boy from the woods looked and acted like. They would see his noble integrity and his non-materialistic ways. They would understand why I loved my summers so much. They would be impressed and finally understand. Best of all, he'd be with me and we could have a few more days of fun.

"Will you?" I asked him.

"Do you want me to?"

"I would love it. It would be really cool. We could go down to the Art Institute and you could see the John Hancock Building too. It would be really great."

"I can ask my parents. If they say yes, I'll do it."

Then to my mom Jay said, "Ingrid, what does Mr. Duncan think of this? Is he all right with this idea of me coming?"

"Oh, don't worry about him, I'll talk to him."

Jay left quickly and was back within an hour saying, "My parents say it's a good opportunity and I can do it. They are giving me some cash to have in my pocket so I don't go empty handed. My mother says she will help me pack a bag for tomorrow morning."

My mom was thrilled. "Oh, this is so great! All right, well, we'll pick you up early then. Is eight tomorrow morning too early for you? You'll see our car. We'll just pull into your driveway so we don't disturb your family."

Jay smiled at me. "Okay, see you in the morning," he said, and mussed up my hair with his big hand. I hugged him quickly and smelled his sweet woodsy scent in his soft hair.

After he left I went to bed with a strange feeling I couldn't pinpoint and couldn't shake.

In the middle of the night there was a commotion and suddenly my parents' bedroom door slammed open. My dad burst out into the living room in just a T-shirt, shouting my name, "Sidney? Sidney, wake up! What is this? Who's this fucking hick with the little prick worming his way into my family? You want this kid in your pants; is that what this is all about? You think he cares about you? You want him to come home with you, bring him home to your bed like a stuffed animal with a little penis to play with? Do you think he cares about you? You think he's attracted to you?"

My mom came padding barefoot out from the bedroom. She stopped in my bedroom doorway holding him back with her hands in from of her at his chest, "Don, stop this. Please Don!"

He grabbed her thin upper arm with one hand, "You think he's after you when he's got this in front of him? Look at this woman. You think he's going to be after you when he's got a beautiful woman like your mother throwing herself at him? You're a fool, Sidney. You're the smokescreen. He's fucking her! They're fucking!"

"Don, for God's sake! Stop talking like that. You've made this all up. Stop it. Go back to bed."

I had no idea what to think. I went to the bathroom and shivered, peeing into the cold toilet. My mind and my heart thought something was wrong about bringing Jay home with us, but I wanted him to come. My parents went back to bed. Preston must have slept through the whole thing. I went out to the living room and kissed Brandy on his nose and wrapped an old crocheted afghan around him.

I got up early the next morning because I wanted to help things go smoothly. Our parents were always in bad moods when we closed up the cabin for the winter but this morning was a new level of torture. The shocking words from the night hung over me, as I assumed they did over us all. Maybe my father had been drunk and didn't remember what he had said. I had no idea what my mother was thinking.

Dad did not like to crawl under the cabin on the bare ground and lie on his back doing whatever you had to do to shut down the little handmade water pump that Grandpa made thirty years before. Dad was not that kind of guy. His parents were merchants from Italy, they were interested in business, in fine things. They were not purposefully heading to the northernmost regions of wilderness for their vacations. He was never at home at the cabin and he didn't like the responsibilities my mom placed on him. When he came to the cabin it was always for just a few days, at most a week. He sought out social opportunities with the local people— taking his Jaguar in to the town garage and standing around with the mechanics while they all "cracked a beer and looked over the engine . . . so clean you could eat off it . . . " He bought a boat and became friends with the marina owner so he could store the boat during the winter months. He bought fishing equipment all the time and made friends with all the canoe outfitters in the nearby town of Ely. Usually there was a beer or a shot of whiskey employed in good fellowship wherever he went. He liked to buy the guys he knew a "nice bottle of Jack Daniel's" and stop in for a visit. He may have had friends up there, but a woodsman and a handyman he was not.

Dad was under the house and Preston and Mom were packing, so I was standing down by the crawlspace door peering into the semidarkness watching my dad on his back lying on a plastic garbage bag, tinkering with the pump and cursing my dead Swedish grandpa.

"Sidney, look at this piece of shit! It's literally made out of a fucking tin can. Do you see this?" In fact the main body of the thing appeared to be housed in a red-and-black old-style metal Folger's coffee can. "Goddamn cheap Swede. Why would anybody come up here to no man's land and build a shack like this. And your mother thinks it's fucking paradise. Leaves me alone to work all summer, drags you kids up here . . . "

I was wondering if we were still bringing Jay. I was too afraid to say anything so I just did whatever anyone asked me to do. I got Brandy ready and carried his blanket and his bag of food to the car. We had a really small car for times like this. I was going to be sitting with a bag of dog food and my little duffle bag under my feet with Brandy on my lap, especially if we were really going to squeeze Jay in. I wondered if Preston knew Jay was coming. I just went in my room and packed my few things and locked the wooden window latches and made sure everything looked the way my mom liked it.

We finally all piled into Dad's car. The newspapers were taped to the windows and the cabin looked ready for the winter. Preston was silent next to me with a book on his lap. I put my arms around Brandy's neck. "It's gonna be you and me this winter buddy . . . " I whispered in his ear. He licked my face and I was so glad he was part of the family.

We only had a half-mile drive before we'd be at Jay's cabin. Had my mom said anything? Nobody was talking.

Suddenly, my mom said, "Don, don't forget we're picking up Jay."

My dad was silent.

Preston blurted, "What?!"

Preston glowered at me as Dad pulled into Jay's driveway. I had never been to the cabin. I had only met his mother once for a second on the road. She was a very nice woman, much older than my mom, much heavier-looking, more like a grandmother, but she was very kind and patient and I knew she was wonderful just by that one meeting and by everything her son would say about her and his father. Still, I didn't want to have to go up to the door. The whole situation seemed so awkward. I didn't feel like I was the one inviting him.

Mom said, "Sidney, go get him. Yes Preston, what does it matter to you? Sidney has invited him to visit with us for the Labor Day weekend and we can't go back on that."

Dad was totally silent and Preston looked concerned as I scrambled out of the back seat. I walked down to knock on the door of the cabin, which was not a cabin at all, much more of a ramshackle but solid year-round home. I stepped onto the porch and peered in through what I noticed was the kitchen door. Inside I could see a big wood stove and lots of wood stacked. There was insulation showing in some places and plywood showing on part of the floor. I remembered Jay saying that his mother would sometimes say that the house of a carpenter is always the last one to get finished. But finished or not, their house looked like a serious fortress made to withstand the northern winters. It made our little cabin look like a silly little playhouse. I had not realized how heavy-duty places up here were for those who stayed all winter.

Jay opened the door with his usual impish grin multiplied because of the upcoming adventure. I tried my best to mirror his enthusiasm. He introduced me in his most formal tone, "Sidney I would like you to meet my father. Come in for a minute."

I followed Jay into the main room. Sitting in a big old recliner chair with stuffing spilling out, was a grey-haired man in work pants and a work shirt, big lace up boots on his propped up feet. A television in the corner was blaring the local news.

The man smiled when he looked at me and said, "Oh she's a looker isn't she? No wonder you're gonna follow this one to the ends of the earth."

I said, "Hello Mr. Mayer, it's nice to meet you."

"Oh no it isn't and you know it. Now you kids have a good time and send him home when you're good and sick of him."

I laughed and Jay laughed.

Jay gave his dad a big hug, "Don't get up Dad. We'll just say bye to Mom and be on our way."

Jay beckoned for me to follow him into the back kitchen, on the lake side of the house. His mother was wearing an old-style apron with flour smeared across the blue in a cloud of white. A wooden spoon jutted from a pocket. Her hair was set in pin curls in the way women used to in the '50s. She was cooking something sweet and greasy on the stove and the strong smoky smell of bacon filled the room.

"Oh now Jay, I have freshly made doughnuts for you all for the road. Hello there Sidney! Nice to see you again. I'm going to give you a paper bag full of my cinnamon sugar doughnuts for your trip. Just a second more here. I've got them ready."

She was fussing with layers of paper towels and there were all these beautiful fresh doughnuts rolled in cinnamon and sugar on cookie sheets on the wooden table in the middle of the room.

She finished assembling the bag of maybe a dozen doughnuts and handed it to me. "Okay now, this is for your family. You take good care of my Blue Jay here. He's gonna need some looking after in the big city of Chicago."

"I will. He'll be great Mrs. Mayer. Don't worry. Thank you for the doughnuts, they look wonderful."

"Well, you can't taste 'em with your eyes sweetie. Here's an extra one for you so you don't have to wait."

She handed me a hot fresh doughnut from the sugar rolling plate and gave me a paper towel. I stood eating it and licking my fingers thinking that my family was going to hate this smelly greasy bag stinking up the car and they'd be mad because we took way too long.

But the doughnut was really delicious.

We said a last goodbye and left the house walking together to the car. I didn't like being seen by my family walking side by side with Jay because it looked like I brought this on everybody. But I knew it wasn't my idea. We had the door open and were getting in the back, when Jay was already offering everyone a doughnut. The sweet smell permeating the car would normally be heavenly but under the circumstances, made me want to gag.

I heard myself saying, "It's gonna be pretty tight 'til we get to Preston's school I guess."

Jay asked, "What's that, like a bit south of The Cities, eh?"

Preston was nice enough to answer, "Yeah, it's like five hours. Maybe six. Let's hope Sid doesn't get car sick. Jay, did she tell you she pukes when she rides in cars?"

"Shut up, Preston."

Mom jumped right in with, "Sidney, don't say those words. Don't start in like that. Please. We want this to be a nice trip. Jay, how are you this morning? Are you excited?"

"Well, yes I am. And how are you Mr. Duncan? Did that tin can water pump give you any trouble?"

No answer. Silence all around.

"Don, please, Jay is asking you something."

Silence. We were leaving the peninsula and turning on to the main road.

Dad decided to say, "Jay, I understand you're in for the long haul with us today."

"Yes, sir, I hope that's all right with you sir."

"Well, whether it is or not doesn't seem to be of any consequence at this point."

Mom threw out a helpless, "Don . . . "

I looked at Jay sideways and shrugged. Jay looked at Preston who shrugged too and opened the doughnut bag.

"Off we go," I said to myself.

The trip was long and we were squished but it was fun to have Jay along and he and Preston were happily joking with each other. Mom and Dad seemed to be okay. Everyone enjoyed the doughnuts in spite of themselves.

Brandy was on my lap and I had to sit with one foot on either side of the bump on the car floor but I was just glad nothing bad was happening.

We arrived in Preston's new town. Northfield had two colleges, Preston was saying. "One college is Lutheran and has a really good music program. The other is known for intellectualism and drugs and student suicides . . . guess which one I'm going to."

Preston laughed and Mom admonished, "Oh really Preston, your father is paying for you to go to this very prestigious school and that is no way to talk about it."

Dad had been there once already when he and Preston drove up from Chicago for an interview. He knew his way around. He and Preston agreed on where to park the car. The car doors were flung open and we all spilled out gratefully. I had the leather dog leash wrapped around my wrist and when Brandy lurched off my lap I realized both my feet had fallen asleep so I had pins and needles. I walked gingerly to a stand of trees for Brandy to relieve himself.

Dad seemed genuinely excited about the school. He and Preston pointed out the beautiful buildings, old and picturesque. The campus looked like a really nice park, with rolling grassy hills and a pretty stone bridge over a brook. For a minute, I wondered what it would be like to go to college. It seemed very free and very romantic. I thought about books and the kinds of discussions Preston and I had about Emile Zola's story over the summer and I realized I was going to miss my brother. I wondered if I'd ever go to college. For a fleeting second I thought about how someone like Jay, for all his good heartedness and innate dignity, was not really capable of that type of literary discussion and maybe never would be.

Mom, Dad, and Preston were carrying his things to the dorm. Jay and I had Brandy who wasn't allowed inside.

We walked the campus and saw some very unusual looking characters. There was a girl in a long embroidered dress and heavy leather boots walking across the stone bridge singing what sounded like an aria in Italian. Wow! That was freedom. There were kids who looked dirty and grimy with cigarettes and unusual hats, beads around their necks; young men with long hair, and scarves at their necks; girls with very long or very short hair, ethnic jewelry, flowing gauzy clothes. I remarked that Preston was going to fit right in.

Before long, Preston had Mom and Dad heading to the car. My brother lost whatever nervousness he had very quickly. He came over to Jay and me and said that his new roommate was a cool dude and that he was pretty sure the kid was high already. Jay seemed impressed. Preston seemed elated. "Okay, well I'll see you guys at Christmas, huh? Right Dad? I'll take the bus home for Christmas?"

Dad nodded. He was obviously eager to get back on the road because we had a long drive ahead of us.

"Preston, you haven't eaten hardly anything all day. Is there going to be a meal for you kids?" Mom was worrying. I hated it when she suddenly decided to play the nice mom act. What did she think Preston did all the months he'd been away from her?

"Mom, yeah, it's college. There are two cafeterias and they're open the rest of the day. I'll probably get my roommate and some of the other guys and we'll go check it out. Okay well, goodbye everybody, thanks for getting me here. Dad, thank you. I really think we picked the best place."

He looked at Jay and then at me. "Okay, well don't get into trouble you two. Bye Brandy, you old stinker."

He started to walk back toward his dorm, we were all in the car, the windows open, Dad slowly pulling out onto the street, when Preston turned and as a seeming afterthought called out, "Okay people. Make it home without anybody getting hurt, right?"

Dad let out a sarcastic laugh and pressed harder on the gas. I could see my brother in the rearview mirror, waving.

We drove a long way in silence. The back seat was

comfortable now for Jay and me. Brandy had been lying on the seat between us, but I got kind of cold and
made an excuse to share Brandy's wool blanket with
Jay. Jay and I sitting near each other for so long stirred
up feelings I hadn't felt in a while. I was getting sort
of euphoric from the proximity. I could smell him and
feel the heat from his strong thigh against mine. I wanted to touch him. I thought he was feeling it too because
suddenly he seemed very taut and alive in his skin
and that's exactly how I felt. I pulled the blanket up
and leaned harder against him. I was no longer thinking straight. I was trying to find a way to touch him to
get closer to this feeling. I became awash in overwhelming love for him. I wanted my face in his hair. I wanted to put my hand between his thighs. I knew how a
woman got pregnant but had no idea of what lead up to
that act of intercourse. I had the vaguest remembrance
of what happened to me with my brother when I was
younger, but I buried that so deeply that I would not
be able to say for sure whether it had even really happened. I was not connecting that incident with this. All
I knew was my hand was on his thigh, under the blanket, and he moved it closer to the place where there was
a bulge, a hardness, and he made a small groan or maybe it was just a sigh. Or maybe I made a groan or a sigh.
My dad suddenly came alive, swung his head around,
the car swerving, then adjusted the rearview mirror to
see me, immediately shouting, "God damn it! What is
going on back there?! Sidney! Get over on your side of
the fucking car. Jay, I oughta pull this thing over and
beat the shit out of you. Get your filthy fucking hands
off my daughter. Sidney if I see anything like that again

he is out on the shoulder immediately. God damn it Ingrid."

My mom turned around and glared at me. I met her eyes. She hated me right then. I was afraid but I didn't really have a handle on what was going on. The whole car ride was becoming a weird emotional journey. I got Brandy back in between Jay and me. I couldn't even look at Jay, I was so embarrassed. What happened? What was I thinking?

As we rode along, I started picturing us back in Chicago all together. I thought about my dad going back to work. I thought about Jay being in Preston's room next to mine. I thought about Mom going shopping and Jay and I being alone together in the house and wondered what that would be like.

Mom had been saying for many miles that we needed to stop and eat. Unannounced, Dad pulled the car into a fast-food barbecue place in Wisconsin. We were all very hungry, having only eaten the doughnuts from that morning and what little snacks we brought from the closing down of the refrigerator at the cabin: a few slices of cheddar cheese, a few leftover bunches of green grapes, a few handfuls of crackers.

Dad asked me to put on Brandy's leash. When he shut off the engine, he immediately jumped up out of the car, bounding around to my side where he opened my door for me, which was such an uncharacteristic move that I was immediately frightened. He reached in and grabbed Brandy's leash and jerked the dog by his neck out of the car. "Dad! Don't! You're hurting him!"

"Shut up you little slut," he growled, "Go with your mother and your stupid hick pimple-faced boyfriend.

Look at them. Turn around and look at him. He isn't even waiting for you. Don't you get it? Don't you get what's happening here? Are you that naive?"

I saw that Jay and Mom were talking and walking into the restaurant together. I thought that was good because Jay didn't hear how my dad was talking to me.

"Dad what are you talking about? I'm not going to let you put him down. He's a really nice person. He's not even my boyfriend. We haven't even known each other that long. It wasn't my idea to bring him."

"Okay Sidney. You're a fool."

I went in to meet Jay and my mom. They were in line and my mom was in surprisingly good spirits. "Sidney, what is with you? Come on, put a smile on your face! Jay is going to start thinking you're no fun at all. Now, I'm ordering us all the barbecue beef sandwiches. Sidney, do you think you should go back out and ask what your dad wants? I do. Quick, go ask before we're up at the front of the line."

I dreaded going back out, but I went. "Dad, Mom wants to know what you want to eat."

Dad was standing under a tree on the side of the parking lot with Brandy, smoking a fat dark brown cigar.

"Just get a dish of water for the dog. I don't want anything."

"Dad, you haven't eaten all day."

"I'm not hungry."

I ran back and joined them in line.

"He says he doesn't want anything."

"Oh, that's ridiculous. He's just being impossible."

I got a plastic cup from the self-service area and filled it with water from a cooler they had set out. I carried it carefully back to Brandy and set it down. Brandy's big face was immediately slopping water everywhere, all over my arm, but I held the cup so he could drink and not tip it over. My dad stood looking on in silence. I trotted back in again, and after a few minutes, our trays of food were ready.

The parking lot was hot and sunny and Mom didn't think Brandy should be left alone in the car. She said I should go get Dad and let him eat his sandwich while I held the dog. Jay and my mom brought the four trays to a table and sat down and I jogged back out.

"Dad, they got you a barbecue beef sandwich and Mom says I should stay with Brandy so you can eat."

"Go back in. I'm not eating, I told you that."

"Please, Dad. Go eat. I'll take the dog."

"Go back in there and have fun Sidney. He's your friend."

I went back and I told Mom that Dad wouldn't come. Jay looked concerned and asked if he should go out and let the family sit together. My mom answered, "Don't be silly Jay. Finish your sandwich. Sidney, here, just bring your dad out his tray and he can eat out there then."

I carried a plastic tray with a sandwich piled high with barbecue beef; a cup of cole slaw; and a paper dish of fries with ketchup on the side. There was a root beer in a plastic cup, with a straw. People brought the trays out to the few picnic tables along the edge of the driveway, so it didn't seem like a bad idea to bring Dad this one.

"Dad, here. Mom says to give you . . . " As I was right up to him he suddenly knocked the entire tray hard out of my hands.

The food flew everywhere. Brandy lurched for the beef on the ground and Dad jerked his head back and kicked at him to get him away from the food.

"Dad!" I shouted.

Dad's face was burning. He turned his back to face the car and pulled Brandy away. I stayed and picked up what I could and carried it as quickly as possible to the nearby garbage can and dumped the mess. My heart was pounding in my throat. My hands shook. I brought the tray in and put it on the stack of used ones.

I went to Jay and my mom. I sat down without saying anything and ate a little but my hands were shaking and the food tasted like sawdust. My mom was entertaining Jay with some silly story and neither of them noticed that I was upset.

The rest of that trip was one long painful silence. Jay came to Chicago for three uncomfortable days. I don't think my parents spoke to each other the whole time. Jay slept in Preston's room, which felt weird and sad to me because I missed my brother. Jay was very sweet and cordial and we had fun, but I was relieved when Mom and I drove him to the bus station. I loved him for who he was, but he didn't belong in Chicago and I needed to get on with readjusting to school and suburban life.

THE ESCAPE

On a sunny warm day in late May, my dad called the school and asked for me. It was the end of my junior year, summer was coming early to Chicago, everyone was sitting outside during lunch break. I had put my mom on the Greyhound bus a month and a half ago. I never talked about my mother being gone to anyone. Sophie was the only kid who knew. I heard my name blasted over the loudspeaker, across the campus lawn packed with teenagers. "Sidney Duncan, please come to the office for an urgent message." My face was red, my heart was beating in my throat. I threw my yogurt container at a trashcan and ran through the double doors and down the winding halls to the office.

The administrative assistant told me I was supposed to call home immediately. She set the big plastic student phone on the counter and told me how to dial out of the school system. I called our house. My dad answered. He talked in an officious phony way. I hated him. "Sidney, I'm sorry to tell you this, but your mother and I are divorcing. You need to come home right now and be with your father. I am destroyed. Your mother was seen in a car with Seymour Hoffman, our old neighbor. They were holding hands. I have hired an investigator. It has been confirmed that she is having an affair with this man and that's why she left."

"No Dad, she's up at the cabin. I wasn't supposed to tell you, but you must know. She's not around here. That can't be true."

"IT IS TRUE! Of course I know where she is! He's up there with her and they're sleeping together! Your mother is a deceitful whore. God damn it she's cheating on me with my friend! One of the few people I counted as a true friend. That bastard. That sniveling alcoholic. How could she? How can she touch him? She couldn't stand by me when things got rough. God damn her."

"Dad, listen, I can't come home, I have a big test today."

"What? Are you deranged? What is wrong with you, Sidney? You need to come home. Now. You need to be here with your father. You don't understand that your life is being pulled out from under you. You better get home here and start figuring out where you're going to go and what you're going to do."

My insides were screaming, alarms were clanging in my head. My life was changing forever? What did that look like? I wanted to say, Dad, be there for you? When have you been there for me? I don't know how to be there for you. I don't know what being there for someone means. After everything you guys have done to each other and to me and to your son, why should I stand by you?

All I said was, "I don't have a pass to leave and I really have to take this test today."

He hung up on me. I tried not to think about any of it. I tried to get my schoolwork done. I tried to do a good job on the test in American History. Then I drove to the ice cream parlor for work.

When I got home late that night, poor Brandy had pooped on the pale-green living room carpet. I cleaned it up and took him out for a walk.

When I got back in, the kitchen phone was ringing. "Sid, thank God."

"Preston?"

"Yeah, it's me. Look what the hell is going on there? I'm taking the bus and coming home in about a week for the summer. Dad sounds completely freaked out. Is Mom really at the cabin? Is she really having an affair with Seymour Hoffman?"

"I don't know what to think, don't ask me. I have a job at the ice cream parlor now and Dad leased me a car so I just do my homework and go to my job. And try to take care of poor Brandy."

"Dad sent me money to come home, but he says I can't return because he's so broke. What the hell? It's gonna be my senior year."

"Yeah, he's been staying out really late. I don't know for sure if this is true but he says he stays out late driving a taxi for cash. Is that true do you think?"

"I have no idea. He says he's going to pick me up from the bus station downtown. I'm supposed to call him on the floor of the exchange. I guess he's still going there every day. He says I can work with him as a runner this summer. What are you going to do?"

"I don't know. I think I have to stay here and work."

"Did you hear that Tommy's in town from Florida helping Dad down at the exchange too? He wants to become a broker I guess and Dad's helping him out."

"Oh great. I hope he doesn't come over here."

"I thought maybe you'd seen him already. Dad says he might stay with us for a while."

"Oh . . . "

"Well, don't worry about anything. I'll be there soon. You can drive me around in your car. I still don't have my license so you can chauffer your old brother around."

"Great."

"Okay, don't worry sister Sid, I'll be home soon."

The next day when I got home from school I could not believe my eyes when I walked in the open front door and saw, standing right in front of me, my awful cousin.

I froze, horrified, as Brandy came over and nuzzled me, wagging his tail. Poor guy was probably really freaked out by this strange character.

"Hey! Sidney! Whoa. Look at you. Seriously all grown up. Wow, your dad didn't warn me that you had turned into such a looker. Whew! Come here and give ol' Tommy a hug!"

I didn't. I was paralyzed.

"How did you get in the house? Is my dad here?"

"Oh come on, why that face? It's just you and me. He went back to the exchange, said I could move my things in, get comfortable, which is just what I intend to do."

"Where are you going to sleep? Preston's coming home in a few days."

"Yeah, well I'm taking his room for now and we'll figure it out once he gets here, okay? Don't you worry your pretty little head over it. The men have it all figured out."

I walked past him in the hall, making sure to not even slightly brush up against him. I went straight for the kitchen phone. Thank God Sophie answered instead of her mother, "Sophie, it's me, what are you doing right now?"

"Oh my God, I'm working on my final project for World History. If I don't finish this thing it's no Miami of Ohio for me. What's going on?"

"Can you take a break and come over right now? Remember my horrible cousin, the one who they said got a sewn-on toupee? He's here . . . in the house . . . alone with me . . . right now . . . he's a total pervert . . . you have to come see what he looks like . . . you will die . . . "

"No way. Is he as bad as you thought he'd be?"

"Worse. Seriously. He's disgusting. You have to come."

"Okay, I'll tell my mom I'm getting the stuff I forgot to get her from the store. I can only stay a little while."

I heard Tommy go up to Preston's room. I couldn't stand the idea of him in there wrecking Preston's stuff right before he got home. Preston had all the things he cared about in there. And his bed had clean sheets on it and a nice quilt that my mom bought him and that I knew he really loved. I didn't want that disgusting guy touching any of it, stinking it up with his awful cologne.

I stood at the front door waiting for Sophie to pull up. She lived close enough to walk so in the car it took just a minute or two. Brandy's leather leash was hanging in the front hall closet. I grabbed it and put it on him and he stood next to me.

Upstairs I heard Preston's door open again. I didn't want to turn around so I kept looking out the door for Sophie, but I could hear Tommy coming down the stairs behind me. I could smell him too. It was as if he had put on every product in his toiletry bag, a combination of maybe coconut suntan oil, herbal hair products, and some terrible manly cologne wafting its way in front of him as he descended the stairs.

Sophie's conservative old grandpa car, a tan four-door Buick, pulled into the driveway. Sophie waved as she shut off the engine. I opened the front storm door. She ran up the walk beaming with glee that we were going to check out this atrocity of a human being together. Sophie was the best for this kind of cruel but funny judging thing.

She was just starting to say, "Oh my God Sidney, I couldn't get here fast en . . . " and then she stopped, speechless.

I was holding the front storm door open for Sophie to come in but as she wasn't moving I turned and looked behind me.

There stood Tommy in his full glory. He was deeply Arizona suntanned. He had huge bulging muscles. His face was coated with some kind of bronzer or concealer probably meant to smooth out his complexion. His only articles of clothing were a pair of shiny gold metallic disco style jogging shorts and striped athletic socks with Adidas running shoes. No shirt at all. Worst, or best, of all was the thick shock of yellow blonde hair hanging over one eye just a bit, perfectly sculpted into place. His hair on the sides and in back was shaved very short and was blonde too. My recollection of Tommy was that he, like my dad and grandfather, and even Preston, had very thin hair that was obviously heading toward baldness at an unusually early age. I had heard that he paid for a very expensive procedure in LA where they actually sew, with thread, a toupee on to the top of your bald scalp. Could it be true? Sophie and I had already puzzled over this. By looking at him, you honestly couldn't tell how it was being held on, but you could for sure tell it wasn't his real hair.

Tommy was eyeing Sophie up and down. "Oh man! Two for one! What, the beauties around here just keep multiplying! Who do we have here? What's your name, you little morsel?"

Sophie was the Junior Miss of our town for several good reasons. She was by far the most beautiful girl I had ever known personally. She made my mom look like a sad long-faced starving horse out to pasture. She was wearing old Converse sneakers, a pink oxford button-down collar shirt, and cut-off denim overalls that were pretty baggy on her because she was so thin. She always wore smudgy eyeliner that perfectly and subtly emphasized her wonderful huge brown eyes, so even in tomboy clothes, she was spectacular. I looked at those expressive eyes and they looked back at me. Our horror was sheer delight. Tommy could not have been weirder. Sophie's intellect was a much bigger delight for me than her pretty appearance, so I was thrilled that she had made it over just in time for us to witness his arrival together.

He was still talking, "Sidney, are you just going to stand there? Don't you have any manners? Who is this beautiful creature?"

Sophie turned to face him and her beautiful brow furrowed. She stepped one foot forward as a gesture of bravery. I smiled.

"My name is Sophie and I came here to see Sidney."

With her chin held high she turned her pretty face to me, "Sidney, let's sit out here on your porch, shall we?"

I could see that we couldn't get past him into the house and honestly it didn't feel safe to be inside with him. Brandy wanted to go out too.

Sophie, Brandy, and I went out to sit on the stoop. Brandy peed on the bushes by the door and then threw himself down in the sunny grass.

Tommy followed us. He stood shirtless, hands on hips, facing us, his back to the street.

"What'd you say your name is, Sophie? So Sophie, how old are you?"

"I'm sorry, but Sidney and I need to talk about something private, please excuse us."

"What the heck is that supposed to mean? I'm her cousin. I'm a houseguest. You're not going to pull some snooty act with me."

His physical presence, standing right in front of us, bare tanned muscled chest, flimsy gold shorts, was too much. Sophie was getting angry, I could feel it. We were going into a fight or flight situation in our guts.

Sophie stood up off the stoop and started talking in a loud brave voice, "Okay, look, we get it. You want us to pay attention to you but we aren't going to, so take your ridiculous self and go back in the house and put some real clothes on and get a life. I don't know who you are, I don't care who you are. I am never going to talk to you. Leave us alone."

I felt myself getting scared as Tommy's face became more indignant. I still had to live with this guy. My dad wasn't home. I was going to have to go back in the house at some point.

He turned and headed toward the gate to the back yard. "You bitches can piss yourselves for all I care. Nice welcome, Sidney. I guess you haven't changed a bit. I'll be out back working on my tan."

Sophie and I looked at each other as the gate slammed shut. We burst into giggles. Sophie had scared him off for now but I was still wary.

The next few days were awful. I was afraid to be in the house alone with the gorilla cousin. Every time I came around a corner, it seemed he was standing, looking at himself in a mirror, no shirt, gold shorts. I was in my last few days of school and working a lot at the ice cream parlor so I had reasons to be gone from the house. Tommy started going down to the exchange with my dad. No one told me anything, but I saw him put on tight pants, a dress shirt and a tie and leave with my dad in the morning. I couldn't believe my dad was okay with bringing this guy who looked like a clown, with him. In a way, it made me think that family meant a lot to my dad because he was helping his nephew start a new career at the worst possible time for himself. But I also thought it was possible that the nephew's presence was somehow helping my dad, I wasn't sure how, but I sort of had a vague feeling that my dad wouldn't do anything that didn't benefit himself somehow. Maybe it was just an ego trip, having this big hulking guy following him around and taking orders. That was probably enough right there.

The house was getting wrecked. The dog was having accidents on my mom's perfect carpeting. Poor guy, I didn't blame him, everything was just so messed up — this strange guy was staying there, and I was gone a lot.

Dad bought a few cans of disgusting beef stew and pork and beans for Tommy and him to eat when they were home. There was no way I was eating that stuff. Dad didn't even put the cans in the cupboard, he just set a stack of them by the stove and a few along the kitchen windowsill bumped up against my mother's custom-made kitchen curtains.

Dad left the ironing board set up in the kitchen and came down in the mornings and quickly pressed himself a fresh shirt. My mom used to stand for hours priding herself on her meticulous ironing of my father's beautiful dress shirts. Now they were getting discolored and frayed and he had lost so much weight, he had his pants doubled over at the back of the waistband, held in place with his leather belt.

When my cousin and my dad came home at night, they sometimes brought one or two more men with them and they would all drink. It wasn't wine any more. It was bottles of Jack Daniel's mostly. I would be in bed when they came in and I would stay in my room, usually with Brandy snuggled up with me until morning when the two men would either be snoring in their beds or already gone. I wasn't sure I could handle much more. Everything felt on the verge of collapse. I was beginning to think I should try to get up North to be with my mom.

One morning the kitchen phone rang. "Hi Sidney, how are you doing honey?"

It was my mom. I was so touched to hear her voice, to hear her call me honey. I suddenly missed her so terribly. I started to cry and poured out as much as I could of what had been happening and how it was for me. She said it was awful what I had to go through and that I should come up there when school ended. I said I had to stay and work over the summer. She said the weather up there was getting nice. It was torture for me to hear her voice, think of the cabin and the lake, wishing I was up there.

My mom told me about a mother fox living under the cabin floor with two little kits who came out to play in the sun every afternoon. She told me that she wanted me to come up there and that I should try to figure something out, and then she had to go but said she'd call again soon.

After I hung up, I wondered about the likelihood of getting to go up to the cabin this summer. I knew Preston would be back any day now. I had no idea how that was all going to go. I decided to try to talk to Jay. I sat down at the kitchen table and called his parents' house. His mother answered. "Hello, Mrs. Mayer. This is Sidney Duncan. Is Jay home?"

Jay's mother was nice and Jay's voice came on the line after just a few seconds, "Hey Sidney! How are you!"

He told me how he had driven my mom out to the cabin and helped her get the place warmed up and livable. He mentioned that there was some "friend of the family" who was there the last time he had stopped by, so he hadn't been back since. "I figured if she needed my help, she knew where to find me."

I didn't want to know if that person had been sleeping there, so I didn't ask and Jay didn't say. I asked him what he thought about me trying to get up there. I told him how weird everything was here in Chicago.

"Why can't you tell your dad you want to drive up and visit your mom?"

"I've only had my license for a little while. I'm not very good at driving on the highway. I'm not sure I could drive all the way up there. It's like twelve hours."

"Just get out a map, and take your time. You could do it. Ask him. It would be great to see you. And your mom would love it if you came, I'm sure."

"Yeah, maybe."

That night, Dad and Tommy and their weird sidekick, the ex-priest, were in the kitchen drinking and eating takeout pizza when I got home from the ice cream parlor. I thought I'd eat a piece of pizza and visit with them a little, to make it seem like everything was good between all of us. The ex-priest was the only one who said hello to me when I walked in.

"Hi," I answered, "can I have a piece of the pizza?"

"Are you paying for it?" my dad shot back.

"Dad. Geez. Forget it. Never mind. Sorry I asked."

"Suit yourself."

I knew it wasn't a good time, but I didn't think there was ever going to be a good time, so I ventured, "Dad, what would you think of me driving up to the cabin for just like a week or something when school gets out? Maybe Sophie would ride up with me. She's a good driver."

Dad put his beer bottle down hard on the table.

"You are kidding, right?"

He looked at Tommy.

"I met that little sass Sophie. She's bad news if you ask me."

"Dad, Tommy is not helping to decide things in our family okay? I'm asking you."

"Well, you might have a better chance of asking Tommy because I have absolutely no intention of letting you take that car anywhere except to your job and back home again. You still have another year of high school left, is that correct? Then you need to keep working and help keep this place going so you have a roof over your head for next winter. Understand? And if you think I am going to give you money to go visit your mother, forget it."

I felt the prison doors closing. I felt sick. Tommy was gloating, I could feel it. I glanced at the ex-priest, but he had his eyes down like it was too shameful a thing to witness. Yeah, Mr. Ex-priest, avert your eyes from the evil around you.

The next night Preston was in the kitchen when I got home. I was thrilled. I was so relieved to have him back, so relieved to see him again. I noticed his face was withdrawn and he looked more worried than he used to, like life was weighing on him. Preston always looked up to Tommy, only because he was older, I thought. He and Tommy were already joking around like they used to when they were boys.

Dad bought Preston's favorite Chicago-style hotdogs from his favorite place in his old neighborhood on the way home from the exchange to celebrate his son's return. There were white paper bags and huge hotdogs smothered with peppers or sauerkraut, each wrapped in its own paper, lying all over the kitchen table. It was a feast. Dad was happy and half-shouting a story to the other guys and everyone was wolfing down hotdogs. "So then this asshole has the nerve to tell me that the Jag needs a new goddamn pump when I'm telling him the pump is brand new and this is a finely tuned machine that does not go a day without a complete inspection by the finest mechanics in the city . . . "

I was happy for the hotdogs and happy to hear my dad telling stories. He was on a roll, talking about things I never knew about his life.

"So I'm driving a fucking cab, and these people have no idea who they're dealing with, they're talking like they know one fucking thing about this city, about the best way to get to the Hancock building from O'Hare at two in the morning in a snowstorm. They have no idea I have a law degree. They have no idea I've held seats on the Chicago and New York Exchanges. They start arguing with me and that's it, Boom, I snap, pull the fucking cab over. They're scared like they think I'm going to rob them, I'm telling you the looks on their doughy pathetic faces was priceless . . . and I'm saying 'Okay, look people . . . '

"So I'm up at her shit-hole cabin that old Gramps built himself, and the water pump, I kid you not, is made out of a goddamn Folger's can . . . am I right? Preston, am I right? Have you seen that thing? No? No, of course you haven't because you don't do a goddamn fucking thing to help, you're just taking the money, getting your high-priced education. You know what you cost me last year? I'm going broke helping you! Why? You know why? Because my parents were too old-country, too provincial, to think their son needed a higher education.

They thought whatever was good enough for them was good enough for their son. Yeah. That's right. Who paid for me? Huh? Who paid my way? Huh? Yeah that's right. Say it. Fucking say it. Nobody. Zero. Not one red cent. I worked all night at Swedish Covenant Hospital as an orderly. Did you know that? No. You don't know anything do you?"

The next thing I knew Preston was saying, "Dad, don't get yourself all worked up . . . "

Dad leapt up to get his hands on Preston and then Preston stood, unsure on his feet. Dad hauled him out into the hallway and started boxing his ears and Preston had his hands up saying, "Dad, no! I'm sorry, stop . . . "

I grabbed my dad's shirt by the back, yelling, "Stop it! Leave him alone!"

My dad swatted me away with one arm. I ran back into the kitchen where Tommy had picked up the *Sports Illustrated* magazine that was lying on the table and was thumbing through the magazine nonchalantly like he was in the doctor's office.

I cried out, "What is wrong with you, Tommy? You have to do something!"

Tommy looked at me and said, feigning calmness, "He's my uncle. I'm not going against him. It's his house. It's not my place."

The scuffle seemed to have quieted down, but while we were still alone looking each other in the eyes, I took the opportunity to say to Tommy, "You make me sick."

I had no interest in waiting for a response. I passed through the now darkened hall to the stairs and safely made it to the bathroom to brush my teeth and wash my face. Before I opened the door again I listened to be sure that my brother and dad had both gone to their rooms. When I was sure there was nobody around, I unlocked the door, dashed across the dark hall at the top of the stairs to my room, locked my flimsy little lock and pushed my dresser in front of my door.

A few days later my school let out for the summer. I got two As and two Bs, which was sort of my usual. I never tried to get As in the classes I didn't really care about. But I tried to never get a C. I realized, as had been the case almost all along, that there was no one to show my report card to, that no one showed any interest. I brought it home on the last day and set it, standing up, on top of its cardboard envelope, on the kitchen table. I thought of the papers that used to be sitting there for my mom to sign. I thought of the times my mom left Preston's report card on the table for "your father to see this when he gets home" as a threat to Preston when he got even one B instead of all As. I wondered if my dad would pick it up when he saw it or even notice it sitting there.

I was officially home for the summer now. I put on my cut-off shorts that thankfully still fit from last summer and a T-shirt of my brother's and called Brandy to come put on his leash. We stepped out the front door into the bright sunlight and I thought about how different it would be to not be in Minnesota for the summer where the air always cooled down at night, where the crystal-clear water was so cold you could barely stand it, but was just perfect by late July. How the sky there was huge and endless and the clouds were so expressive and you saw the weather at all times playing out in a majestic drama. The lake itself had so many moods. The water could express joy and be light and frolicking or it could be fore-boding and dark. There were no boys like Jay in Chicago either. I'd gone to the public schools since kindergarten and I had never met any who were as down-to-earth and as closely connected to nature. There were really no girls like me either. Some of the more sophisticated intellectu-al girls were sort of like me, but they usually weren't as tomboyish or they would never understand, ever in a mil-lion years, my fondness for a boy like Jay. Most of them weren't used to spending as much time alone as I was. Most of them probably didn't know what it felt like to have nobody care about them all that much.

Brandy and I walked all the way to the forest pre-serve on the other side of the high school. Some peo-ple said that girls shouldn't go in there alone, but it was the only woods I had now and Brandy was pret-ty scary-looking to most people. We walked through the coolest, deepest part of the woods and I thought that it would be very hard to stay home all summer and have this be the only slice of nature. It got really hot in Chica-go and summer had barely begun. The kids in my neigh-borhood went to the public pool a lot. I had been there once or twice at the beginning or end of summer, but I thought it would be pretty sad to have that be where I went to swim instead of the big cold northern lake with the rocky shore and the crashing waves, and the canoe, and the dock, and the dreamy long days and possibly, fun nights with other kids up there.

I walked back home slowly, Brandy panting and moving slowly. I talked to him, "We've got a long summer ahead of us, buddy. If you're hot now, what are we going to do in July?" He and I sat down for a few minutes on the grassy corner across from our house. There were no sidewalks in the fancy neighborhoods so I sat on the cement curb and Brandy lay down and rolled over on his side in the grass. I stared at our house. Plain white. My mom always talked about the dormer windows on the second floor. She loves the house. Her parents only had an apartment in Chicago and the little cabin up north so it was the first real house she'd ever lived in. I didn't look at it with love. I hated the celadon green inside and I hated the three sterile bushes planted painstakingly across the front under the picture window.

I hated the bad memories, and there were plenty. I looked at the garage and remembered Dad yelling at us for scratching one of his precious cars. He lined us all up, even Mom, and interrogated us about how the passenger side of his two-door Jaguar got scratched. What a freak! I had good memories too. I remembered how I would decorate the dormer window in my room every Christmas. I set up my portable record player by my desk near the window and plugged it in to an outlet that was triggered by the light switch next to the room door. I set the record player needle to the Mormon Tabernacle Choir's rendition of "Joy to the World." I also plugged in a desk-sized, white plastic Christmas tree with tiny pastel lights that my mom had bought for me, in the center of my window so people could see it when they drove by. When anyone entered my room during the holidays they would be regaled with the blasting music and they'd see my little tree. I thought the whole thing was very wonderful.

I crossed the street slowly with Brandy in tow. He didn't want to walk but he was probably thirsty so we had to go inside. We entered the house and everything was quiet. We were the only ones home. I looked at my mother's precious house. Her carpeted stairs that I had vacuumed a million times were now damped down, soiled. I looked at the living room picture window with white divided enameled panes. Mom usually had the window-washing spray and paper towels out almost daily to wipe the place where Brandy sat and smudged the window. Now you could see the shape of his body where he leaned against her celadon-green, silk full-length curtains, resting his slobbering chin on the white enameled windowsill. I walked into the kitchen where cans of beef stew were strewn around the sink, the dishes only half done, the ironing board blocking access to the stove and the cupboards.

My parents' pub sign they loved so much was even harder to look at now. Bitterness was on my tongue as I recited, without having to read, "Money's the root of all evil, it's treacherous, slippery and vile, but the baker, the banker, the preacher and I don't think that it's gone out of style."

I filled Brandy's dishes with water and food. I patted his soft head. He drank his water and sighed, settling down in his bed in the corner. What a good dog. So unassuming. "I love you Brandy. I promise I won't let you down." I crouched down next to him in the corner, behind the kitchen table. I sat down in the corner on the floor next to him and rested my head on his back and put my arms all around him. I saw how the world looked through his eyes. Water, food, someone to sit with him. What the hell else was there? I kissed him on his nose and eased up out of the corner and headed to my room. I wanted him to eat so I didn't invite him up with me.

I got to my quiet room and saw my guitar in the corner and knew that was the answer. It had been the answer for a while, and it would be this summer too, I was sure. I sat cross-legged on my bed with the acoustic guitar my grandparents gave me for Christmas when I was eight, when we still had big fun Christmases. The guitar was a big surprise, not necessarily something I had asked for or even had thought about wanting. I was the one grandchild they gave a guitar to—don't know why they did. I picked it up and played it. I started reading the songbooks and figuring out the little chord diagrams that came with the case. I started writing songs of my own too, because when I heard other people singing theirs, they were relaying their own feelings out to the world. They weren't being interrupted or shut down. They were having their say. I thought that was extremely wonderful. The idea of sitting on your bed with your guitar and singing the exact perfect words that exactly fit your situation seemed like the most glorious experience I could dream of having. So I went after it. I played other people's songs because they were better than mine. I played my own songs because they were mine.

The sky was growing dark outside. It was getting late. I had nothing else to do so I kept playing until I became aware that the phone rang and then stopped and then rang again. I stopped strumming. I listened for the ring of the kitchen phone. There it was again. I didn't answer that often because it was mostly bill collectors or people asking for my dad. But there it was again, two or three rings and then hanging up. I started to think it was someone trying to message me that I should answer. I scrambled off my bed and ran down to the kitchen. I stared at the phone on the wall. There it was again.

"Hello?" I said into the receiver.

"Sidney! Oh thank God!"

"Preston?"

"Sid, this is bad. Really bad. Dad's gone crazy. He's been drinking. He's really mad. You gotta come get me. He went crazy. He pushed me out of the car. I'm all cut up. I tried to stay in, the car was going. I fell out. I rolled onto the gravel. I'm all cut up."

"Preston, where are you?"

"I'm in a phone booth on the tollway. Two or three stops from our house. The tollway, you know what I mean right? You gotta come get me. I'm all scraped up from the gravel. Bring some towels."

"Okay, I'll come right now."

"No Sid, don't hang up. We can't go back there. Dad went crazy. He fired me. He started screaming at me on the floor of the exchange. He's crazy. It's bad."

"Okay I'll come right now."

"No Sid. We gotta leave. We can't go back. You gotta get out of there. You have to take whatever you can and get Brandy in the car and we have to go to Mom. We have to get away from him. If he comes home he won't let you come get me. Run around and grab whatever you can. Get me some pants and a shirt and my jacket. Get Brandy. See if there's any money on my dresser or Dad's dresser. Hurry! Shit! You gotta get out of there!"

I hung up and grabbed Brandy by his collar. We went to the closet and I put on his leash. I ran with him out to my car. I left the garage door shut. I ran back to the kitchen and grabbed his dog food. I ran that to the car. I ran up the stairs two at a time. I threw on my thick hooded sweatshirt and changed into my jeans. I ran around grabbing stuff in my arms. Cash from the dressers. My guitar. My flute in its black case. My book of sonatas for the flute. My songwriting notebooks. The quilt our great grandmother made by hand. I ran down and stuffed things in the trunk, leaving the trunk open. I ran back through once more, got Preston's clothes. I thought about what was important to our mom. I had a brainstorm and ran into the dining room and found the wooden box containing my grandmother's good silver service. I ran that to the car. I couldn't think of anything else.

I prayed that I'd make it out without Dad seeing me. I pressed the garage door opener and prayed. "Please God don't let him be here . . . "

The coast was clear. I backed out the Volare and pressed the garage door shut. I looked up and saw the house, already abandoned and very dark. No outside or inside lights were on. When Dad pulled up he'd know I was gone.

I pulled out and drove fast to get out of our street, our neighborhood. My next thought was that if Dad wasn't home by now, maybe he was going back to find Preston. Maybe he felt bad and was already picking Preston up and I'd get there and never find him. I thought about what I'd do then. In a way, I could feel my heart lifting at the prospect of the drive to the cabin, like the good old days. This was when we always went, when I got out of school. And my mother was there so it wasn't like I was doing something wrong. I was just going up to see my mom at our family cabin. That sounded so normal. I started telling myself that I'd go whether or not Preston had changed his mind.

The tollway was well lit. I got to the first tollbooths and peered off to the side where there was a sign for a public telephone, but no Preston anywhere. I didn't want to hang around in case Dad was on my trail.

I drove farther to the next set of tolls. This was the only place Preston could be if he wasn't at the last one. I knew if I didn't find him here I never would, so I pulled way over and slowly drove along the shoulder. My heart leapt into my throat when suddenly there was a figure frantically waving his arms at me and running toward my headlights. I leaned into the windshield to try to see. I would hit the person soon if I didn't swerve or stop. Preston's face, distorted with shouting, white as a ghost. I stopped and unlocked the doors. He jumped in. "Go! Go! Put the pedal to the metal! We gotta get out of here!"

"We have to go through the tollbooth. Take it easy."

"No! Fuck them! Step on it! Bust through the gate!"

"Preston, stop it. I don't see Dad's car. There's nobody around. Just let me pay the toll."

I threw my coins in and the gate went up and we were on our way. Preston was talking really fast. "Dad was so crazy! He started hitting me as he was driving and then we slowed down to go through the toll and he reached over and opened my door and shoved me and I was hanging on saying, 'No Dad, no!' He just kept hitting me and shoving me and I fell out into the gravel on my face. Am I bleeding? I was bleeding really badly I think."

Preston started crying hard, sobbing. I tried to look over at him and I could see some blood on his face. "What the hell is the matter with him? Jesus! I'm his son.

We were buddies. I was gonna work with him, get the business back on track this summer. Fucking Tommy, that faggot. What the fuck will he do now? Just follow Dad around, say yes to anything. Fuck him."

"Preston, do you think you need stitches any place? Do you need to go to an emergency room? Should we pull off and check your face? Dad's never going to find us at some random exit ramp."

"No! Are you nuts? He will kill us if he thinks we're going to take this car and go to Mom. He'd fucking rather kill us himself than let that happen."

"Look in the mirror. It has a light I think. See if your face is okay."

"Sid, God, shut up about my face. My face is fine. Do you realize what's happening here? He's probably got the police out looking for us by now. We stole this car."

"That's ridiculous. He got this car for me and I'm driving it. I didn't steal it. We're his kids. He can't say it's stealing."

"We have to get across the border to Wisconsin, Sid. You gotta drive faster! Is this as fast as you can drive? What are you some stupid pussy driver like Mom?"

"What are you talking about? You don't know how to drive at all and you're like twenty years old."

"Yeah, I'm not crazy enough to get behind the wheel of one of these death traps. You're my brave little sister who can do anything. Come on Sid! Push this thing! What a piece-of-shit car! Dad's such an asshole. We gotta get out of Illinois."

I got going about as fast as I could handle, maybe seventy miles per hour, and just tried to keep my eyes on the road.

Preston fell into silent contemplation, staring out the window. As I drove I thought back for a moment to the house, the fancy stuff of my mom's that I left behind. Stuff in my room, stuff in my closet. I felt good that I didn't care about any of it. Brandy, my guitar, my flute, were all I needed. My brother. Preston fell asleep. I thought about what was ahead for us. Mom didn't know we were coming but she'd be glad to see us I was sure. I was happy that the way to get there was very clear in my mind. I knew we had to go to Wisconsin Dells first, through Janesville. After that it was up through Spooner and Rice Lake in Wisconsin. After that Cloquet, then Virginia, Minnesota. Before we hit the tiny town where we did our grocery shopping, we turned off onto the lake road. We had a long way to go. I didn't care. All I had to do was watch the white line, stay on the road, mind my own business, not try to pass anybody. Stay well back from any other cars or trucks.

I hated the big semi trucks. The night was very dark outside the city and the trucks were going fast. They barreled down on us out of nowhere every few minutes. The highway was two lanes going in the same direction. The other side of the highway was pretty far off to the left so it wasn't like we'd get hit head-on, but I had definitely heard people talk about truckers on the road at night nodding off and crashing. I was keeping my distance.

Many miles went by. Preston and Brandy were both sound asleep. I was tired but not that tired. I knew I could go to sleep in my cozy pink room when I got to the cabin. I was determined to drive all night and make it there by morning. We would probably be there by ten.

That would be great. Mom was going to be so surprised and happy.

The next time I checked, the dashboard clock said it was four in the morning. We were somewhere outside of Rice Lake, where we used to stop at a pancake place with Mom and Dad. Those were very different times.

I had to pee and get something to drink. Brandy needed water and a chance to go out too. "Preston, wake up."

"Shut up!"

"Preston, seriously, I'm stopping."

"No, shut up, don't stop. Dad is probably following us."

"Oh my God. What is with you? There is no one anywhere for miles around. I have to go to the bathroom."

"Piss in the woods. You can't go into one of these truck-stop places. Dad will have police looking for us."

"No he won't."

"Yes! He will! I'm not going with you. I'll go in the woods. If they capture you, I'm making a run for it. They're not gonna get me."

"Preston, have you lost your mind?"

I took the next exit with a sign for gas, pulled into a service station and parked the car in front of a gas pump.

"We need gas, too."

I counted the cash I grabbed from the house. Plenty for fuel and some drinks. I wasn't good at pumping gas. I had only filled the Volare tank a few times because I didn't drive very far back in Chicago, just to the ice cream shop and back most of the time.

I managed to pump the gas and went inside to pay. My legs were a little stiff. Dampness in the air and a fine mist made me feel like we were getting closer. The air here was like the Northwoods already. The clerk was asleep when I walked in. I cleared my throat a few times. He was a kid not much older than me. He looked surprised when he woke up and saw me standing there. He took my money for the gas plus two cold cans of root beer from the store's cooler. I got a paper cup from the self-serve counter and filled it with water from their drinking fountain.

"I'm just going to set this stuff here, okay? Can I use the restroom? Does it have a key?" The kid looked confused. "No, it doesn't have a key. It's right there."

I saw the door marked for women and went in to use the toilet. When I came back out I could see Preston outside with Brandy on his leash, slinking around behind the car. The sleepy kid behind the counter smiled. I smiled back and said, "Okay, well, bye. Thank you."

We climbed back into the car. I pulled the Volare back out onto the entrance ramp, foot on the gas pedal, thinking of my driver's ed drill sergeant, pressed harder on the gas, merged.

I was having fun. I was glad this was happening. I loved this drive. With every mile the landscape became more remote, wild, wide-open, beautiful. Dense dark stands of tall trees against the starry sky. Majestic outcroppings of granite. I saw several deer standing off to the sides, some with sweet fawns. The faint light of the coming morning was way off in the distance beyond the horizon as I drove.

I had a pang of guilt, a tug of compassion, for Dad. I kept picturing him coming back to the house and seeing the dog gone, his daughter gone, his son gone. I wanted to tell myself he deserved this. I kept wanting to replay the bad scenes in my mind to keep my conviction up but I didn't really blame him for how he had treated me. He wasn't that bad to me. Whenever my mind went down this path, I remembered the flute story.

A while back I wanted an open-hole silver flute because my beautiful fairy godmother of a flute teacher, who had studied in Paris under a very famous flutist and spoke French in what I thought of as the most divinely feminine manner, had decided I was ready for this rite of passage. My flute teacher was a person I never wanted to disappoint. My mother said we couldn't afford the special flute my teacher said I needed, and that my rental flute from the school marching band was good enough. Mine was pretty dented and didn't really take to polish much. Some of the keys got stuck when I played. My teacher said that the tone would never be right no matter how well I played it. The more advanced girls in the orchestra all had the open-hole flutes by now. Even a couple of girls below me did.

At dinner one night, I told my parents that I wanted the new flute for the big concert coming up. I was thirteen. We were still riding around in Jaguars. I didn't have any idea that money was an issue. My mother was arguing with me, saying that we couldn't afford it, that I didn't need it, that I was never going to be a serious flute player so I should be happy with the one I had. I pointed out that my flute teacher had an older student selling an intermediate flute that we could get a really good deal on, and so we wouldn't have to pick one out at the store. I didn't think my dad cared. I didn't think he was even paying attention to what my mom and me were saying.

A few days later, when I came downstairs in the morning, there was a check on the kitchen table for the amount I had said I needed for the new flute.

I brought the check to my next lesson and soon I had the new flute. The teacher worked with me on adjusting to the new fingerings. She showed me how to clean it. She was as excited as I was. I was happy. It was the right thing. That evening when my mother picked me up right in front of the flute teacher's house for once, I was beaming. "Look, Mom!"

I jumped into the front seat and immediately opened the elaborate casing to reveal the gleaming article of craftsmanship in all its sterling silver brightness and glory.

"That's beautiful Sidney. I hope you realize your father sold his favorite hunting gun for you to have this."

"Oh."

"Yes, he had those two nice hunting guns and that one was worth a lot of money. He took it downtown and sold it yesterday to write you that check. I don't know how many fathers would have done that."

"Wow. I love it so much. I'll tell him when he gets home. He'll see how wonderful it is. I can play you guys a little concert."

"Well, I don't know that we need that. The important thing is you had better be practicing and I better see your room neat and you had better be on extra good behavior with a smile from ear to ear from now on."

My dad buying me the flute stayed with me. I couldn't say I knew why he did it. I didn't think my mom put him up to it. She wouldn't have cared one way or the other whether I had a better flute. I often thought about my dad making that decision for me.

The sun was climbing above the trees as we hit Cloquet, a sleepy town in northern Minnesota. The local paper mill gave the whole place a distinctive odor that smelled like everyone in town was making oatmeal at the same time. I pulled into the weird but super cool-looking Frank Lloyd Wright-designed gas station and a guy pumped our gas and cleaned our windshield and our headlights, which were smeared with the multicolored fluorescent splattered guts of many dead insects. Brandy was crying to get out so I got his leash and we walked over to the roadside strip of grass.

Preston was waking up and looked disheveled and bruised. I watched him walk around to the back corner of the garage and I turned so I didn't have to watch him urinate on the bushes. After that he took Brandy for me so I could go to the bathroom. I went around to the back of the cinderblock building and held my breath while I peed in the fly-infested bathroom's grubby toilet. I washed my hands and got out of there as fast as I could. I went inside the station and saw that they had powdered sugar doughnuts. I bought a box and some orange juice for my brother and me. Preston looked happy when he saw what I was carrying.

Back on the road, the last stretch up to the cabin was a narrow highway through the encroaching woods on either side with only a thin yellow line saving you from every drunk and every nodding off trucker out there.

Preston wolfed down more than half the box of doughnuts and gulped orange juice out of the cardboard container. He fumbled around getting something out of his backpack. He started thumbing through a magazine, front to back, back to front, looking for something.

I looked over and realized the magazine was full of pictures of naked women.

"Preston what are you looking at?"

"What? It's *Playboy*. I got it for the interview with Jack Kerouac. It's unbelievable. They have great articles. Everybody says that like it's a joke, but it's no joke. There's an interview with Jack Kerouac. Seriously, this shit Kerouac is spitting out, it's like fucking performance art. He keeps saying this great line about 'up your ass with Mobil gas,' fucking brilliant. And what about the pictures? You, intimidated by beautiful women? You're as hot as these chicks. A lot of them are smart like you too. Seriously, Sid you could be making us some dough off those breasts of yours."

"Preston!"

"What? Seriously! You could do wet T-shirt contests and you'd win hands down. Most chicks only have big tits 'cause they're fat or fake. You got the goods, Sid."

Preston read some of the Kerouac quotes from *Playboy* out loud to me. He was getting really animated. He kept looking up and interrupting himself to tell me to drive faster. He was suddenly all pumped up about how I wasn't driving fast enough. He wanted me to pass the semi truck in front of us. We'd been happily going along at my idea of a safe speed all night and I never had to pass anybody.

"Shut up Preston, I'm doing a good job. Just go back to sleep."

"Sid come on man, this is bullshit! Fuck this guy! These roads are made for passing! Grow some balls Sid!"

"I'm not passing."

"God damn it Sid, this guy is ruining our time! We were doing great!"

"It's not a race Preston, shut up."

"Pass him! Put the pedal to the metal and fucking PASS HIM!

"I don't want to!"

"Come on, sister Sid! You can do it! Don't be such a little coward! This guy's a load! Do it! Do it!"

I pushed down hard on the gas pedal and felt like closing my eyes. The Volare had a spot where it wouldn't get any faster unless you really pushed hard on the gas so I shifted my weight and shoved my foot forward. Our car lurched forward into the left lane. The yellow line was divided where I crossed but a double line was coming, a hill was coming, over the hill a pack of cars was coming and suddenly Preston was rolling down his window. As we came up alongside the trucker's cab, Preston lifted his body out of the passenger window, had only his legs still inside, with his butt lodged on the doorframe. He was waving both his arms over his head and shouting something that at first I could not decipher, but which turned out to be: "Up Your Ass With Mobil Gas! Up your ass with Mobil gas you fucker! You think you own this road? Get out of my little sister's way!"

I was screaming, "Preston cut it out, you idiot!"

Brandy sounded the alarm by standing up and barking. We got well past the trucker and I pulled into the right lane ahead of him. Preston was back in his seat rolling up the window, laughing hysterically, then suddenly he was crying.

"Preston, what's wrong? What is wrong with you?"

"Sister Sid . . . why is this happening to us? Why is this happening? Why does Dad have to be such an asshole? Why is Mom so fucked up? I can't stand it. It's like a John Steinbeck novel. All his people are always getting fucked with by life, by other people. Steinbeck makes it sound like it's all some epic thing like the Bible. God is testing us little sis. God is testing us. Why are you so strong? I think you turned out to be a good person all on your own. How did you do that?"

"I didn't. I'm only seventeen."

"Yeah you did. You already did it. I'm glad we're doing this. I'm glad I'm with you. Brandy's glad too. Look at him."

We both turned and looked at Brandy's big head sticking up between us from his perch in the back seat. He licked Preston's face and nuzzled his neck until Preston was smiling.

After a while Preston started telling me, "I have one more year of college left. Dad says he can't pay for it. I might not be able to go back."

"Oh no, that would be really bad."

"Yeah and what about you, Sid? Isn't this going to be your senior year?"

"Yeah next fall."

"What will you do?"

"What do you mean? We'll probably go back with Mom right?"

"I don't think so Sid. I don't think anybody's going back. I don't think there's going to be anything to go back to."

I tried not to think. I kept driving. The morning sun was coming straight over the endless trees to the East as

I drove along the outskirts of the big mining town of Virginia and then out onto the last highway to the cabin. The trees were towering and crowding the road and the sense of the power and magnitude of nature was evident. True wilderness, long stretches unclaimed by human beings. A sense of peril filled me as I contemplated how far we were from easy salvation. We had no way to call anyone for help out here. There wasn't a phone booth anywhere but in the middle of the bigger towns. There were no houses for many miles and no gas stations for many more. I wondered how my mom was feeling about being up here for so long by herself.

Summer was just beginning in this far northern land and it was still chilly on this morning drive in early June. The foliage was fragile, a shade of light bright green on the white birch bows, on the quivering aspens. The hint of what was to come, what Mother Nature had in store as we drew closer to the lake, was evident in the tall exposed sheets of blackish bedrock, so unlike anything seen in Illinois or Wisconsin. These outcroppings of ancient rock, seemingly as old as glaciers and dinosaurs, made me want to pull over, lie flat, resting my cheek on the cold surface, be one with the deep energy of the lake area, the woods, the wilderness. I wanted to hug and kiss every tree. The pines heralding our arrival were so tall, so strong, so numerous. Silent conquerors. This primal place brought out the best in a person. I looked for a small handmade sign around the bend that had been standing for as long as I could remember. Yes, there it was. Someone had fashioned this plaque of sorts—a sheet of plywood stained black, and white birch twigs attached probably with small finishing nails, so well made that it had been withstanding the extremes in weather year in and year out. The small sign read, "Why Live In God's Country Without God?" Underneath that, in smaller letters, was the faded and barely legible name of a church. I had no idea whether the church existed still or not. I had the feeling that the church had been disbanded long ago. The saying was just as strong without a church to go to. Stronger. I loved it. I believed it. I agreed with it. This sign beat the hell out of the one over our kitchen table in Chicago—which my parents lived by.

We made it to the next roadside station for gas and provisions and I pulled in to fill up our tank one last time. I opened the car door and was bowled over by the intoxicating aroma of pine and earth and freshly unfurling leaves. The air was as crisp as an icicle. The sky was crystalline blue. My God, what a place. Preston and Brandy were both out, Preston holding Brandy's leash and both of them peeing on the same bush simultaneously. I pumped gas and went inside to use the toilet.

When I came back to the counter to pay, I saw that there were fresh baked goods from the town bakery. Since Preston had eaten all the doughnuts, I bought a big white paper box of cinnamon rolls with white icing for us to take to Mom.

I thought the woman running the counter was someone familiar from past summers but she didn't seem to recognize me. I had spent enough time up here every year that most of the people looked familiar even if I didn't know them.

We were back in the car, with the heat blasting now because it was a whole new level of chilly as we turned out onto the lake road. We crossed the old dam and the water was higher than we'd ever seen before, roaring over the dam in a great waterfall, high with spray. Many times in the past we crossed barefoot, balancing at the crest of the dam over the tiniest trickle of water. But that would have been mid or late summer. Preston knew the river that emptied into the big lake much better than I did. One summer when he was younger he convinced our mom to drop him off with the canoe at a place up north on the river. He canoed back to the cabin over several days, camping alone with a pup tent, and portaging the heavy canoe around the dam. Preston had always been an adventurer.

Once we passed the dam, we were home free. I couldn't believe we were almost there. The night had gone so quickly and I wasn't even feeling tired. I was so excited to be there in that beautiful land, God's Country. Yes, it was.

Last stretch, trees and tall grasses lining the crude blacktop road.

Last turn, grasses lining a gravel road wide enough barely for two cars to pass.

Last several hundred feet were only a packed down dirt trail for car tires with grasses growing up between the tire tracks.

Last stop, our old driveway of tall grass and wildflowers, just beginning their summer jaunt, the old red truck parked out in the open, old tarp thrown off, old sticker of a cheerful black bear on the driver's side door.

I switched the engine off. Preston let Brandy bound out unleashed. Brandy started barking. I decided to honk the horn. I started honking and Preston jumped out and started jumping up and down with his arms over his head.

Our mother, a truly beatific look of overwhelmed joy on her face, came out into the high grass covered with dew, an apron around her waist, her arms out to see her son.

I opened my door and got out and went to our mother and she hugged us both to her and I felt we were right to come. I felt we were loved and had done the impossible and had succeeded in making the long drive. I had delivered us. Everyone was happy and Brandy was making us laugh, racing in circles, running down to the lake and back up, running rings around the entire cabin. He knew how to express himself thoroughly. I felt like doing the same and I began to run and he ran with me. We ran down to look at the magnificent lake, sprawling in its wide unmarred excellence, its unspeaking divinity, its godly grandeur. I dropped to my knees in the sweet tall grass and gave Brandy a hug as he licked my face. "We made it old buddy. We made it."

MY NEW JOB

Days at the cabin unfolded with quiet deliberation, each of us rapidly seeing our futures unfold. Preston started working at the nearby resort tending the grounds; raking the beach, mowing the lawns, cleaning the fish house. He didn't love it but he needed the money and he could walk down every morning and back in the afternoon. Mom had installed a phone and the phone was ringing a lot.

Every morning Mom talked to a lawyer whom she obviously liked a lot. She would get off the phone and tell us about this guy. He had an office in downtown Chicago. She had never met him in person, didn't know what he looked like, but she loved his attitude. She kept calling him "a real roughrider." He was saying she needed to "get her ass back down to Chicago" right away and reclaim her place in her home. He had a viewpoint that none of us had considered: that

Dad could sell the house and take off and Mom would be high and dry. As it is, she didn't have any income and Dad had frozen her access to their joint checking account. Mom said she was afraid to go back, that she was going to have to go back on the bus again and be in the house. We were scared for her and for ourselves.

Dad was calling her a lot. At first when we arrived he called about us. He and Mom had a big argument but in the end it seemed right that since Dad had been so horrible to Preston that we would want to go up and be by our mom especially since we usually spent our summers at the cabin anyway. Dad wouldn't stop calling though and Mom got to the point where she was hanging up on him and he called back over and over. Mom told us that he was threatening to come up and kill us all.

If I answered the phone, thinking maybe I could talk some sense into him, he would start swearing and yelling. I couldn't really tell what he wanted at that point. Everything he yelled over the phone was a threat. It seemed like he hated us. It seemed like we hated him.

I knew I needed to make money. My mom had heard that the biggest resort on the lake was hiring girls my age for cabin-cleaning and waitressing. My mom drove me over to the resort one morning so I didn't have to go alone and because I was a little scared to ask about a job.

Inside the old lodge I spoke with the owner—a big man with a playful joking personality who said his family was all from Chicago. I liked him right away. He must have thought I seemed okay because he introduced me to Margaret, the cook in the lodge kitchen and told her to show me the ropes. She was not sure about me at all and she made that clear to him and to me. Margaret showed me around the 60-year-old log kitchen and the stool I could sit on by the big warm stove with many burners and three ovens. In the mornings I was to peel potatoes from a huge burlap sack into an equally large tin pan filled with water. That sounded like an okay job to me. I had peeled many potatoes for my mom and knew just how it was done with a metal peeler. I could picture myself doing that and even kind of enjoying it. She showed me how the tables were to be set for the fishermen's breakfast and again for dinner.

She brought me out to the back and introduced me to her daughter-in-law, Jeannie, who was in charge of the rental cabins. Jeannie walked me through a couple of cabins, talking as if I'd been scrubbing toilets and wiping dust off the tops of light bulbs all my life. Although I knew how to clean a toilet, I had never considered wiping the dust off the top of a light bulb and it had never occurred to me that dust would accumulate there. In each cabin bathroom there were exposed lightbulbs over the sink and they all needed dusting every week. Who knew?

Jeannie was cute and sassy, maybe thirty years old at most. She was married to the cook's son who was the groundskeeper for the resort. She told me they had two little boys, and that they lived in one of the cabins on the resort property. Her husband was out chopping wood in a far corner and she waved at him as we walked briskly from cabin to cabin. Jeannie walked with a sexy fun air of confidence and enthusiasm. She had a tight thin body, and it made sense to me when she mentioned that she had her own horse she rode in barrel races in a pasture

at the other end of the property. She had red hair in wonderful natural waves and bangs that hung just a bit over
her bright blue eyes. She had light skin and freckles. She
wore a calico-print cotton blouse tied in front at her mid-
riff, and high-waisted flare-legged jeans that were too
short but somehow looked great with her lace-up brown
work boots. I thought she was wonderful.

I followed Jeannie back to the lodge to see where I
would pick up my cleaning supplies when I arrived at
work. We saw my mom sitting on a bench near our truck.
"Mom, this is Jeannie. She's in charge of the cabins and
she's showing me how to do the cleaning on Saturdays.
It looks like I have the job!"

Jeannie extended a firm hand to my mother and I
saw my mother hesitate.

"Hello," my mother smiled her fake demure smile at
Jeannie. "Sidney, what? Oh, you'll be cleaning? Are you
sure? I don't know . . . that's very hard work . . . "

"Yeah Mom, that's the job. Helping in the cabins and
in the kitchen and in the dining room. It's great." I was
happy about it and I wanted to make sure Jeannie understood that.

Jeannie jumped in with her impatient manner, "Yeah,
well, Sidney seems excited about it and she's willing to
give it a shot so let's just let your daughter see what she
can do. If it doesn't work out she can quit . . . unless she
gets fired first! Ha ha, right Sidney?"

I wasn't afraid. I thought it was perfect. It actually
sounded fun. I would have to be there at six in the morning every day. I would peel potatoes and set tables. Then
I would serve the fishermen their breakfasts. After that
I cleared the breakfast dishes and reset all the tables.

I would have to wash the dishes some days too. Then I could go home on weekdays and not come back until four. I would help serve dinners some evenings. On Saturdays I would clean cabins.

I started the very next day. I drove over in the Volare. It was only about three miles down the road toward the town.

Margaret did not suffer fools gladly. When I got there the first morning she acted like I should just jump in and do everything she asked, but there was a lot I didn't know. She taught me how to run the old-style dishwashing machine, which had racks for the dishes on a conveyor belt that you manually shoved along until the dishes were under the spigots for the burning hot water and spraying dish soap. You yanked down the sheet metal doors with wooden handles on either side of your rack of dishes and let the burning water and stinging green soap do its magic. Then, without burning your hands or forearms you hoisted up the metal door on the far end and pulled the clean dishes out onto the end of the conveyor belt where they cooled. Margaret was disgusted that I was afraid of the hot water and the dirty dishes. She showed me how you picked up every dish and scraped it clean into a big metal garbage can at the front of the line and I felt like I might vomit when I saw all the people's discarded food. I didn't want to touch their dirty dishes.

The cook snapped at me, "I've never worked with a spoiled city slicker before and I hope you won't make me regret it now. I'm giving you a chance here. Maybe you can learn to make something of yourself. If you can't, I'll fire you. I have no time for spoiled little rich girls."

"Well good because I don't either," I answered. I thought I saw her smile.

I felt great about working every day, making a paycheck and tips. The people around the lodge were nice; the fishermen, the older couples who'd been coming every year since the '30s. The owner from Chicago was a big out-of-shape guy who didn't seem capable of running such a labor-intensive operation. He and his wife had only owned the place for a few years. His wife was tiny and smoked and drank coffee all day and switched over to some kind of brown liquor in a lowball glass every afternoon. She wore well-made wool skirt-and-jacket sets with nice dress shoes and silk stockings the way older women in Chicago did. She seemed to have no desire to adapt to the Northwoods. Somehow she knew something about me, because every once in a while she'd throw out some clever comment or quote or French phrase, and she'd look at me. I would usually get what she meant and she'd say, "Right Sidney?" And then she'd wink. Her husband would joke, "Well good thing you're here Sidney because more than half of everything my wife says is completely lost on the rest of us." They made a strange couple but they seemed to genuinely like each other and to enjoy their circumstance.

The owners must have bought the place and kept the staff because Margaret the cook knew more about everything and had been working there forever. Margaret would tell the owner and his wife how to do things and they'd do it. The cook was the one who was really running the place and she knew it and she was always mildly disgusted and looking down on the rest of us, the city slickers. It was a nice coincidence for me that the owners and I were from Chicago, and that they too were obviously urban people by habit. Margaret was always taking an "us against them" viewpoint. She felt that she and the other locals were more hardworking. I don't know whether that was actually true. But she had herself convinced and she'd go out of her way to convince me.

There was a white enamel teapot that sat on the stove back burner. When the dining room was open, Margaret spent all her time facing that stove. Looking right at it. Constantly moving pans around, flipping things on the griddle, stirring pots of soup. I was instructed to fill the teapot with water before dining room service began and to turn it on and heat up water for tea if anyone requested it.

One evening early on in my apprenticeship under Margaret the cook, someone wanted tea so I ran into the kitchen and turned the gas flame on under the kettle. The dining room was very busy and I was the only server on duty.

I was running back and forth from the kitchen to the dining room helping the guests when I suddenly remembered the tea.

I went back to the stove and saw the kettle spewing black smoke, the flame under it still burning. No steam was coming from the spout. All the water had boiled away and the once bright-white enameled kettle had turned black.

I gasped.

Margaret was standing there observing my reaction and it was obvious that she had watched the kettle and seen what was happening. With one of Margaret's oven mitts I took the now blackened kettle and refilled it with water from the sink. I put it on high and ran out to tell the customer the tea was still coming and that I was sorry it was taking so long.

I came back and set up the cup and saucer and the individual teapot for the water. I brought the tray, filled the little pot and grabbed an assortment of tea bags. The customer finally got his tea and I forgot about the whole thing.

The dining room was busy and I was kept running all evening.

Eventually things quieted down and we were getting ready to close the kitchen. Margaret said, "Sidney, you're going to have to make time to scrub my teapot white again. I don't want my teapot looking like that."

"Sure Margaret, of course. I'll do it as soon as I finish the dishes."

I carried in the dining room dishes and went through the usual process, scraping, stacking the washer trays, dragging them through, stacking the clean hot dishes on the shelves on the other side.

I was ready to go home and Margaret had thrown her vinegar on the griddle, which steamed up and gave a feeling of finality to the day's work. "Sidney, I hope you aren't planning on leaving without getting my kettle cleaned up."

"Oh gosh Margaret I forgot. Can I do it tomorrow? I can do it after I peel the potatoes. I don't have anything else to do then."

"I don't want to start my day out looking at that thing all black like that, no thank you. You can stay now and get it over with."

I was upset, but I thought "fine, I'll just do it really fast and go."

I started with the steel wool scrubbing pad. The black on the white enamel didn't budge. It looked like it would wipe right off. I scrubbed harder. It didn't look any different. My heart sank. Good old Margaret was watching over my shoulder.

"Not as easy as it looks, huh?"

"No. Am I using the right thing? Is there a better way?"

"You're using the right thing, but you aren't using any elbow grease. Elbow grease is the key ingredient."

"You mean just scrub harder?"

"Yep."

So I scrubbed as hard as I could for about thirty seconds and I could see some white starting to show through the black. This was going to take forever.

"Margaret, how much did this kettle cost? Do they have them in town? I can just buy you a new one. I'll give you the money from my paycheck."

"That's an easy answer isn't it? That's the lazy city slicker answer to everything. Throw it away and get a new one. Well, I don't want a new one. I want my white kettle and I want it back to looking clean and white. The only way you're gonna learn not to forget something on the stove is to clean that kettle until it's gleaming white. You've forgotten the kettle before you know. Do you realize that?"

"No. I don't remember ever leaving it on before."

"No, of course not. That's because I've been covering for you. You've been running around sometimes like a chicken with its head cut off and I knew you weren't going to remember so I'd just shut it off for you."

"Oh. Thank you. I didn't know."

"Well, the time comes when you can't rely on everyone around you to cover up for your mistakes. The time comes when you have to take full responsibility."

"Okay. I get it."

"I'm going home now. When that kettle is good as new, all you have to do is turn off this light and pull the back kitchen door shut tight on your way out. Good night, Sidney."

"Good night, Margaret."

I stayed and cleaned it.

The kettle was white when she came in the next morning.

Margaret smiled at me when I came in and I smiled too.

MOM GOES BACK TO CHICAGO

My mother's lawyer, the rough-rider, was insistent that my mom should go back to Chicago and stake her claim. I had no intention of going with her. I felt like I had left the celadon hell-house for this knotty pine sunny heaven. Preston felt even more strongly that he and Dad had made some kind of permanent break and that we'd seen the last of our father forever.

One morning Jay came over and I was surprised to see him. He brought my mother an eight-track tape of Bob Dylan's *Highway 61 Revisited* album. He wanted her to hear the song "Like a Rolling Stone."

My mom had an eight-track player sitting on a table next to the stone fireplace and she and my brother had been listening to some tapes; my mom had the Bee Gees and the Kingston Trio, my brother had The Doors and Uriah Heep. I didn't know where those things had come from, I didn't have any recorded music of my own. When I left Chicago I left behind my few cassette tapes: Cat Stevens, The Moody Blues, the first Rod Stewart album. Jay showing up with Bob Dylan recordings was a revelation to me. I had never understood who Bob Dylan was. I'd heard "Lay, Lady, Lay" on the radio in Chicago, but I didn't love that song and I didn't connect the voice from that recording with the voice from songs like "Blowin' in the Wind," which I never liked much either.

This "Like a Rolling Stone" song really resonated with me. Dylan's singing was intense and sincere. The music was freewheeling. Mostly it was the colorful words, and I could see that my brother, my mom, and Jay thought it should be my mom's anthem. I agreed but somewhere in my heart it was mine too.

I walked into the cabin from my morning work and there they all were, huddled around the tape player. When they got to "Like a Rolling Stone" they got really animated. Jay knew all the words and yelled out the ones he thought were relevant to my mom's situation. Preston was jumping and dancing around. My mom was clapping along and dancing from foot to foot. I saw the breadth of Bob Dylan's words and got a glimpse of what was happening to us. I cried as I sang along and so did my mother and Preston. Jay was with us in solidarity. We were all alone together at the top of the world.

Soon after, my mother boarded the bus bound for Duluth and then for Chicago. She had only a small overnight bag with her that she could easily carry. Her plan was to stay with our Aunt Evelyn the first night, then go to the house the next day. The lawyer said it was urgent at this point. He thought my dad or maybe even the bank had put the house on the market. Either it had gone into foreclosure or maybe our dad was trying to sell it fast and get out while we were all away. Mom promised to call us from Aunt Evelyn's apartment.

In the meantime, Dad called the cabin, usually late at night. He called one night very late soon after Mom had left. I was so exhausted from work, I stumbled out into the living room and answered before I could think to strategize about not answering. He immediately started asking me a million angry questions. I wasn't sure how to answer any of them. He was swearing, telling me I was crazy to be up there with my mother, didn't I understand what she was trying to do, to ruin him? To divorce him and marry that bastard, Seymour Hoffman? I hadn't seen Seymour Hoffman nor did anyone mention him so I kept telling Dad that he must be wrong. He was shouting, "You're a fool! She's using you! You don't think she actually gives a shit what happens to you, do you?"

All I could answer was, "Dad, honestly it doesn't seem like you do either. None of you do. I have a job. I'm doing what I need to do. I have to go to bed. I have to work at six o'clock in the morning. Goodbye. I'm hanging up."

He called back the minute I hung up. "Dad, I'm sorry, but I'm not going to just stand here and listen to you scream a bunch of mean stuff at me, goodbye."

I hung up and he called again. I answered. He was screaming at me, calling me names. I decided to fight fire with fire. I started screaming back, calling him an asshole and anything else I could think of and as I screamed I wondered whether I was acting or whether I had truly lost my temper, or my mind. It was like fake it 'til you make it. I didn't want to call him those names and everything I was saying felt sick and bad coming out of my mouth, but I felt like I had to try shocking him out of calling because I didn't want the phone to keep ringing and I didn't want him to keep screaming at me. I yelled some more mean things and slammed the phone down in its cradle. The phone rang again immediately. It rang and rang. There was no answering machine, no way to get it to stop. I picked it up and shut it down again. It started right up again ringing. I walked to my bedroom door as it rang, not stopping, and back out to the living room one more time, wondering how Preston could sleep through this, and I took the receiver off and stuck it in my grandmother's old sewing basket next to the dining table. After a minute or so it started making a loud buzzing alarm that was meant to notify you that your phone was off the hook. I left the receiver in the sewing basket, thinking that the alarm would eventually stop and I'd be able to sleep.

I had finally fallen back to sleep in my narrow pink bed when I heard a siren. I couldn't remember ever hearing one come down our road.

To my horror, the car with the flashing lights and siren came flying into our driveway. From my bedroom window I saw it turn and plunge down into our front grass, driving right up to our cabin windows, siren still blasting, headlights glaring into the cabin windows.

Preston was stumbling around in his room. I grabbed a sweatshirt. I was shaking all over.

The beam of a blinding spotlight was blazing from the car, searching our house's interior. A man's voice came over a megaphone. "If you are armed, come out with your hands up."

Preston and I both stumbled in the blinding light onto the kitchen porch and walked slowly toward the lights with our hands up.

The light shut off and only the headlights of the car showed the police officer and his squad car. There was a second officer in the driver's seat.

"You kids the only ones here?"

Preston spoke, "Yes officer. What's the problem? We didn't call the police. We were both sleeping. There's nothing wrong here."

"Well, a man named Donald Duncan has called us with an emergency report from Chicago. Do you know that person?"

"Yes, that's our father."

"Mr. Duncan called us tonight around one a.m. saying he tried to get a hold of his family by phone but that there's been no answer and that the phone line is out of order as of late this evening."

Preston didn't know, so I said, "It's not out of order, Officer."

"I'm going to come in and take a look around, kids."

The officer, with his gun out and pointed in front of him, walked up to the porch and said, "You kids come on in here with me and we'll just have a look around." He motioned to the other guy in the car who got out and started looking around the cabin with a flashlight and a gun.

Preston and I stood in the living room and watched the policeman poke around. "Where's the phone?"

Preston said, "It's usually on the table, but . . . "

I watched as the officer traced the cord from the wall to the phone base on the dining table bench. Then he followed the curling cord from the bench to Grandma's sewing basket and pulled out the receiver.

He looked from Preston to me.

"The phone don't work too good like that," he said, the receiver in his hand, a wry smile on his face.

I just stood there.

Preston just stood there.

He put the receiver back on the cradle on its base.

"Let's see if we can get through the rest of the night without any more calls from Chicago. How does that sound?"

I was relieved.

He turned to leave, had his gun back in its holster.

At the kitchen door he turned. The other officer was right behind him on our porch.

"Are you kids up here alone?"

Preston quickly answered, "No we aren't. Our mom is up here with us. She went back to Chicago for just a few days and she'll be back later this week."

"How old are you?"

"I'm twenty-one. My sister's seventeen."

"Okay, well you kids be careful and stay out of trouble, ya hear?"

"Yes Sir. Thank you, Officer. Sorry for your trouble, Officer."

After they left, Preston who had slumped down in one of the two upholstered chairs in the living room said, "Holy shit, that was bad. What the fuck is up with Dad? What was that brilliant thing you had going with the phone? What was that supposed to do? That guy's face was pretty funny. 'Oh, I see, the phone receiver's hidden in a sewing basket.' What the fuck? Sid, have you lost your mind, what were you doing with that?"

"I put it in there because Dad was freaking out and he kept calling and I have to work at six and I told him not to call any more and he just didn't listen. Then I took it off the hook but the alarm thing went off and it kept buzzing so I stuck it in there."

"Funny. Next time just take the jack out of the wall. Just undo the phone completely."

"I don't know how."

"I'll show you. Here." He walked over and unplugged the phone from the wall jack. "See? Just do that. Then there's no phone at all. Okay? I'm hitting the sack."

"Yeah. Me too."

"Good night. That was scary."

Over the next few days Dad didn't stop calling and he insisted we return the Volare. I didn't really care any more. I didn't want to drive it anyway because Dad said he had cut the insurance. One day we received a letter from a lawyer saying that the Volare was to be turned in at the Hibbing Airport by a certain date. Preston and I read through to the bottom. The car was to be surrendered tomorrow. We were pretty shocked but I told myself I didn't care.

Preston was upset. "Fuck Dad and fuck his ugly rental car. Piece of shit. Fuck Dad and fuck his fucking Volare."

"Preston, what do we care? Who cares? We don't need his stupid car. We're doing great."

"Sid, we're doing great for like another month. Then what? I have one more year of college. How am I going to finish now? And what are you going to do, stay here? Do you realize what this place will be like by October? This is the fucking tundra line. It'll be snow up to your eyeballs by November and it's the coldest place in the entire goddamn fucking country. The Coldest Place. You don't even have a winter coat. This place is not insulated. You haven't even graduated from high school yet. We are fucked. Dad has fucked us over for leaving. But what were we supposed to do? Stay with him and get the shit kicked out of us? We had no choice! We're his kids and he's fucked us over! Why is he being like this? I was trying to help him. We were going to turn it around. I know Dad really wanted to save his business and save the house and everything and drive up here and bring Mom back, but obviously that isn't what happened by the way he's acting. You know he wanted Mom to sign some papers last winter? Do you know about that?"

"Know about that? Oh my God, that's all I heard about every night. They came in my room every night trying to make me the referee. They are the worst parents in the world. I hate them both. I really don't give a shit about either one of them. I hope they kill each other when Mom gets down there. I'd rather be an orphan."

"We pretty much are orphans. Have you taken a good look at our situation lately? Those papers were Dad trying to use the money from equity in the house to infuse the business with cash so he could make some new investments and make a bunch of money and bail us all out."

"That sounds like gambling in Las Vegas to me. That's what Mom said too."

"He was trying to save his business and save his marriage and save his family, his house, everything.

That's all Dad ever wanted. He only wanted Mom and he wanted to give her everything she wanted."

Preston started to cry. "But the stupid asshole. He fucked it all up. And now he's fucking us over."

We were out in front of the cabin near the road. I still had the letter about the car in my hand. Preston sat down in the tall grass and put his hands over his face.

I put my hand on his shoulder. "Dad's a jerk. Mom said he should just give up on having his own business and go back to working for EF Hutton."

"Shut up, Sidney."

I went down to the cabin and thought about how to get the car to the airport in Hibbing by tomorrow. I called Jay's house. I got lucky and he answered.

"This is weird, but I have to take the Volare to the Hibbing airport by tomorrow to get sent back to Chicago. Can you meet me there and give me a ride back?"

Jay was nice and sensible as usual. "Yeah, well, no problem but I'd have to do it tonight."

"Okay, well it says it can be dropped at the Hibbing Airport any time and that the keys get dropped to the twenty-four-hour desk clerk. So any time is fine."

"Okay, I'll come at seven tonight to your place and you can follow me."

"That's great cuz I have no idea where the airport is."

"Yeah, I figured."

I hung up and heard the first crash. Broken glass. I ran to the kitchen door and listened, my heart pounding in my throat. Another crash. I told Brandy to stay in and I cautiously walked up to the road toward the sound. I heard a gasp like someone was about to start screaming or sobbing. Preston. Then another crash. The Volare came into view, parked as usual in front of the carport. Preston was standing in front of it, a big rock from the woods over his head. He whipped it hard with both hands just as I came around the corner and it smashed into the windshield. Glass flew. The windshield was shattered in two places. I watched. My brother had tears streaming down his wet face. The sky over him was clear blue. The trees were towering and fully green, leaves shining in the sunlight. "Why Live In God's Country Without God?" I thought to myself. My brother's hands were meant for writing. He had slender fine-boned fingers. His hand gestures were expressive and intelligent. He was no football player, even though he'd been a good one. He was no fighter. The heavy rocks in his hands, the shattering of glass. His face was full of tenderhearted pain over love for his father. I knew Preston loved Dad a lot. Honestly, Preston loved Mom a lot too. Preston loved them both, and understood them both, and was hurt by them so much more than I was.

"Come on Sid, get a rock." Preston smiled through his tear-stained anguish.

I smiled. I went to the edge of the woods and saw that back when the road was made bigger they'd left small piles of rocks along the edge. I picked up a rock and threw it toward the car but it didn't even reach the car much less damage it.

"Oh my God, Sidney. That's pathetic. Get your arm into it."

I smiled again. I picked a smaller rock that was more comfortable for throwing. I hurled it. It landed on the front hood with a thud.

"Come on kid sis! I'll show you how it's done."

My brother chose a rock the size of a softball and pitched it hard. Glass flew everywhere.

"Geez Preston, I'm gonna have to drive this thing to the airport you know!"

He moved around to the back, picked up more rocks and pulverized the rearview mirror on the passenger side. I was sort of laughing. He was crying and laughing.

I went back inside because I didn't want Brandy to be scared. Brandy sat on my lap in the big chair with the duck-print fabric. I patted his big head and he licked my hand. We listened to the sound of glass breaking and metal getting pounded and every so often, a sob.

That night Jay showed up in his trusty pickup truck. He came down to the cabin door with astonishment on his face.

"What the hell happened? Are you guys nuts?"

Preston just looked at Jay and shrugged. I said nothing.

Preston rode with me and we followed Jay in his truck all the way to the Hibbing airport about fifty miles away. Preston helped me brush the broken glass off the front seat and the dashboard, but once we got going, little bits of glass kept hitting us in our faces as we drove. Good thing it was summer, but it was still pretty chilly with the wind right in our faces. I kept slowing down and Jay was patient and went slow too. A few times we hit a cloud of tiny bugs and we both held our breath and squinted so we wouldn't get them up our noses or in our mouths or eyes. The drive took forever because I was afraid to go any faster than about thirty-five miles an hour.

When we finally made it to the airport, we chose a spot for the Volare pretty far away from the front entrance, hoping no one would notice what shape the car was in. I went inside and asked the night clerk if he knew I was dropping off a car. He said he did so I gave him the keys and told him it was parked out front. That went better than I expected.

I came back out and Preston and Jay were just looking at the car and laughing. I felt bad. I didn't want to even look at the car.

"Let's go, you guys."

Two days later our dad called and I answered.

He was really mad. He immediately asked, "Do you know anything about how that car got vandalized? Where did you park it? Was it okay when you dropped it off?"

"What? Yeah. What are you talking about?"

"The people from the rental agency went to get the car and found it smashed. The stereo ripped out, the leather seats all slashed. Would your stupid hick friends do something like that?"

"No Dad. I don't know what happened. I guess we shouldn't have left it there."

"God damn it."

When Preston got back from raking the resort beach that morning, I told him about the additional damage. He was almost disappointed, "Geez. That's pretty funny. So what we did looked like nothing compared to what somebody else did."

"Do you think Dad will have to pay for it?"

"What? No way. He doesn't even care. The car company has to take it on the chin because we dropped it off just like we were supposed to."

"Okay."

"God, Sid. It's not exactly a good time to start feeling sorry for Dad. Have you heard from Mom since she got down there?"

"No."

Later that day I went down to the dock to swim before I had to go back to the lodge. I had the old red truck to drive so I went back and forth easily, not having to walk the three miles, not having to wait for Mom to pick me up. From down on the dock I heard the phone ringing. It hung up and started up again. There it was again. Someone was trying to get us to answer. I ran up the old stone steps, ran up through the grassy path in the yard and slapped open the screen door. I ran to the phone and answered a breathless, "Hello?"

"Sidney, it's Mother."

"Hi Mom! How's it going?"

Soft crying on the other end.

"Mom? What's happening?"

"I went to the house. It was all locked up. The locks weren't the same. My key didn't work in the front door. I tried to look in the front window. There were price tags on everything. Oh God. Oh God. It's so terrible. Oh God . . . "

"Mom, what are you saying? Who did that?"

"My lawyer says this is what he was afraid of. Don has either put the house up for sale and is selling everything in it, or the bank has taken it and they are doing this. I don't know. The lawyer can't get a hold of your father. I don't know where he is. I don't know if he's living at the house."

"Okay, well what should we do?"

"You? You are not having to deal with this. You're

up there at that beautiful cabin. What are you saying, you? You aren't down here having to sneak around your own home. You have no idea what I'm going through, no idea . . . "

"Mom, okay. Okay Mom. I'm sorry."

"You don't know what I've been through the past few days! I thought I'd be able to get in the house and that I was to sleep there to reclaim my half-ownership. But with the doors all locked I didn't know what to do. I took the city bus out from Aunt Evie's apartment. I walked over to the park and just sat on a bench and cried. I didn't know what to do. Then I thought, 'no this is foolish. This is my home! I've lived there for ten years!'

"I walked back and I took one of those nice white stones we have that lines the landscaping in the front, remember what they're like? They're pretty big. I picked one up and I smashed through one side of the picture window! I couldn't believe what I was doing! It was so awful. The glass flew everywhere inside onto the carpet. I climbed through and I saw that the carpet was ruined anyway. Everything looked terrible. There are price tags on all the furniture and the paintings . . . my paintings I chose so lovingly for my beautiful home! Oh, it's a nightmare!"

I listened to my mother sobbing her innocent girlish sob. I was broken-hearted for her and myself. Everything inside me hurt for us. I wanted to turn off and disconnect and be completely done with my parents and their tugging on my heart. Why was I always feeling for them, thinking of their plight, considering their circumstances? When had the tables turned? When did they stop doing that for me? Had they ever done that for me?

She was still talking, "And poor Aunt Evelyn has had such a terrible time. I don't know if she can take this at her age. I've been sleeping on the floor, and you know how tiny her apartment is. She answered the phone one night and it was Don. You know she always liked him so much, even when we were dating she always liked him. And he started yelling at her on the phone and she just couldn't take it. She broke down in tears. Her health isn't good and she shouldn't have to be going through this. She is worried Preston won't be able to finish college."

"Yeah, well he says he can get loans since it's only for the one last year. Tell Aunt Evie that, Mom."

My mother and I somehow wrapped up the conversation and she said she'd call again when she knew more about the house.

I came in the cabin one morning after my early shift. It was Saturday so I had peeled the potatoes at six and then cleaned with Jeannie until ten. I was planning to take off my denim skirt, T-shirt and running shoes uniform and put on my bikini for a swim in the lake. When I got to the bathroom, it was occupied. "Preston, how long you gonna be in there?"

"What? All day it looks like."

"What? Why?"

"I got a problem with my butt and Mom says I have to soak in a tub of Epsom salts."

"How am I supposed to go to the bathroom?"

"I don't care. Go outside."

"Outside? What if somebody comes?"

"Just go outside. Nobody's coming. My asshole is

falling out and I gotta sit here in privacy. I got like a serious plumbing problem. Mom says it's stress related. God is testing us sister Sid."

"God, Preston."

"What? This is a fucking disaster! I can hardly walk, much less do all the stuff they want me to do down there. Those people are crazy. They want me to do the work of like five guys every day. They're killing me."

"Did you tell them you can't do that much? Tell them you're getting sick from it?"

"I can't tell them that. They think we're spoiled kids. I think they're making me work extra hard. I swear to God they have something against us. Maybe it's from the years when Dad came up here with his Jaguar and his big cigars."

"Probably."

"Yeah, probably."

I went outside and peed around the back of the woodpile where Brandy liked to poop so nobody could watch him.

THE UNRAVELING

Another phone call from Mom. "Oh Sidney, I'm afraid it's all bad news. The lawyers told me I had to get over to the house myself with papers that proved that they could not go ahead with the bank's liquidation of our property. There was an estate sale going on. Our home! Everything in it! There was a rude woman at a table in the front, on the driveway and our own neighbors, those people! How could they do it? They were buying our things! Carrying things out and walking right past me! They wouldn't even talk to me. I was pleading, begging them, 'please, they don't have a right to do this, please stop.' They walked right past me with my beautiful paintings, the horse sculpture, the lamps from the family room. I remember when we bought those brass lamps and how your father thought they were so terrific. How could he let this happen to his family? I told him!

I told him! I was begging! Oh God, I shook the papers in front of that woman's face and she said she didn't know anything about it and I ran into the house. I got on our phone, as people were just swarming the place looking at all our things. I called the police and told them they had to help me. They came and stopped the sale but by then so much had been taken already. I just collapsed in the driveway and cried. Oh Sidney, your toys, your beautiful doll from Italy that your grandmother brought back for you."

"Did they take my bike?"

"I don't know. I didn't see that. Is that all you care about? Your bike? Your mother is telling you of this ordeal I've just been through and all you can think of is your bicycle?"

"Do you think we'll get the house back?"

"I don't think so, no. Sidney, don't you think I'd give anything, anything to be back in my beautiful home again?"

"I'm sorry, Mom. I really am. Preston and I have been talking about what we should do and everything. Do you think we can find out what's still in the house? Preston wants his winter coat. And he told me I can have his down coat and down vest if you can bring them up."

"Bring them up? What do you think I'm doing down here? I am not going to be back up any time soon. Sidney, you need to get realistic."

"Realistic? Mom, I'm seventeen years old. You're telling me we have no home there any more. What am I supposed to do? The summer's almost over."

"I don't know. Aunt Evie is falling apart over this. I've been crying in her apartment sleeping on the floor every night. She can't take this. I have no idea what you're going to do."

After that conversation, I saw my future different- ly. Everything felt strange. Bad strange and, surprising- ly, good strange. I felt like everything around me was tingling with possibility. I wasn't sure where this was all leading but I felt excited. The air was getting cool- er. In the mornings, as August progressed, there was a real chill in the air. Some days it stayed very cool and Preston made a fire in the fireplace at the cabin. There was a big woodpile, some of the wood very old, some of it newer from fallen trees that Mom had paid local people to split and stack. The cabin had an old furnace under the floorboards, sitting on cement blocks on the dirt. It had no cellar, and was built on footings on slop- ing land. At its tallest, the space under the cabin, where I had seen Dad crawl in to fix the pump, was about five feet. That was on the side that faced the lake. On the low side where the cabin faced the road, the floor- boards were just about right at the level of the bare ground. The furnace was nestled in there near the lake- side, an old oil-burning thing, with an oil tank. Preston was telling me things about the cabin that we had never thought about before.

"Sid, I'm leaving soon. I got my loan money, you knew that, right? I'm heading back to finish college. I have to. You could maybe come with me and stay in my room. That'd be kind of cool. What a dude you'd be if you were like a stowaway in your big brother's dorm room at college."

"Yeah, that'd be cool. But I have to finish high school."

"Mom says you can take the bus to Chicago and stay with Aunt Evie."

"What? When did she say that? She didn't tell me that."

"Well, she probably thinks you'll flip out."

"Yeah well she's right. Where am I supposed to go to school then?"

"There's a high school right across the street! Remember?"

"That's a city school. I'm supposed to go there where I know no one? Those kids will probably hate my guts because I'm from the suburbs. I'd get beaten up for sure. I transfer there and then what? Mom and I both sleeping on the floor in Aunt Evie's one-bedroom apartment? Forget it."

"This is why she didn't tell you. Her other idea is to get an apartment near your school, near our house, well our old house, and the two of you live there and she'd get a job to pay the rent. And you could finish at your same school."

"I'm not living with her. I hate her. She's a pathetic whiner. I am not telling people there about this whole thing. They bought our stuff out of our house! They probably know that Dad has screwed us over. I'm not going back there and answering all their nosy questions. And what about this whole Seymour Hoffman thing? Where is he in all this?"

"I don't know about him. No idea. Maybe Mom's fucking him. I have no idea. I don't see why she'd want to, except if he's got some serious dough holed up someplace. He's old. He's like a World War II veteran. He's fucking old."

"Gross. I don't want to see any of them or any of their crap."

"Wow. Sounds like you're taking a stand."

"Yeah. I guess I am. Didn't Grandpa die up here? I can stay up here until I die too. Grandpa stayed up here all winter, right?"

"Yeah, but he died doing it."

"No, he lived up here for a few winters, not just the one when he died."

"True. Three winters. But by the third one, he keeled over in the snow."

"Okay well I wouldn't have to stay forever. I could stay this one winter."

"You could try applying to go to the school in town. There's a high school. We drive by it. That old brick building. That's their high school. There's probably a school bus that comes out to get the kids who live on the lake."

"You think there are other kids living out here who go to high school there, really?"

"Yeah I'm sure of it. Let's go to town and see about signing you up. You could graduate with their senior class next spring. That would be a badass move sister Sid. Incredibly badass move."

Preston rode into town with me and I went into the old high school building. There was a light on in the office. To my surprise there was a cheerful-looking man in a black suit with white shirt and nondescript tie, spectacled and balding, talking to a middle-aged woman in nice office attire, seated at a desk in the center of the room. They looked at me with kindly interest and surprise.

"Hello," I said, "sorry to interrupt."

The man spoke, "No, not at all. What can we do for you?"

"I wanted to inquire about attending school here this fall."

They both raised their eyebrows simultaneously.

"The school year is starting up in about ten days."

They looked at me with very serious faces. I didn't flinch. I thought they could see that I was determined.

"You'd have to really get on it. I can give you all the forms to fill out and we'll have to have your parents' signatures if you're under eighteen."

"I'll be eighteen in February."

"So what grade do you think you'd be in?"

"I know for sure I'm starting my senior year. I only have one year to go."

"We'd have to request your transcripts from your previous school then. If you fill out the forms and everything looks okay, I can get on the phone with your old school and get everything squared away. But you'd have to get right on it."

Again they both looked me over. I stood my ground.

The man went on, "My name is Mr. Harlan and I'm the principal. This is Mrs. Briggs and she's the secretary. You'll be dealing with both of us. Are you sure this is something you want to pursue?"

"Yes. I'm sure."

"Okay well, then Mrs. Briggs will help you get all the papers together and go over them with you. Once you bring everything back signed, you and I can discuss what classes you'll need to graduate. We have pretty high standards and we pride ourselves on our academic excellence, well, to the best of our abilities with our budget and all."

"Okay, sounds great."

Mrs. Briggs got up and started bustling around opening drawers and getting papers out. "Where did you last go to school?"

"In Chicago."

"Have you ever moved before?"

"No but I'm not moving really. My family has had our place on the lake for fifty years or more. I'm just staying on for the winter this year."

"But you're not there alone?"

"No, no, of course not. My mom will be going back and forth from Chicago. And my brother will be back from college for the breaks too."

"Oh, your brother goes to college?"

"Yep, in Northfield, Minnesota."

"Oh. I see."

"I'm sure we can get this all together for you. What is your name?"

"Sidney. Sidney Duncan."

The kindly principal extended his hand, "A girl called Sidney. That's pretty interesting, Sidney's a man's name around here. A trailblazer, huh? I like it. Nice to meet you, Sidney. It won't be easy switching schools at the beginning of senior year. The kids all know each other very well. There are only about fifteen students set to graduate this coming spring. It'll be a small group. There'll be a lot to adjust to. And I hear Chicago is cold, but it's nothing like these northern winters. But if you're determined, I'm here to help. And something tells me, with a name like Sidney, you're up to a challenge."

I couldn't believe they were taking me seriously. I couldn't believe what was happening. I took the papers and ran out to the truck.

"They're going to take me! I'm staying!"

Preston looked happy and surprised and slapped my hand saying, "Way to go, little sis!"

My heart pounded in my chest with excitement, "This is going to be so cool!"

Once I'd made up my mind to stay, I started looking at everything differently. I talked to the resort owners and they said I could stay on as long as they had work for me to do into the winter and if things went well and they kept the lodge open all winter for dinners I could keep helping as a server at least a couple nights a week.

Preston pressured Mom to send his winter coat and some other things he wanted from the house. She was trying to get the lawyer to make the people who hosted the estate sale get the stuff and ship it to us. One day Preston told me that the goods would be delivered to the cabin in the next day or two. Preston was going back to college in just a couple weeks. He needed his clothes. I was hoping they'd send my bicycle because I loved my bike and I could picture myself riding it to work instead of driving all the time. He said we wouldn't know what they sent until we saw it with our own eyes because they could ship anything they wanted. There was nobody from our family telling them which things to work with. Unless maybe Dad himself was in charge of these people. We didn't know for sure. Maybe Dad was directing them. Would Dad send our favorite things or ones we didn't care about, on purpose, to be mean? Preston kept talking about what would be in the boxes.

One morning a truck pulled in to our driveway. I ran up from the cabin to talk to the driver. They said they had a delivery in our names and I said, "Yep, that's us!"

Preston had just woken up and he was sleepily coming up the path but he was so excited that I knew he'd be right behind me.

The truck driver and his partner both got out and came around to where Preston and I were standing. One guy had a clipboard full of papers. "I'm gonna need a check and a signature. Is one of your parents here to take care of this?"

Preston stepped up. "No, our mom's not here. She had this stuff sent for us from Chicago. It's our personal belongings. I'm twenty-one. I can sign for my own stuff. And my sister's."

"Well, it's not that simple. This stuff was shipped COD."

"What?! That's a mistake. That's not possible."

"Yeah, it is. I got the orders right here. It all got sent at the expense of those receiving on this end. I'm gonna need a check before I can open up that door."

Preston was getting really tense.

"How do we even know for sure if that's our stuff if you don't open the door. What do you mean you can't open the door. You can at least open the fucking door and let us see if that's our stuff."

"No I can't and I don't have to stay here and talk to you if you're going to be unruly."

"Look. This stuff is important. My sister's gonna be here all winter. Alone. She needs the things that were coming. What do we owe you? How much is it?"

"It's near a thousand dollars son."

"A thousand dollars?! Let me look at that."

Preston grabbed the paperwork on the clipboard. He peered at the figures on the paper. "God damn him. God damn him. Our own dad sent us our stuff COD for a thousand fucking dollars. It's not fair! We can't pay this. We shouldn't have to pay for our own shit we already had. Look, just open up the truck so we can figure this out okay?"

"Sorry, buddy, but we can't do that."

The truck driver took the clipboard and turned to walk. Preston grabbed him by the back of his shirt.

"Open the fucking truck, you asshole!"

"Get your hands off me boy or I'll get your ass put in jail."

I was yelling, "Preston! Preston don't!"

Preston stopped, he put his head down. When he lifted his eyes again they were full of tears. "Listen man, I'm sorry. This isn't your problem and it isn't your fault, I know that."

"Yeah, we been driving all night to get here and now we can't make this delivery so we gotta get this stuff of yours to a storage place before we can get back on the road. So it ain't no picnic for us either."

"What happens if we get the money together?"

"If you can get the money, great. Your things can be delivered same day at that point. We'll see that it's stored real close by for you kids. I can see this ain't what you had in mind. It's a tough spot you're in, way up here in the middle of nowhere. You kids don't have a parent here at all?"

"No, we don't. Not right now anyway. But our mom may be able to get the money. What do we need to do?"

"Just get on it quick 'cause the storage is gonna be expensive. Every day it's in storage the price goes up. This could get so expensive it wouldn't be worth it to pay. It'd be cheaper at some point to get yourselves some new stuff."

"Yeah, well nobody's going to give us money for new things. The best we can hope for is to get this. Thanks, and sorry I got so worked up."

"It's okay, we see all kinds, you know. Here's your copy of the delivery notice so you have the numbers to call if you get this straightened out. Good luck to you both."

Preston went in and called Mom.

He came out looking optimistic.

"Okay, she says the lawyer's been telling her she can take some money from the bank up here because she owns this place outright. She's going to take out some kind of loan. We're going to drive in to town tomorrow and get a cashier's check for the amount of the truck and storage bill. Then we better pray to God that the stuff on the fucking truck is worth it. Jesus Christ! What a fucked-up deal. Fuck Dad. God is testing us like in *The Grapes of Wrath*. Where's John Steinbeck, man? I should be taking notes, writing this shit down. God's fucking handing me the chapters. You can't make this shit up. This story's writing itself."

Mom came through and the next day we drove to town and got the cashier's check. A day later the truck drivers came back. Same guys. They had driven all the way to North Dakota and back since we saw them last, but here they were with our stuff and here we were with their check.

The paperwork was a breeze and one guy jumped up and opened the sliding side door wide. We could finally see in.

Preston craned his neck to see and asked, "How much of this is ours?"

"Everything left on the truck is yours. We got rid of all our other loads. All this is yours."

"Oh man. I don't know where we're going to put all this. I don't know where there's room for it."

I looked in the truck. There must have been about twenty boxes and some of them were big like they could house an appliance. The two truck drivers started pushing boxes closer to the edge of the truck nearer to the opening. Now we could see that there were loose things as well.

We could see Preston's weight-lifting equipment. "Holy shit, they sent all my weights and the bench and everything? That's insane. Was this by weight? Yes? No wonder it was so expensive. I swear to God Sid, Dad did this on purpose to fucking ruin us. Do you see your bike? There it is! You got it!"

One of the drivers lowered my bike down. I tried not to cry. I wiped my eyes. I tested out the hand brakes. I loved my bike as much as ever. I saw that in some ways it looked wrong here, and I wasn't sure how I would store it for the winter, but I didn't care. I could put it in the cabin in my room if I had to, or it could go down in the old bunkhouse by the water.

Preston was discussing the options of where to put everything and the drivers were getting antsy. The driver tried to explain, "Look, we are not authorized to carry all this down to that shed. It's way beyond the guidelines for distance from the truck. You'd have to pay more if you wanted us to carry all this down there."

"Okay, shit. We can't have the cabin all full of boxes. We won't be able to walk around. We gotta leave it all right here in the yard and we'll figure it out as we go. Okay, Sid?"

"Yeah, okay." It seemed bad to have the front yard all full of boxes and a weight lifting set. I knew Mom would have a heart attack if she saw all this in the front yard. But there was nothing we could do about it. As they came down off the truck into the grass I started opening boxes, looking for things I might want. I ripped the tape off box after box, realizing there were a lot of books.

Preston said goodbye to the guys. They jumped into their truck and waved. As they drove away I felt like that was the last vestige of civilization, watching us get smaller in their rearview mirror. We were alone at the end of a peninsula in the middle of North America, specifically in one of the consistently coldest places in America. And Preston was bound for his last year of college—leaving in just a few days on a Greyhound. And even after that, he'd be getting on with his life. I was staying. I was staying indefinitely and I had no plan B. I went back to ripping tape off boxes.

"Preston? Have you looked at these boxes yet? I hate to say this but it sure seems like a lot of books. And like not even very interesting books. Are these yours?"

Preston looked into a box. He looked into another, and another.

"Oh Jesus. This is unbelievable. This has to be a purposeful thing. I mean the weight set? And now these books? These are Dad's old law books. He knows goddamn well we don't want these. Either he sent us these to make it more expensive and fuck us up, or he had absolutely nothing to do with it and this is just random stuff. But no way, because we said the things from the children's rooms. The children's personal things. No one could have thought these law books were ours. Fuck them all. Fuck them all."

We combed those boxes for everything we could find that was of any use to either of us. We moved some of the weights and boxes down to the bunkhouse. We got Preston all packed up ready to go back to college. Before we knew it I was driving Preston to the bus station in Virginia.

He was scared about his loan. "Sid, you know I took a loan from the Dallas Cowboys guy that Dad was friends with. I told him everything and he sent the check. One check for the whole year all at once. It's all paid for already, tuition, room, board. Boom. Bullseye. Done. Incredible. But he made me send him a letter promising to pay every penny of it back over the next ten years after I graduate. Shit. I hope I can do it. I don't know. I mean what's he going to do to me, send somebody to break my legs?"

I had no idea what a huge pro football guy with a ton of money would do to somebody who owed him money. I thought it was such a big relief that Preston could finish school and graduate that I didn't care about what would happen after. "Preston, I don't know, but you'll figure it out. Don't worry about that now. Just get good grades and graduate!"

I sat in the truck and waved until Preston's bus pulled out. He sat in the last seat waving back to me. He was wearing a red-and-black plaid flannel shirt and his black wool beret from France. He had his black wool pea coat that he got out of the boxes. He had buttoned the top button of his shirt and he looked great, very studious. Ready for anything. I watched and waved until the bus turned to head out to the highway.

LABOR DAY WEEKEND

August was over. In a few more days my new school would start. I dug a few of my clothes out of the boxes in the yard. It had rained a couple times already and the boxes were getting soggy. I knew that if anything was really important I had to get it now. Preston and I had dragged the most important stuff down to the bunkhouse. Dad's books were sitting in the yard. It was eerie to walk down after I parked the truck past the boxes. I knew I had to keep making good decisions as I went forward. I knew I couldn't make sense of any of it yet. I didn't try.

At night I lay in the narrow pink bed and prayed to the only God I knew. I sang myself into fitful sleep on the Liturgy from my childhood in the Lutheran choir, "O Christ, thou lamb of God, that takest away the sin of the world, have mercy upon us . . . "

I would wake in the night wondering if I had made

the right decision. I prayed that I'd be safe and would fall back to sleep. Brandy lay out on the sofa all night keeping watch.

During the day I was going through the motions, going to work, working as many hours as they'd give me. When I had free time I picked up new songs on my guitar. I wanted to learn many Bob Dylan songs so I could sing them easily by memory. That was all I wanted.

Jay was the one who had introduced my family to Bob Dylan. I hadn't seen him in a long time. I knew that by now he would have gone back to town where his family had their other house. Jay had become more of a drinker and smoker over the summer. I didn't like stuff like that at all. I hated being around people who were drinking. I hated it. Jay came by once before Preston left and they smoked some marijuana together and drank a lot of beer. I was very unhappy. Their giggling laughter, so unlike both of them, made me feel sick inside. When I walked past them on the porch they mocked me for not joining them. I hated that. Preston apologized the next day. But Jay was going back to town and I didn't care whether I saw him again or not. Now that I was alone, I wanted to believe he'd be there for me if I needed him like he'd been there for my mom when she first came up on the bus. So much had changed since last April.

My mother called one morning. She said she was coming up over Labor Day weekend to see me and to check on things. I was so relieved. But I also dreaded her arrival. I looked at the cabin and tried to remember how it was supposed to look. I knew everything was a little dingier than when my mom was around, but I couldn't quite tell what wasn't right. I put away anything that wasn't supposed to be sitting out. I brought in arm-loads of wood and stacked the wood box high. I brushed Brandy and washed his bowls so they looked fresh. I put away all the dishes, even the clean ones in the drying rack. I went to work, came back home and went to bed, all the while waiting for my mother's arrival.

In the late afternoon, when I was sitting close to the fire with Brandy, playing my guitar and writing a song idea in my notebook, I heard a horn honking. I went out to the porch. Brandy barked and ran up to the driveway. I saw the wet boxes and cringed. I saw my mother get out of the passenger side of a car I didn't recognize. Then a man stood from the driver's seat and I realized it was Seymour Hoffman, driving my mom. Damn.

From that moment my head was swimming. I lost all my bearings. Everything I had been handling with confidence was swept out from under me. My mother's eyes were on everything. She looked at me, not at me but at my body, my clothes, my hair.

"Sidney, what are you wearing? Where do you go looking like that?" and as I looked down to figure out what was wrong, and to try to remember what I had on my body, she followed with, "You remember Mr. Hoffman?"

Of course, I remembered Mr. Hoffman. I wished so badly that Preston was there right then. "Yeah, of course." I mumbled.

"Well, aren't you going to say hello?"

"Hi."

"Brandy, oh my God, I can't believe how heavy he's gotten. He's all bloated. What have you been feeding him? You know he has heart trouble. Have you walked him at all? Oh God, I should have known. I should have known."

I tried to answer that Brandy was fine. I watched my mother's face.

She looked at Seymour with an "I don't think I could face this without you" look. She walked over to him and took his arm. I looked at the two of them standing there arm in arm and I thought I would cry or burst into flames or vomit. The Mr. Hoffman I remember would never have been wearing a cotton turtleneck and a leather bomber jacket. Never in a million years. He was the kind of guy who wore old door-to-door salesman kind of clothes even when he wasn't at work. She had him all dressed up. I couldn't look at them.

I thought to myself that my mom and I should have hugged by now, but I decided I wasn't going to try. It was too late already.

I turned and headed toward the cabin. I heard them following me through the fallen leaves.

"No one's even bothered to pick up a rake. And these boxes, how am I supposed to move them now, look at this, these waterlogged books? I can't believe this."

My mind was racing ahead, my eyes darting, trying to guess what else would be wrong. I couldn't guess. I felt bad about Brandy, but honestly, he didn't look different to me and I just fed him normal dog food. My mom always made rice and ground beef for him from scratch but we hadn't been doing that ever since she left the first time. Who was going to make that? There was no way. Brandy didn't seem to care.

I walked inside the cabin and my heart sank. I couldn't pinpoint what was wrong but I knew it didn't look like it did when my mother was in charge. She came in and took off her coat and just started changing everything. I was glad. I was relieved. Mr. Hoffman said he'd go back outside and see about moving the boxes.

I couldn't deal with any of it. They had some bags of groceries and they came back in with those. My mom got mad about the old milk in the refrigerator. I said I had to go to work.

She said, "I suppose you're just going to hop in that truck and drive off. Boy have you been spoiled. That's my truck and it's my only means of transportation up here. You better get an attitude adjustment little missy and stop thinking you own this place. I can see I didn't come back a moment too soon."

I drove to the resort in the truck. I went into the warm kitchen. Margaret was there. I went over and stood by the stove. My eyes were filling with tears. Margaret was watching me.

"You okay, Sidney?"

"My mom came back."

"And I take it that's not a good thing necessarily."

"Well, I thought it would be."

"Do you want to take the night off? You've been a real hard worker all summer. There won't be many diners tonight. You could go home."

"Please don't make me go home."

I lifted my eyes that felt swollen with tears. I looked straight into Margaret's stern honest face. She straightened her shoulders and wiped her hands on her apron. "No. Okay. That's fine. You stay and work. Let's see. I know what. Maybe tonight's a good night to get some extra cleaning done in the back room. I've been meaning to get you on that job. What do you say? It'll take quite a while and once we start we can't quit 'til it's all put back in order. How does that sound?"

I smiled. I loved her right then. I was fighting to keep the tears from coming to my eyes as I answered, "Okay, yeah, great."

My heart was filled with gratitude as we headed back to the big walk-in pantry and switched on the light.

That night I got home very late. The cabin porch light was on as was the one in Preston's room. It felt good to know someone else was there besides just me. Brandy met me at the door. I gave him a hug and he headed through the living room toward the master bedroom. I was afraid that Mr. Hoffman was sleeping with my mom and I was horrified to see his shoes as I got inside the kitchen door. I wondered why I hadn't noticed his car. I went back outside to check. He had driven his car down into the grass and parked it by the woodpile where you couldn't see it from the road. They didn't want people to know he was there. No. Neither did I. It's not like a lot of people were driving by our cabin now at the end of the summer, but if someone wanted to drive out to see what was going on with my family, a strange car would be of interest for sure. I got ready for bed and went to sleep in my little room with the door closed. I dreaded the morning.

The next day, Mr. Hoffman was already awake and dressed when I got up. "Hello, Sidney. What do you have planned today?"

I liked the way he asked me.

"I have to work but not until about four."

"Your mother tells me you've enrolled in the school here."

"Yeah. I did."

"I have a couple of ideas to help you get this place ready for the winter. Your mother and I are going to town to buy a wood stove today. They fit right into the fireplace. I'll have to fit some kind of seal around the opening once we get the stove in place. It'll make all the difference in the world once the cold sets in."

"Okay, cool."

"Yes, well, warm I'd say." He gave a friendly chuckle. "We're going for heat, right? While we're in town, we're going to order an extra supply of wood, already split, really great burning stuff, it'll get delivered and stacked and we'll get a tarp for it. It's going to take a lot of wood to keep this place going all winter, but it isn't impossible."

"Okay. Good."

I was not used to anyone talking to me about what was happening. And he wasn't mad at me and he didn't look at me funny, like he was judging me. I was starting to like him in spite of myself.

I went out to the kitchen where my mom had the oven going and something cooking already. It was cinnamon rolls.

"Hi Mom."

"Oh Sidney! I made your favorite. And there's scrambled eggs too. And bacon. Help set the table for all of us will you please."

This was so weird and wrong but I really was grateful, so I went along with it.

I ate quickly, my mother eyeing my plate to see what I'd eaten and how much of the cinnamon roll I'd eaten compared to the scrambled eggs. I hated her scrambled eggs. I loved her cinnamon rolls. I could have eaten the entire pan of eight rolls. I could have vomited from eating even a forkful of the eggs. The bacon was great. I drank some orange juice and stood up announcing that Brandy needed a good long walk.

No one could argue with that so I hooked on his leash and took off. When Preston and I had gone through the boxes before he left, we had found the bright red down vest and light blue down coat he had promised me. I was already starting to wear the vest and I was glad I had it when Brandy and I turned up onto the road. The trees were getting just a tinge of yellow to their leaf tips. The sumac that jutted out in the midst of the undergrowth along the edge of the road was turning red. Wild grapes were dark purple, the vines turning yellow and brown and red where they had been only green a few weeks ago. Field mice, blind moles, chubby chipmunks all dashed across the road in front of us, their mouths filled with seeds, fruit, nuts to be stored for the winter. I thought of the time we arrived at the cabin in the early summer and my mother was so guilty and saddened when she showed me how the mice had carefully made neat little separate piles of grains and seeds of many varieties, including the bright blue pile of the tiny mouse poison pellets. I vowed that no mouse would be killed during this winter when I was in charge.

That made me think about what was happening with my mother and Seymour Hoffman. Were they staying? It didn't sound like it. Was my mother understanding that I wasn't going back with them? I resolved to have a talk with her when I got back.

I walked into the cabin and my mother had her makeup on and was wearing her jaunty denim trench coat, so they were heading out.

"Mom, I don't really get what's going on. Are you guys staying here? Is Mr. Hoffman staying? Are you guys going back soon? I mean, I just want to know. Do you know that I signed up for school here?"

"Oh Sidney, do we really need to get into all this right now? We're just heading out the door to go to town. We're going to buy one of these wonderful wood stoves. Did you see the brochure? They're really terrific."

"Yeah okay. Mr. Hoffman told me."

"I think he wants you to call him Seymour . . . Seymour? Is that right?"

I looked at him, but tried to not look into his eyes. I focused my eyes on his turtleneck sweater collar, as he answered, "Yes Sidney, I think you should call me Seymour."

I couldn't stand any of this. "Okay. Seymour. Fine."

"Well good, so we're going to town. Will you be here when we get back, to help?"

"I have to leave for work at four."

"Oh Sidney, really, we've been here less than twenty-four hours. Don't you think you could take time off to help when your mother is here?"

"I need the money. I mean, that's what I'm trying to ask. Do you guys have a plan? Do I just go ahead with what I have planned at this point? I mean, does anybody know what's going on?"

"Sidney! I've been through so much. You have no idea. And don't you talk that way to me. And Seymour has done nothing but try to help."

"Okay, so I'm starting school in like two days okay?"

"I think we understand that."

"Okay, and how long are you guys staying? Is Seymour staying? Are you staying?"

"I have to get back to Chicago. Your father has left us in a terrible situation and Aunt Evelyn really can't be left alone right now either. Her health is not good at all since all of this, you know that. No. I will be here as long as possible, but I have to get back if there's any hope of getting any resolution with all of this."

"Okay, just asking."

I went in my room and closed the door. I heard them walk off the porch and up to Seymour's car. I heard them pull out and head down the gravel road. The day was coming, and it was coming soon, that they'd pull out and I'd be alone.

I got home from the resort early that night and the two of them were in high spirits. The new wood stove was burning bright. Seymour showed me how to use it. He pointed out how the iron was pressed with whimsical designs; the figures dancing in relief, hand-in-hand wearing woodland garb. He pointed out the deer facing each other with matched racks of antlers, the tall pines lining the trim around the base. The stove had a glass window in the door that allowed you to watch the fire and check its progress. The rest was all black cast iron. Seymour showed me the trivets that sat on top for warming a pot or a kettle. He demonstrated how you used the wired handle to unlatch the door, hopefully without burning your hand, and how you had to carefully fit the logs in so the door would shut. The stove had its own narrow metal pipe chimney that went through a hole in the asbestos liner, which Seymour had fitted over the mouth of the stone fireplace.

I made a joke about us all dying of lung cancer and Seymour answered, "Well, without the asbestos you'll freeze to death long before you could ever develop the cancer, so at least this way you'll make it through 'til spring. You know what they say, we can make it to spring if we can just get through the mattress."

"Nobody says that."

"How do you know?"

I was beginning to like Seymour.

The next day Seymour and my mom had a handyman from the town come to help out. He knew how to "take up the dock" so he did that first, with Seymour's help. I watched as they first went down to the water and hoisted all the wood pallets, which made up the decking, up onto the shore. They fastened hooks and metal cables that were in the woods on the old winch. Then they cranked the frame on its big iron hinges until the dock hung suspended over the water at a forty-five degree angle.

I felt sad. My decision was closing in. It was only the beginning of September. Why were they doing all this so soon? I would no longer be able to bring the canoe down and get it in the water. The stone steps were inaccessible with the dock cables in the way.

I went to my room and strummed my guitar. I thought about what kind of song I could write to express the way it was all going down. But then I heard Seymour and the handyman right up on the porch by my window so I went out to see what they were up to next.

"What are you guys doing now?"

"We're putting plastic up on all the windows to keep the heat in better."

"Does everybody do that?"

The handyman answered, "Yep, if you want to have any kind of comfortable feeling in this place, this has gotta be done."

I watched for a while as they stapled plastic sheeting that really wasn't completely see-through, and then they tacked wood strips all around the edges to hold it in place. I went back in my room and it felt like I was in a goldfish bowl that hadn't been cleaned in a while.

Luckily, they decided to leave the picture window that looked out over the lake uncovered. From there you could see the big thermometer that Grandpa had used to chronicle his winter experience. He had a journal that sat by the window and wrote about any birds he saw and what the temperature was on each day. He recorded that the thermometer bottomed out a few times because it only went to forty below. Only went to forty degrees below zero. Fahrenheit. I couldn't imagine it. I knew that people and animals lived through it every year. I knew my eighty-year-old grandfather did it for several winters in this very house. I was so excited about the little school and the new kids, and so glad I didn't have to return to Chicago, to the scene of the crime, that I was happy to tough it out.

I was excited. I liked bundling up. I liked ice-skating. Ice-skating. I went out on the porch, passed the two men working on the windows, walked up to look one more time through the soggy boxes in the yard. Didn't Preston hold up an ice skate and laugh? I dug through. There. Very pretty white leather ice skates. They weren't mine.

They must have been my mother's from a long time ago. I brought them down and closed the door to my room. The laces were white too, very new, like nobody had ever worn them before. They were hard to slide into at first but once I got them on it was like they were made for me. I stood up with them on and looked at myself in the dresser mirror. They were great. I held up each foot behind me to see them better. Cute! I wondered when the lake would freeze. I wondered if I'd be able to find a way to get down to the water easily enough to put skates on. Another thing to look forward to. I took off the skates and hung them tied together by their laces on a nail on the knotty pine wall. This was going to be so cool.

That night Seymour said goodbye after dinner and headed out to his car.

"Where's he going?" I asked my mom.

"He's found a place to stay in Virginia. He doesn't want to upset you by staying out here. He thinks you are disapproving."

"Mom. You're still married to my dad right?"

"Well, the divorce is in process."

"I don't really get why you and Dad aren't going to try to get back together. He always said he'd love to live up here and teach law at the community college. Remember that?"

"Sidney, what's wrong with you? You're the one who put me on that bus and had me shipped out of town. You're the one who had me leave my own home. Now you're trying to take it all back? It's too late for second thoughts."

"Mom, are you kidding me? I'm seventeen. You're like forty-five. You're blaming all this on me?"

"Well who was it that just had to get me on that bus, just had to push me out?"

"Oh my God. I was trying to help you! He said he was going to kill you! I ran over to the neighbors to try to get help for you! You were crying all the time! Waking me up at night with fighting!"

"All right that's enough. After everything I've been through, how dare you? I wouldn't have ever talked to my mother this way. My mother died when I was your age. I had no one. You have no idea what hardship is. And Seymour has come all this way to help us, to help you. And this is how you act? You're just impossible. Everyone's done everything they can for you."

I went in my room and shut the door. I got out my guitar, but I didn't want her to hear me playing it. If she got mad enough she might try to take it away. I lay on my bed looking out the blurry darkened window at the evening sky. It was getting dark earlier each night.

I saw the headlights of a car come creeping along toward the cabin on the road. I thought maybe Seymour had changed his mind. I thought I might even have liked that because I got along better with my mom when he was around. I felt safer with him there. I watched, expecting to see him get out. But, no. This car was long and black. Both the front doors opened. Two men stood. My heart dropped. My father.

My father was standing in the driveway. On the driver's side, Tommy my cousin. I watched as Tommy stretched his arms over his head and looked around. I wanted to run away. I wanted to hide under the bed. My heart was pounding in my chest. The two men walked down the path to the kitchen door. I thought to warn my mother, but was too afraid to speak. I could see them clearly now; absurdly, improbably, dressed in tracksuits, my cousin in green, my father in black. Both had loose silky jogging pants with white stripes down the sides. Both had a zipper jacket of the same fabric with stripes down the arms. I had never seen my father dressed like that in my life.

They banged on the door and my mother's gasp was audible through the wall. I couldn't let her take them on alone. I went out there, stood in the living room looking into the kitchen. Oh God, how the hatred welled in me as I laid eyes on Tommy! He looked bigger, more muscular, more suntanned, his fake hair standing on end like a cartoon version of a professional wrestler. My disgust was stronger than my fear and I could feel it rising in me. My righteousness too. I was afraid to look at my father, afraid we'd make eye contact. I saw him standing in an aggressive stance. I saw that his eyes were red, his face flushed. I saw him look at us as if he had caught us doing something wrong. What we were doing was not wrong. We were left with these circumstances by his dishonesty. His brutality. We were trying to have peace. We were trying to live without trauma and fear. I stood in my spot in the living room with my head held high.

My mother was pleading, "Please, we just want to be left alone. Haven't you done enough damage? Haven't you hurt everyone enough? What do you want here? We have nothing. We don't have anything for you. We have nothing. You always called this place 'your dad's shit hole of a cabin,' well this is our home now. Please, please just leave us."

My dad began with, "I've told my daughter that I want her to come down to Florida with us and go to private school. Sidney. You know your mother's crazy. You know she'll abandon you up here. You can't survive this. I know you think you're so tough but this is insanity. Tommy and I are on our way to the relatives in Florida. Sidney can go to a good school and graduate on time. Get your things together, Sidney."

"I can't, Dad. I already signed up for school here. I don't want to go to Florida. I don't trust you or Tommy and I'm not going with you guys. I'm staying here. I have a job and I'm starting school."

"Don't tell me. Don't you stand there like some goddamn privileged little bitch and tell your father what you're not going to do. Get your ass in gear. Get your things. Your mother can stay here and freeze. And where's that coward, that loser, that old man you're fucking, Ingrid? Where is he? Hiding in the coat closet?"

My dad lurched across the room and flung open the rickety closet door, which slammed to the wall.

"He's lucky he wasn't in there, I'd have killed him right now with my bare hands."

My mother was in the living room now, crying, wiping her eyes on her apron she still had around her waist from doing the dishes. She came over and put her arm around me. I felt good that she was standing with me that way, until I realized that Brandy was slowly walking toward the two men.

Brandy was walking over to see Dad. He loved Dad. He had realized it was him and was wagging his tail and approaching him.

That's when my dad said, "Tommy, grab the dog. Grab his collar. Get him out of here. Take him up to . . . "

"Dad, no!"

Tommy was afraid of Brandy, I knew. He was hesitating. My mom started wailing. I had to think fast. They couldn't take Brandy. He'd die. They wouldn't know about his heart problem. I turned my body, looking for something, I don't know what, when I had an idea. I threw myself suddenly to the floor, flat down, letting my head hit hard. I lay flat on the living room floor, unmoving.

My mom went nuts. She started screaming, "Look what you've done! Oh my God! Look what you've done to her! Let go of that dog. You get out of here! Both of you! We don't want you here. Get out!"

My mother was crouching by my head stroking her hand over my hair, "That's right! Get out! Get out of here and leave us alone with your terrible bullying! You've hurt us all enough now. Oh my God, she's fainted."

I heard Brandy's collar and I felt him licking my face. I felt my mom's hand on my back. I heard the old wooden bells that hung on the door start chiming.

And then the kitchen door slammed.

Two sets of heavy footprints on the porch floor.

Two car doors slamming.

The engine starting.

My mother went to the window to be sure they were gone and said, "Sidney honey, you fainted. Are you okay? That was so frightening, I don't blame you. Oh, they're driving a Lincoln Continental. I can't believe him. That's so like your father and his tricks. What a terrible scene. Are you okay?"

I was sitting up on the floor, hugging Brandy.

My mother came over to me and looked down into my face. "You were so frightened that you fainted and fell to the floor."

I smiled then.

"No I didn't. I did it on purpose," I was smiling bigger now, a big wide mischievous grin was taking over my face as I said, "I faked it."

My mother plunked herself down on the upholstered ottoman and untied her apron. She looked at me with awe.

"You are really something Sidney. I never would have thought to do something like that. No one would have. What made you think of that right then?"

"I don't know, I didn't think. I just went for it. I couldn't let them take Brandy. I wanted to tell you I was okay when it was happening but I was afraid you'd blow it."

"I probably would have, you're right! Good thing you didn't. You mean like if your hand reached out and touched my ankle or something? I probably would have just screamed or something stupid and ruined the whole thing. It was really an Oscar-winning performance all around. Absolutely incredible. You should be an actress. An unforgettable performance."

"Thanks, Mom."

The next day was the day before school was to start. The school bus that drove out to the Indian reservation had added me to its route. I was looking forward to the bus coming down the gravel road for me. I was supposed to walk down to the turnaround at the old lodge so the bus could easily turn and head back to town. I felt like things were really falling into place.

Around noon, Seymour came to see how things were going. He and my mother asked me if I wanted to ride with them into Virginia, the biggest nearby town, and see if there was anything I needed for school. I jumped at the chance. We all rode in Seymour's stodgy salesman-looking sedan, but hey, I wasn't picky about anything any more. The fact that Seymour had a reliable car and that he was a kind person, was beyond my expectations. On the way, I got to talk about my dad and Tommy showing up and how scary it was and how they tried to take me and then, Brandy, but I freaked them out by pretending to pass out on the floor. Seymour seemed very concerned at first but by the end of the story I had him laughing. I liked him and I didn't care any more what it all meant.

We went to the mall in Virginia. My mother said I needed better shoes. I'd been wearing flipflops or running shoes all summer. I had the red down vest, which fit me well, and the light blue down coat, which was big but would go over the vest perfectly when things got really cold. I picked out some cute shearling-lined hiking boots with bright red laces. I put them on and put my running shoes in the box and wore them out of the store. I felt like a lumberjack in a very good way, like I could take on anything. We went to a teen clothes store and I fell in love with a white cotton flannel blouse that had a Victorian look with a high collar, white lace trim, and buttons all down the back. It was a perfect prairie girl kind of thing. I spotted a bright-red wool sweater that had two white reindeer facing each other and a white snowflake pattern knitted in to the sleeves. My mother suggested I get a plaid flannel shirt as well so we did. We walked out of the store with all three items and I was elated.

Lastly, we went down to the far end of the mall to the Fleet Farm store, which had workmen's supplies. I picked out a women's one-piece wool long underwear, a union suit, in red. I didn't need it then, but Mom and Seymour said I'd be needing it soon enough. They sprung for chopper's mitts, which were a set of oatmeal colored rag wool mittens fitted into tan leather outer mittens. You could wear them together or separately. Just before we left Seymour laughed about the big fur trapper hats near the check out counter. But I wasn't laughing. The store had small, medium, and large and the small fit perfectly, so we added it to the pile. I was going to be the cutest Northwoods girl ever. I loved all of it.

Seymour took us to Mr. Steak, a restaurant by the mall, and I ordered the fried shrimp and steak combo. It came with a cheesy twice-baked potato and a salad.

I was all smiles. Life was beautiful. I was ready for anything. On the way out of town we stopped at a drug store and I bought a three-ringed notebook and a big package of loose paper with holes punched in it; a package of two Bic pens; and a set of pencils with their own erasers and a sharpener. I was ready for school.

SCHOOL STARTS

The next
morning was
sunny and bright,
the third of September.
The high would be near seventy the radio
had said, but I had to be at the bus stop by
six-thirty so it was cold, forty-five degrees.
I wore my new red plaid flannel shirt,
my jeans, my new hiking boots and a
cream-colored cable-knit fisherman's
sweater that had been my grandmother's. I found my red backpack
from last year that was in good shape.

I had been told by the principal that my
bus stop would be at the old turnaround for the
lodge. The lodge was someone's private summer
house now, and there was no one there, but it was the
only place where the road could be plowed with ample
room for the bus to turn around and head back toward the
main road.

I waited in the early morning quiet of the woods until
I heard the chugging and wheezing of what could only

be the school bus coming to get me. When it pulled up I was shocked at the poor condition it was in. It looked like it was from the '50s and it probably was. The door swung open and I got my first glimpse of the bus driver who would be ferrying me every morning over the coming winter. He wore a flannel shirt and a hunting hat. He had big long fuzzy sideburns sort of like Elvis Presley. He introduced himself right away. "So you're Sidney the new girl, huh? I'm Corey. I'll be driving this baby all winter so we might as well get acquainted right off the bat."

"Hi. Nice to meet you."

I turned to step inside and could see that the bus was more than half full. I went to the first seat I could find and tried not to look uncomfortable. A few other girls around my age got on at the various stops. Some of the girls were nice and smiled at me and even said hello. Some just seemed like they hated school or their lives. I smiled at everybody. I liked them already. Most of them seemed to know each other but I didn't feel bad about any of it. The kids at the back of the bus were rough-housing and the bus driver yelled at them a few times. They were from the reservation. I thought it was sad that they were all together at the back of the bus but it seemed to be their choice to sit back there.

When we got to school I saw the principal, Mr. Harlan, again and he seemed in high spirits. He was joking with everyone in the halls, making the boys remove their hats, teasing the girls. I noted that he talked to the kids who came from the reservation with the same affection and respect that he had for the other kids. He seemed to love all the kids and his job.

I went to each of my classes and met the teachers. For the most part, I felt it was going to be easy. The only bad thing was that the English teacher was a young woman who was the women's gym teacher and looked the part. She practically admitted she knew nothing about teaching an English class and she immediately set to handing out grammar worksheets, which we sat and did in silence the rest of our very first class with her. What a disappointment!

On the other hand, the history teacher was an incredibly funny and highly verbal guy who in just the first few minutes had me wondering what his story could be because he was bright and funny and sophisticated, and all the kids loved him and he loved them back. He explained that he was the hockey coach and the history teacher. Apparently he had been so good at hockey in high school that he had won a full sports scholarship to Harvard. So he went to Harvard and played hockey and graduated with a history degree. Then he came back to this godforsaken tiny town up near the Canadian border of northern Minnesota and got this teaching job. And he'd been here ever since and said he didn't ever regret it one bit.

These people were wonderful. I got off the bus at three in the afternoon. The sun was shining. The leaves were colorful and the drive down our narrow gravel road was beautiful.

I kicked through the grass down to the cabin and Brandy was happy to see me. My mom was cooking a duck with wild rice stuffing for dinner. Seymour was in a chair reading the local paper. I thought this might all work out.

My mom laughed as I told her that I joined the band, the orchestra, and the choir. I sang for the choir director and he said I should try out for the fall play. They put on plays! In Chicago I sang in the church choir and was able to do solos often. But at the big high school everything had been quite specialized. You couldn't take band and choir because the schedules conflicted, but if you played an instrument you could be in the band and the orchestra so I played my flute in both. But then when it came time to try out for vocal parts in the school musicals, I was seen as a flute player from the orchestra and they never gave me a chance. The girls who were in the school choral program were always being groomed for the parts in the musicals. Here in this tiny school I felt like I could be anything and everything and they were for the most part glad to have me along.

I also told Seymour and my mom about the mayor of the town being the calculus teacher. The mayor and the principal were joking around in the hall, saying that they were going to have to show this city slicker . . . me . . . what a real education was all about. The school had received my transcripts from Chicago and they were impressed with my grades. The mayor, who looked a lot like the wizard in the original *Wizard of Oz* movie said, "Well you haven't come up against my calculus class yet, Miss Smarty. We'll see how smart you really are."

The principal just laughed and shook his head when I answered, "I never said I was good at math. I'm not good at math! I shouldn't have to take calculus. I didn't take math all last year. I opted out of math."

"Opted out of math!"

This only made the two jolly men laugh harder.

The principal gave a speech, "No student is going to graduate from this fine institution on a college bound track without calculus. We have standards! We have standards!"

I didn't have any faith that college would be a possibility next year anyway, so I just laughed along.

My mother and Seymour seemed to find the stories about the people at the school to be very amusing. "You know, that new school of yours is an education in and of itself, regardless of what you learn or don't learn in their classes," Seymour commented.

I happily went to my room to organize my new notebook and do my first homework assignments.

I quickly got into my school routine and within a week I felt well acclimated. The kids and the teachers were fun, with the exception of a grouchy business teacher who didn't like me but didn't seem to like anyone else much better. I'd get home every day and Mom and Seymour would be planning some kind of great dinner so I was happy to go in my room and work on my schoolwork until dinner was ready. My mom didn't pick on me or make me do much. They seemed to want the time alone and I was fine with that. I found myself wishing that things could keep going this way.

But soon my mother was talking more about what was happening in Chicago. She called her lawyer a lot but wasn't sure that everything was being done to get the divorce cleared and the money issues sorted out. One day she said that Seymour was leaving to go back to Chicago for his own business affairs and that she thought she should go with him. She was worried about Aunt Evelyn, who had been having trouble breathing at night and was feeling weak. My mom thought she needed to go to a doctor but Aunt Evelyn wouldn't go alone, so my mother was to make an appointment and take her once she got back.

When my mom left she cautioned me that Brandy was an old dog who needed to be watched carefully. He needed to be walked and I had to keep the wood stove going as best I could so he'd stay warm. If I stoked it up when I left in the morning it would burn a pretty long time and the coals and the iron would stay warm hopefully until I got home in the afternoon. She showed me how to turn on the oil furnace too, but the tank wasn't very big so it had to be used sparingly.

When Seymour came to pick up my mom, he came in and asked if I'd speak with him for a moment in my bedroom. I thought that was really weird, but I did it. My mom was up by the road, packing her things in Seymour's car. "Sidney, I have this for you and I want you to have it while we're gone. He reached in his inner breast pocket of his coat and pulled out a pale blue-gray felt bag. It had a silk cord drawstring closure. I watched intently as he pulled open the drawstring and pulled out a very small silver gun. It was a pistol. I couldn't believe my eyes.

"I'm not saying you'd ever have to shoot it. If you do have to, hold it out in front of you with both hands and pull the trigger. It's loaded. It's only got three bullets in it. But three would do it. Mostly you can just show someone that you have a gun and they'll turn around and run. That's what it's for. An emergency. Keep it here in your room. Make sure you always know where it is."

Just then my mother came back into the cabin and Seymour quietly stepped out into the living room. I thought he didn't want her to know. I was okay with that. I didn't say a word about it. When I picked up the pouch I was surprised how heavy it was. I put it in the pink desk drawer.

I walked up to the driveway with Brandy at my side. We watched as Seymour got in his car and started it up. My mom came over to me and hugged me and I tried not to cry. "I love you Sidney. I'm sorry this is happening this way, but you know it was what you wanted. You could be coming back with us to Aunt Evie's. I know, you don't want that. Well, I'll be back as soon as I can. Take care of Brandy. And be careful."

Brandy and I watched them drive out of the driveway and head out down the road. I went back in the cabin, threw a log on the fire, sat down and cried.

I was happy at school in the coming days but sad on the weekends alone in the cabin when all the other kids lived in the town for the most part and did things together there. I would hear stories and wonder about their social lives. I still worked at the resort but it was quiet now, with just a few of the regulars at the bar and a few couples coming through on fall getaway weekends in the dining room.

One Friday the girls my age who rode the school bus told me they were going to a party later that night.

"You should come too, Sidney," said the nicest girl, Jennifer, who had big cow eyes and a chubby figure. She was gentle and kind, always watching to see how other people were feeling. I knew she was a safe person to be around.

"I have to work, but I could come after if it's going to go late."

"It will! Come! There are these boys, they're brothers. They play guitars and sing. You will love them. They'll love you. They're so cute. They're the cutest boys we know. They're much cuter than any of the boys from school."

After working a few hours and picking up my much-diminished paycheck, I drove in the old truck over to a campsite along the lake where the kids were having the party. I had never seen anything like this before. All the cars were backed up to a roaring bonfire and all the car radios were tuned to the same station so the rock music was blasting.

Everyone was leaning up against cars or sitting on the tailgates of pickup trucks. Every kid had a can or a bottle. I walked in from parking my truck up near the road. I was alone so I wasn't sure how I'd be received but as soon as the girls from school saw me they came running over. They were kind of drunk and silly. They asked me if I wanted something to drink but I said no thanks because I really didn't like the taste of beer and I'd never had a drink before, so I was afraid of something bad happening.

They were bringing me around, pulling me by the arm, introducing me to kids who I either hadn't met yet from other grades at school or kids who went to other nearby schools. I wondered about the guitar brothers. Where were they?

As I was thinking about them, another set of headlights came busting down through the woods, the car was low and making its way unceremoniously over roots and branches and rocks until it was squeezed into the circle. The sunroof opened and a boy pulled himself out through the opening. A window opened and another lithe boy emerged. Everyone was laughing and congratulating them on squeezing their car into the circle.

My new favorite girl, Jenny, came over to me, "Sidney, those are the boys I was telling you about, the Parker brothers. Aren't they divine? Do you see that sweet car? Isn't it cool?"

"What is that kind of car called? It's like half car-half truck."

Honestly, I thought it looked kind of stupid and hick, but I was definitely in the mood to like everything so I went along with her enthusiasm.

"It's an El Camino. That's the coolest car you can drive besides like a Camaro I think. And in the daytime you can see it better; it has a sweet custom paint job. See? See the sides have flames painted? Oh, they're getting their guitars out!"

The brothers had fancy-looking guitars in big cases. They kept them in a special trunk latched down on the flatbed. These guys were like big fish in a very tiny pond. Everyone was gathering around and all the radios got shut off. The woods were silent except for the crackling fire as they tuned their acoustic guitars. I watched them carefully, deciding what I thought of what they could do. So far the music I'd heard from the kids at my new school was pretty low-quality. Their singing wasn't great and their abilities on the instruments in the band and orchestra were disappointingly elementary. But these brothers were making a big enough deal out of this that I thought I might be in for something special.

They launched into their first song. Their style of guitar-playing was not something I was familiar with, nor were the songs. One brother was taller and had very dark thick hair that hung over his eyes. He had a wide grin and twinkling eyes. Everyone liked him. He seemed very gentle and kind. He was playing a twelve-string, which I thought was probably harder, but I wasn't sure. He was doing a lot of fast picking. The other brother was younger, not as tall, a little more mischievous and slightly strange-looking. He was playing a six-string that was a little more beat up and he was mostly thumping out a lower bass-like part. I asked one of the guys from school who seemed especially into the song what kind of music this was.

"Yeah, its bluegrass! Aren't they great? They usually have a washtub bass too. The song's from the Ozark Mountain Daredevils. That's their favorite band."

They were singing the chorus now and their harmonies were thrilling.

I loved it. I loved them. I stood alone listening carefully to every song, every melody, every lyric. Some songs I knew. They played some folk and some rock. The bluegrass stuff was the most fun.

I yearned to sing along. I wanted to get my guitar and play too.

I stood still in the crowd of kids, thinking about it all.

Then Jenny and some of the other girls came over and grabbed me and dragged me up to the brothers.

"Dale, Greg, this is Sidney."

"She's from Chicago."

"She plays guitar."

"She sings really well too."

"She's living out here on the lake for the winter."

Dale, the older brother, put down his guitar and

jumped down off the hood of the car where they'd been sitting.

He put out his hand for me to shake, which was charming, "Hello Sidney, I'm Dale. It's a pleasure to make your acquaintance."

I laughed.

"Thank you Dale, it's a pleasure to make yours as well."

The younger brother squeezed in and got in front of him.

"Hi Sidney, I'm Greg the 'little brother.' Which is not actually accurate if you get my drift." Everyone laughed. Kids started goofing around again. The radios went on again. Dale stood next to me looking at the scene.

"Are you having anything to drink?"

"No, I don't really drink. I don't like the taste of beer. And I don't want to get drunk."

"I know what you mean. I don't like to drink myself. My brother loves to drink, I mean, *loves* to. But my dad gave it up and he says he's a better man for it so that's good enough for me. Why go through the misery just to find out what somebody else already learned? That's how I see it."

This Dale guy could not be for real. He was so chivalrous and earnest. It was like he was not meant for this earth. What a sweet guy! You could just see all the way through him straight to the center of his soul, and it was all clear blue skies and sunny days all the way. A diamond in the rough maybe, but a diamond with no ugly flaw of charcoal buried inside to ruin it. I knew it from the minute I met him. I could see that everyone felt the same way. He was just true blue to the core.

Dale turned to me, "Excuse me Sidney, I'm going to go over and say hi to some kids I haven't seen in a while. You're welcome to join me if you want to be introduced around. Maybe we can talk guitars later or if you want you can play some of your stuff. You could use mine."

"Thanks, yeah, we'll see."

I was standing alone. An awesome song came on the radio and the kids cranked all the car stereos louder. Tom Petty sang "Refugee" and then all the kids joined in on the chorus.

Now, the little brother was back, and handed me a brown bag crushed around a glass bottle. His eyes were shining bright and his lips were pink and wet. "Here Sidney . . . Sidney? Is that it? Is that really your name? That's like a guy's name. I mean, like no offense. I like it. It's sexy. You're sexy. You are very sexy. I think my brother likes you otherwise I'd like you. But I think I'm gonna let my brother have this one, you know, it's the least I can do for the guy. Ha, ha, yeah like I have a chance, right? Do you want some of this? It's delicious. Try it. Come on. Don't be a baby. Just swig it down. Just like this. See? That's not so bad. Come on. Live a little, Sidney."

I thought, and maybe I said out loud, "Oh, what the heck."

I took a sip. It was good. It tasted like Hawaiian punch.

I liked the little brother. He was funny.

"Come on, Sidney. Let's sit down on those stumps by the fire and get to know each other a little better. I'll share this with you."

I sat down with him. I couldn't believe how great everything was. I loved the party. I loved the music. I thought Dale was so wonderful. I was happy to be with his brother because I felt like I was like an insider with him, like I was closer to Dale, closer to the music. I let Greg pass me the bottle and I kept drinking from it. I let him tell me stories about their antics as boys together. I just sat happily watching the fire start to blur.

At some point the brothers were both sitting with me. They brought over a guitar. The radios went off and I played a couple of songs. On the second one, the old John Denver "Country Roads," the brothers joined in and we sang the rest in three-part harmony. I got to do a higher descant at the end and then the other guitar came out and Dale and I sang some more songs we both knew. I felt so wonderful. The music sounded like heaven. I was surprised by how easily I remembered all the words and just sang effortlessly, not embarrassed or hesitant at all.

After a while the brothers told everybody they had to work early and were going to leave.

Dale asked if I needed a ride. I said I had my truck. I sat a while longer listening to the songs playing on the radio and staring at the fire. I was aware then that Dale and the brother had left. I got up to go pee but I couldn't walk straight. No one was paying attention. Everyone who was still there was probably very drunk. I was pretty sure the girls I knew had said goodbye and left long ago. I stumbled into the woods.

I pulled down my jeans and squatted. The fire was going out and it was pitch dark. I knew no one could see me. I didn't think there was anyone left that I knew anyway. I pulled up my jeans and stood. I was dizzy and I felt like I might vomit.

I started to head back for the fire, but then I knew I was going to throw up so I turned and bent forward, heaving onto the dry leaves in the woods.

I walked a few steps and knew I had to lie down. I had my sweatshirt on and I pulled up the hood and tied the strings as best I could. I sat down in the leaves. I couldn't keep my head up and I lay down with my head on my arm and curled up my legs. I fell asleep. I must have been asleep for hours. I heard footsteps and I sat up, startled, my heart pounding.

It was Dale. "Oh geez. Somebody didn't make it out alive."

"Hi."

"I saw the red truck. Lucky for me I was driving by this way. Lucky for you too, I guess."

"I got drunk."

"I see that."

"It's your brother's fault."

"Well, see now, you're already catching on. Everything's always my brother's fault. Let's get the leaves off of you and get you in the warm car. You must be frozen."

"Luckily it was such a nice clear night. God, that was so stupid."

"You could have been eaten by a bear or a wolf."

"Geez."

"Do you remember me telling you that I don't drink much?"

"Yeah, vaguely."

"Well, it's because this kind of thing is what always happens. It's just inevitable."

We walked to his running car and he opened the passenger-side door for me.

"You stay here and warm up. You got your keys? Let's see if that baby starts."

I got the keys out of my pocket and handed them to him.

His car was warm and he had more than one of those silly pine tree-shaped air fresheners hanging from the rearview mirror. It was overkill on the fresh scent, but it was still nice to be in his well-kept new car.

Dale came back and got in the driver's side.

I saw the exhaust from my truck in the cold morning air and was glad it started.

"I can take you home and we can get the truck later if you want."

"No I'm okay. I am really embarrassed. I never drank before. It tasted really good. What was it?"

"It's the stuff my brother always makes when he's going to try to pick up girls. He calls it Wanderer's Punch. And he says 'makes 'em wander right into my arms.' I don't think he was trying to get you drunk though, honestly, he's gonna feel really bad when he hears about this. Of course, we were supposed to work together today and he didn't get out of bed."

"You guys seem like you make a good team."

"Yeah, except when he's hung over in bed. He's in the same shape as you this morning. Well, not really, yours was beginner's luck. He should know better by now."

I looked at my truck running and realized I had to get home. I had no idea what time it was, but the sun hadn't hit the road yet so it was probably still very early.

"Well, thank you so much. I better go home. My dog's been alone all night. I'm gonna take a hot bath.

Luckily I don't have to be anywhere today. I really like your music. I'm glad I met you guys. I hope I can hear you play again sometime."

I opened the car door and stepped out into the frosty air, which seemed so much colder after being in his warm car.

"What do you say I come by and take you out for a decent dinner some night? I'm making good money in the mine and I live at my parents', so there's plenty extra to show a girl a nice evening."

"I'd love that."

"Okay great. I'll swing by your place later and see how you're doing. If you're up to it, we could get dinner tonight. You're out there after the Johnson place right?"

"Yeah, the one with the turnaround driveway."

"Yeah, I know it. Okay see you soon."

I ran to my truck. He had the heat blasting. I shifted into drive and swung it out onto the frost-covered asphalt, heading for the cabin. I was excited to be going on a date. I was excited about singing harmony with guys who could sing. I thought about what I could wear that night once I got cleaned up. My head was throbbing though and I knew that the first thing was to take the hot bath and a long nap. Poor Brandy would need attention first. He'd been alone all night.

Dale must have driven all the way back to his parents' place and all the way back out to my cabin because he showed up showered and well-dressed in a black cowboy-style shirt and dark blue jeans, dark brown cowboy boots, and a grey wool jacket. He looked great. I was wearing my flannel prairie dress, fitted at the waist and flaring out down to the tops of my nice Frye boots. I had my old faded jean jacket, which wasn't warm enough but looked really cute over the dress. My hair was a little longer now and I liked it that way.

We made a cute couple when we walked into the old Daisy Bay Supper Club on the lake. Dale ordered a steak and said I should get one too so I did. We had fun. When he brought me back to the cabin he kissed me on the cheek as I jumped out of his car. He honked as he headed out. I was glad he didn't try to come in, but I hoped I'd see him again soon.

AUNT EVIE

My mother called from Chicago late one night crying hard into the phone, "Sidney, Aunt Evie died this afternoon. She went down to get the mail. I was out when it happened. She climbed the three flights of stairs and sat down at her kitchen table. Preston had sent her a letter. She just laid her head down on the table with his letter in her hands and died. I read Preston's letter. It was sweet, telling her how school was going and that he loved her. It's a very beautiful way to die. No hospital. No pain. She was feeling just fine when I left in the morning. And she loved Preston so much. I don't know what to do next. They came and took her body already. I'm going to have to close up her apartment and get rid of all her things. Oh dear! It's really going to be a lot. Oh dear! Well, how are you doing? Is everything all right up there?"

"Yes. I'm fine. I feel bad about Aunt Evie."

"Well, feeling bad isn't going to help. You feel bad? What do you mean by that? I don't think you understand what she meant to me. After my mother died, my Aunt Evie was my family. She was the one person who really cared about me. I was only eighteen. My father remarried right away and I was pushed out."

"Okay Mom, I get it."

"No, you don't get it. "

"Yes I do Mom, don't say that. She was my aunt too."

"Your aunt, too? She was your great-aunt. Yes, she was that. And she did everything she could to make you happy. She brought you down to the Christmas lunch at Marshall Field's. Do you remember when we did that for her employee lunch? You were so enthralled with the Christmas Fairy?"

"Yeah Mom, of course I remember. That was one of my favorite things ever."

"But when poor old Aunt Evie came to stay with you when you were older, when I was so terribly sick in Florida, how did you treat her?"

"Mom, she thought the refrigerator was blowing up every night."

"I don't care. How did that make her feel? You and she never had the same relationship after that. No, I'm not surprised that you aren't crying over her death. That's just who you are."

"Please Mom, don't say that."

"Good night Sidney. I'm hanging up now."

"Mom, please . . . "

She hung up. I turned around and stared at the

empty living room. I looked at the doorways to the three bedrooms and the bathroom. I looked out the picture window at the dark autumn night. The sky had been overcast when the sun went down so there were no bright stars, there was no bright moon. Most people who had places along the lake shore had closed them up and left for the winter and there were only two places with electric lights visible on the far shore. There were no lights down our point until the old lodge that was now somebody's summer house, which had a big floodlight that stayed on all the time. The resort I worked at was further out on the main road and its lights were obscured from my view by an island that sat uninhabited most of the year, black as the night. Aunt Evie was dead.

I got ready for bed. I tried to wash my face in the bathroom but I felt like somebody was behind me every time I tried to wash the soap out of my eyes. I kept opening my eyes and looking into the mirror to be sure there was no one. My eyes were stinging. I went into my room and for the first time realized that the knotty pine was very dark and had shadows from the knots that looked like faces. I thought of all the times my mother would say that the fireplace stones held the faces of Indian spirits. I went back out into the living room to check on Brandy. He was curled up in one of the duck-print chairs with his nose tucked under his paw, which I knew meant he was cold. I tucked in the big warm wool blanket that had been over the back of Grandpa's favorite chair around him. I stared at the fireplace stones. The fire needed stoking. I added two more logs and, through the glass window, watched them get enveloped by the flames. I looked at the stones again. The spirits' faces were visible tonight. I could see them clearly and they were laughing with wide open grinning mouths, "ha ha ha." I left both living room lamps on. I went to the kitchen door to be sure it was locked. There was a padlock with a metal hinge you could flip and then put the heavy free-hanging lock on the metal loop. I did that for the first time. I left one of the electric wall sconces lit in the kitchen. Aunt Evie was dead.

I closed the kitchen door to help keep the heat in the living room. I kissed Brandy one more time on his soft forehead. I went into my room and got out the gun. I didn't open the soft felt bag. I just held it and looked around my room for a better place to keep it. I decided to pull the pink wooden desk chair over next to my bed and place the gun on its seat.

I looked at myself in the dresser mirror. I was wearing my long flannel nightgown from Chicago that I luckily found in a box. My hair was longer now because I didn't think about it and it just grew out. It looked pretty good, it was more blonde from the summer sun.

I hoped my figure was okay, that I wasn't gaining weight from living up here. Again I felt someone was watching me. I looked behind myself in the dresser mirror. The knotty pine walls were dark and shadowy. I turned and looked all around me. I slowly walked the few steps to the small closet and opened the door. There hung my few pieces of clothes that had been salvaged. My pretty black flowered party dress with the Saks Fifth Avenue label inside. My long layered floral skirt and a silky cream-colored, peasant-style blouse. And thank goodness I had my Frye boots. They were my one "nice" pair of shoes, and with my boots and my tweed jacket

I could go anywhere. Except that up here, I wasn't sure there'd be many opportunities to wear these things. Every once in a while one of the girls in town came to school all dressed up, probably an outfit from going to a wedding I guessed. Maybe one day I'd get to wear my prairie skirt and tweed jacket for school. Also, I liked Dale a lot and I thought he would like it if I wore that outfit if we went out together again.

Okay, I felt better. Thinking about clothes always cheered me up. Thinking about Dale made me feel safe and happy. I shut the closet door. Nothing scary in there. I felt like I was back to normal so I shut off the light on the dresser and climbed into bed.

I didn't remember my room ever being so dark once the light was off. I closed my eyes and to my dismay the feeling of being watched came back immediately. I told myself it was stupid. Brandy was sound asleep. He'd know if anyone was nearby even outside. He'd never sleep through someone being near the cabin, especially at night. I lay on my side and stared at the gun. "There's nothing to be afraid of, go to sleep," I told myself several times. In my head there was only one refrain: Aunt Evie is dead.

I fell asleep for a while, I don't know how long, when I woke up suddenly and found Aunt Evelyn in the pitch dark, at the foot of my bed, watching me.

I opened my eyes and there she was.

I closed my eyes and opened them again and there she was. I stared back at her and our eyes met.

I closed my eyes and pulled the covers over my head.

I lay for a long time not moving, praying, praying, "Please God, make her go away. Make her leave me alone. Make her be gone."

I peeked out from under the covers and there she was, still standing, staring, blinking from time to time. I knew why she was there. She blamed me. She blamed me for putting my mother on that first bus and making the decision that lead to the demise of our family, for the end of my parents' marriage, for my mother having to sleep on the floor, for my dad calling her screaming, for Preston having to take a loan for his final year of college, for my living up here in the cabin alone as the winter was setting in.

She blamed me for all of it.

She blamed me for her death.

In some way it was all true.

What I did by putting my mom on the Greyhound bus that day, killed Aunt Evelyn. What I did that day killed my parents' chances of getting back together. What I did that day killed our family.

I woke up the next morning to no ghost, just silence, and then the click of Brandy's nails on the wood flooring as he came into my room to wake me. I got dressed and took him out into the cold morning for a walk.

THANKSGIVING

The days were full and I was enjoying my new life. Dale was becoming my closest friend and sort of boyfriend. He worked in the taconite mine during the week and played with his brother and their band in bars around the Iron Range region on weekends. He lived with his parents so he had plenty of money and was saving money to, as he said, "either take some college courses or do something nice for somebody someday." He was a whimsical sort of soul, not intellectual at all, but with a deep sense of empathy and morality. I knew that there wasn't a nicer person on the planet. Dale was unlike anyone I'd ever known. He was unafraid, unfazed by hard work or hardship. He had low expectations of what life was going to give him and he was full of wonder at what he already had. He loved his parents, his brother and sister. He was utterly remarkable to me. His presence in my life was a balm to everything that had been wrong.

By late November, he felt comfortable enough with our relationship to stop in unannounced at the cabin on a weekday evening. I heard his car on the gravel first and smiled as I was sitting at the kitchen table doing homework. Brandy looked at me and wagged his tail, knowing it was Dale just by the sound of the engine, the opening and closing of the door. By this time, Brandy was having trouble getting up and down out of the furniture so he stayed curled up in the chair and just wagged his tail and grinned at me.

I heard Dale's footsteps at the door. He knocked and I jumped up to answer. There he was at the door, so tall and handsome, with cheeks pink from the cold. He was wearing the army surplus pea coat I suggested he buy. He liked clothes and had taken me into Virginia a couple of times to help him pick things out. He said he was so glad to have met someone who knew how. He would always insist we go to the women's shop I liked and he bought me something as "payback."

He came in and gave me a wrapped paper package that held a bouquet of fresh cut roses. He was really into stuff like that.

"Dale, Wow! These are beautiful. Thank you!"

"Beautiful flowers for a beautiful girl. For the best girl I know."

The thing about Dale was that he could say things like that with no sense of cynicism or irony because he had none of either. Honestly, he probably didn't know what those words meant.

I put the roses in an old cut-crystal vase that sat on the stone mantel over the fireplace. The mantel held a wooden plaque of a mounted, unusually large small-mouth bass, caught by Preston when he was a young boy. "Beginner's Luck" was the caption under the photo that had appeared in the small-town newspaper the next day. The heavy cement mantel extended out like a shelf on the big stone chimney. On the mantel's face, etched red letters, that had become faint with time, read "Life Is Too Short To Be Little."

Another sign. My family liked signs I guess. Slogans. Manifestos.

I walked over to put the roses on the mantel and said, "Dale, the one thing you have to remember is . . . "

"I know. I got it. Don't tell me. 'Life Is Too Short To Be Little'."

"Dale I know you didn't remember. You're just saying it now because you're reading it."

"Well that can't be true because you know I don't know how to read."

"Dale."

"Sidney."

"What are you going to eat for dinner?"

"A sliced apple with peanut butter."

"No you're not. We're going out. Put on your coat. Where do you want to go?"

"Burger King."

"We can do better than that."

"You decide."

"Okay let's go to the Black Bear Cafe. You can get a bacon cheeseburger there. They're a lot better than Burger King."

"Sweet."

"Yes, you are."

We drove in his warm car to the Black Bear and I was cheered by the cozy old-time atmosphere. I was surprised to see many of the booths full on a weeknight. We had a fun dinner and Dale paid the bill, not willing to take any cash from me.

We drove back and Dale came down to the cabin again. I had to help Brandy get out of the chair to go outside. He didn't like to because it was cold and he wasn't doing well.

I helped him down and herded him to the door. He didn't need a leash because he certainly was of no mind to run off on his own.

He did what he had to do and shuffled as fast as he could back inside.

Dale asked about him. "He has had a heart problem for a long time and it's getting worse and he doesn't really like it up here. It's not a place for boxers. It's more for golden retrievers or huskies."

Dale said his family had never had a dog so he didn't know much. He patted Brandy's head while I put food and water in his bowls.

Dale made several trips out to the woodpile to bring in four or five heavy armloads of wood and stacked them in the near empty wood box. We stoked the wood stove and he started playing my guitar.

We sang and talked about doing some songs as duets for his band's next show. I had never played a public stage or bar show that was not about religion or a talent contest. I was thrilled at the possibility and said I'd surely do it if they asked.

Then the guitar got set aside and we picked up where we left off the last time we were alone together. I was so conveniently alone. He could have stayed all night and no one would have known. My body and my heart wished he would. If I could have, I would have had him stay with me all the time. I wanted to curl up in his warm arms and sleep without bad dreams, without visits from ghosts, without fear of intruders or crazy fathers. But I thought I would regret losing my virginity to the first guy I dated after running away to the Northwoods and living alone out on a lake in the middle of nowhere. I didn't want to be slutty and so predictable in a trashy way. So we kept our clothes on and made out feverishly as the night wore on, until his hard crotch was pressed up against mine for so long and in such an insistent way that we came to some form of glorious climax that came as a great surprise.

After he left, I rinsed out my moist and sticky jeans in the kitchen sink and hung them up to dry by the fire. On the bookshelf, I found a book that I remembered seeing years before called *The Victorian Erotic Reader*. I remembered flipping through passages describing sweaty bodies grinding together. I wasn't interested at the time, but I was now. With no siblings, no close friends from childhood, no parent, and no access to the rest of the world, I had nowhere to turn for information besides my grandfather's bookshelf. Thank goodness for the *Erotic Reader* because it described just what was happening to Dale and me, and there was much more detail about what could happen if we decided to take our clothes off. I wasn't ready for any of that yet, but kept the book next to my bed, alongside the pistol in its felt bag.

When I was at school the next week, I walked by the glass doors of the school office and both the secretary Mrs. Briggs and the principal Mr. Harlan motioned for me to come in. They both looked very concerned. "What? What's wrong? Did I do something?"

The principal looked at Mrs. Briggs and she frowned and looked back at him and at me. "Sidney, step into my office please."

I liked Mr. Harlan and I figured that if I'd done something wrong it couldn't be that bad because I couldn't think of a single thing I'd done.

"What's going on?"

"Sidney, a man is calling us saying he's your father, I believe he's telling the truth."

He got out a piece of paper. "What's your father's full name?"

I answered.

"And his date of birth?"

I answered.

"Yes, I do believe it's him. You know I have known since you started here that you were out there alone. I could have reported you to social services, had you put into foster care. I knew you had good intentions. So far, you've been a great addition to our school community. You're a good student and a good person. I think you're really going to amount to something some day. We all do. I'm sorry to make this unpleasant for you but your father has said some things to the secretary and I have to ask you some very personal questions. But first of all, when will you be eighteen?"

"Not until February."

"Okay. That's not that far off. So, the big thing is that your father is calling us saying we are helping you cover up the fact that you are pregnant and trying to seek an abortion."

My face immediately got hot. I was embarrassed, and angry, "My dad has no right to call you. My mother has custody."

"Okay, that's good. That helps. Could I get your mother on the phone and would she say that too?"

"Yes. Of course. The only reason she isn't here the whole time is because of the divorce and stuff."

"I see. Of course. But Sidney, is what your father saying about your situation true? I'm sorry but I feel I need to know. I feel responsible to some degree because you are enrolled in my school under the pretense of proper supervision at home when I know that there is none. At least none right now."

"I'm a virgin."

Silence. His eyes met mine. I did not look away. He eventually dropped his eyes.

"Good for you. Not many of those in this school, I hate to say."

"No. Frankly, I've noted that myself."

"All right Sidney. I'm going to make a call to a lawyer I know, but when your father calls, he asks to have us take you out of class to speak to him. He is very irate and irrational. I believe you are under no obligation to speak with him. I believe we are under no obligation to require you to speak with him."

"I don't have to talk to him. Number one, he's not my custodial parent. Number two, he's an asshole."

His mouth started in a slight smile, but he remembered himself and frowned.

"Sidney, please refrain from using vulgarities when addressing your superiors."

"Sorry. It's not like the other kids never do."

"Again, Sidney, we think you've got a bright future ahead of you."

"Yeah, okay, sorry."

He rose from his old wooden desk. He came around and put a hand on my shoulder. "We'll handle your dad. You keep your mind on your studies so you can get your diploma and move on to bigger things."

"Not sure what that'll be, but whatever . . . "

"Don't worry, Sidney, everything's going to work out."

"Thank you."

Thanksgiving's long holiday weekend was coming and I got a call from my mother saying she and Seymour were coming up and bringing groceries. They arrived the day before Thanksgiving and I helped carry in bags of fresh produce, breads, pastries from my favorite bakery in Chicago, and the turkey. My mother was quiet and seemed irritable. She saw Brandy get slowly down off the chair and shuffle over to greet her and immediately started, "Oh Brandy. Oh you poor thing. Sidney, what have you done to him? What have you been feeding him? Have you given him his pill?"

I fed him just the way she told me to, but the pill was hard for me to remember and hard to get him to swallow so sometimes I skipped it, especially in the mornings when I was in a hurry to get to the bus stop.

"Yes, mother, I've been giving him everything."

"Well, this is it you know. He's not going to make it. He can't go on like this. He's suffering."

"No, he's not Mom, he's fine."

"Sidney. What is wrong with you? Open your eyes! Look how he's changed! He's so bloated and lethargic."

"No he's not Mom, stop saying that."

"Well, after the holiday I can drive in with him to Virginia to the veterinarian we like there. We'll see what he has to say."

On Thanksgiving morning, with my mom and Seymour both in the kitchen working on stuffing the turkey, I decided to try something I'd been too scared to do with no one around. I got the white ice skates down from the nail on the wall. I'd hidden the gun back in the pink desk before my mom got there, and the chair was back tucked in at the desk. I put on my red union suit, my jeans, my new white blouse with my red sweater over it.

I got my chopper's mitts and my new rabbit-fur earmuffs I bought with Dale. I put on my vest and coat, but it was very sunny and there was no wind, so I wasn't sure if I'd need my coat.

I headed out the door with Seymour explaining that there was thin ice too close to the shore and too far out and that I'd better stay close to the cabin so they could hear me scream if I went through. I knew how deep the lake was and I wouldn't go out past where I could stand up. I'd heard from the kids at school that people had been venturing out onto the ice so I wanted to try.

There was a dusting of snow, but it wasn't deep, so I could easily walk out to the edge of our property and look over to see where to try to climb down the rocky bank to the water's edge. Our yard up to the edge was grass and scattered trees. Once the bank began to slope it was rocks and brush and trees all growing at an angle in the slope to the water. I picked my way along, using the chair as I went as a steadying tool. I made it down and slid the chair out in front of me.

The ice was clear and I could see small fish swimming in the shallow water. I could see that the ice was fairly thick, I had heard you only needed it to be three inches thick to support a grown man, or even a car. I pushed the chair and it slid a long way. The ice was so smooth! I shuffled out in my hiking boots pushing the chair until I was out of the shade of the shoreline trees and in the full sun. What a glorious view! I could look all up and down the point we lived on, and I could see way out across the widest part of the lake toward town where my school was. I could see all the small and larger cabins on the far side of our bay as well. With no leaves on the trees, everything was exposed. Along our point, it was disconcerting to see all the other cabins with their windows boarded up or covered over in newspaper and only our brave stream of smoke rising and our windows bright with electric lights in the living room and kitchen.

I sat down on the chair and laced up the skates. I stood and got my bearings. I had skated a fair amount as a child in Chicago. There was an outdoor rink near my house that I remembered walking to with my skates over my shoulder along with the kids from across the street. I skated carefully, one foot in front of the other, worrying that if I fell down I might go through the ice.

But the ice was strong and the day was bright. I was surprised by how warm I could get skating along on the clear ice. I felt like I was getting a sunburn on my cheeks but I didn't care. It was as if the entire lake was a huge private skating rink. I could skate forever! I could skate out to the nearest island and all around it. I could skate to the farthest island and around that. I had heard that there were parts of the lake that were spring-fed or had some kind of difference in the current which didn't freeze as solidly. I heard stories of people out on snow-mobiles going through the ice even in the deepest winter. So I stayed in front of the cabin and skated back and forth. I waved up at the kitchen window from time to time and my mother or Seymour waved back. My mother seemed to be really getting a kick out of seeing me out skating and I felt happy. It was so quiet, not the slightest breeze. No leaves rustling as in summer. Stillness and glorious bright sunlight ruled the day.

My mother came out on the kitchen porch in her apron. She was speaking in a normal voice like we were in the same room and it was so still that I could hear her perfectly, "Oh Sidney isn't this a spectacular day? Did we ever think we'd see a beautiful scene like this? You look so great! Are the skates okay?"

"Yeah, they're perfect! This is the best ice rink in the world!"

I got more confident in my skating abilities and started doing my amateur versions of figure eights and twirls. I skated and skated until I hoped it was time to eat. After a while I took off my skates, leaving the chair down on the ice so I could come down after dinner and skate some more.

The three of us sat down together to eat the feast. The turkey was in the center of the table steaming hot and golden brown. My mom said a prayer. She had each of us say things we were thankful for. I said I was thankful for both of them being with me for the holiday, thankful for the beautiful lake, thankful for my new school, and thankful for Brandy. Thanksgiving dinner was as good as I'd ever had and I felt that I was right where I was supposed to be.

Bad news came Monday afternoon when I got home from school. Brandy wasn't at the kitchen door to greet me. He wasn't curled up by the wood stove. He wasn't in his favorite chair. My mom was in her bedroom. I asked where he was. She said he was really sick in the morning when she woke up, long after I'd left for the bus. She said he couldn't even walk and she and Seymour carried him out to the car. She said he was holding out until she was there for him. They brought him to the vet in Virginia and the vet said he was in some kind of coronary distress and that there was no point in taking him back out to the lake to suffer so they put him to sleep.

They put him to sleep without giving me any warning. I didn't get to say goodbye or kiss his soft nose or tell him how sorry I was that I had killed him by being too stupid and lazy to keep up with his medication and that I didn't make the ground beef and rice every day and just gave him dry dog food. I killed him and I didn't even get to apologize.

Their other news was that they were leaving again. The next morning.

The worst thing about Brandy was that my mom and Seymour had brought his body home to the cabin but the ground was too hard already when they tried to dig a hole. So they wrapped Brandy's body up in the plastic wrap the vet had given them and again in a big old army blanket of Grandpa's, and they stuffed his body up in the rafters of the old carport where we parked the truck. Seymour assured me he'd be just fine up there. He promised they'd bury him properly in the spring and I suggested we have a real funeral and my mother and Seymour liked the idea.

CHRISTMAS

The days between Thanksgiving and Christmas were just a blur. School was fine during the day and Dale often visited in the evenings. But the cabin was very quiet and scary at night. Aunt Evie's ghost took up residence at the foot of my bed. She had loved Brandy. She had even more now to hold against me. Sometimes I would wake in the night and cry as she stood unmoving, unsmiling at the foot of my bed. I would say, "I know. I see. I can't do anything about it now. It's too late. It's all too late. Brandy's gone. Leave me alone. There's nothing I can do. What do you want me to say? I'm sorry. I am sorry. I am so sorry." Many nights I lay in bed and cried and prayed, and cried and prayed.

Christmas Eve arrived. I was dressed in my flannel calico prairie dress and my Frye boots and my tweed jacket. I was going to wear Mom's big beautiful shearling coat because it was gorgeous, warm extravagant fur, she wasn't around to get mad and somebody should get to enjoy it in this cold. I think it ended up at the cabin by accident. She would have wanted it in Chicago if she had her mind together, but it was in the closet so I put it on. It had real animal bone (or maybe they were antler), toggle closures and a huge fur-lined hood. The outside was tanned suede. The coat was amazingly glamorous and at the same time utterly primitive. I couldn't believe my good fortune to get to wear it for Christmas Eve.

I'd been invited to a distant relative's home. He was from Chicago—my grandfather's nephew and was living year-round as a new experiment with his much younger wife and their two adorable towhead toddlers. I was told the children were maybe my third cousins or something like that. This relative made a lot of money at one point, then divorced his first wife and took up with this woman and started a new family. The wife was Southern, very bright and serious. They had built a modern, year-round, log-construction home on a windswept and isolated rocky lookout. I didn't know them well but somehow they found out about me and the whole family stopped by the cabin unexpectedly the Saturday before and ended up inviting me for Christmas Eve dinner. I said I'd bring cookies. I baked a batch of star-shaped sugar cookies, sprinkled them with sugar, and wrapped them in a red-and-white cloth napkin. I packaged the cookies in a red wooden box that was in the kitchen cupboard. That would be my only gift but they turned out well so I was satisfied.

I went to their house in my red truck, which had real mistletoe that Dale had bought for me, hanging from the rearview mirror. The mistletoe was frozen solid, like everything else by this point in late December, but it was cheery and made me feel good. I made a suitably festive entrance coming down the drive in my bright red, old Ford pickup truck. They heard my truck on the gravel. Every noise was amplified in the crystal silence of the frozen landscape. The whole family was at the open door as I walked from the perfectly shoveled path to the door. I handed the little girl my gift. The couple greeted me warmly. The wife was dressed in a taffeta plaid long skirt and white blouse, the husband in a reindeer sweater. I was glad I got dressed up. The house was lit with candles and decorated with fresh pine boughs on the staircase and the fireplace mantel. The fire was blazing. I was grateful to be with them.

I was offered some dark red wine, which I didn't like, but was happy to sip to be festive. We exchanged pleasantries about the winter weather, about how different the lake was in winter. Everything was cozy and beautiful. The dinner of a dressed and roasted goose with many lovely side dishes looked delicious.

When we sat down to eat, I was so thrilled with the dinner and the sips of wine and the warmth of the charming family that I didn't notice the conversation shifting. It was as if they were starting to hone in on their real reason for inviting me. Their polite questions became more pointed. I realized they had serious questions they wanted answered.

They were determined to get to the bottom of how I could have ended up alone at the age of seventeen on Christmas Eve fifty miles from Canada in the middle of nowhere with no parents and no exit strategy. I didn't blame them honestly, but they couldn't shut up. They knew nothing of what had transpired with my family in the past year; that was obvious.

When the husband asked, "So Sidney, what did you say your parents are doing tonight?", I saw the immensity of the chasm between us.

My brain was screaming, "Oh my God, do you not get that your question doesn't come close to even beginning to capture the situation? Just give up. You are not going to be able to wrap your heads around this. Don't even try. There's too much to tell. Don't make me try to tell you."

I could hear myself saying, "Yeah, well I mean it's just a really difficult situation, but you know we're all handling it pretty well, I think."

What was I saying? I had no fucking idea how my dad was handling it. I didn't actually know where Preston was right then. My mom was probably having sex with her new boyfriend as we spoke. What am I supposed to tell you? The truth? You think you really want the truth? Do you want to hear about how guilty I feel? Do you want to hear about how petrified I am? Do you want to hear about how the ghost of my great-aunt who you probably used to know is now haunting me every night? Do you want to hear about how terrible I feel about not taking good enough care of our beloved family dog who's dead now because of me? Or, how about my biggest concern right now, which is whether to give in to my primal urges and lose what's left of my virginity to a not very bright but extremely kind young man who works as an unskilled laborer in an iron ore mine?

These thoughts were on the verge of becoming words, but luckily I found a way out of the interrogation. It was my little cousins who saved me. Their Christmas tree was huge in the high-ceilinged living room. The scent of pine from the freshly cut tree and the boughs everywhere plus the smell of the wood from their new construction was wonderful. We had all eaten heartily. The children's eyes had been bright with anticipation as they ate their dinners and finally they were allowed to leave the table. Just as their parents' interrogation became too much for me, the two of them came over and took my hands and started trying to pull me up out of my seat.

I laughed and let them pull me to the tree. They pointed out all the many wrapped gifts. The little girl was dressed in a wonderfully voluminous taffeta dark green party dress. The boy was in dark green suede lederhosen style shorts and wool knee socks, with a crisp white collared shirt. They were darling with their chubby cheeks and affectionate gestures and distracted me from the scrutinizing gaze of their intelligent and cultured parents who were never going to get what was going on with me. The parents and I cleared the dishes from the table. A Christmas Yule cake was served. A few gifts were opened. I was given a hand-knitted pair of pretty cream-colored mittens with a matching long scarf and beanie cap. Everyone had one of my cookies. Finally it was time to say goodnight.

I left with a lump in my throat. It was hard to leave their warm safe beautiful home. I cried as I drove on the dark long path to my little cabin that was so desperately empty without Brandy. I went to bed on Christmas Eve with the light of my wood stove twinkling in the main room. Aunt Evie appeared at the foot of my bed way after the stroke of midnight with her same unfeeling countenance, her accusing eyes. I wished her a Merry Christmas and turned over and put the pillow over my head. The gun, now that Brandy was gone, was next to my pillow.

On the afternoon of Christmas Day I went skating down on the lake. As the winter was progressing the snow was not cooperating. I kept my desk chair down there with a red shovel that Dale had brought over for me. I had to shovel the whole thing off every time I skated and the sides were getting very high with snow. The rink was getting smaller too as my conviction faded with the ever-heavier snowfalls. Some mornings I came down to discover that a snowmobiler had run right through the middle of my rink, usually got stuck, usually put some gouges in my perfect ice, and usually made a mess of my rink after trying to escape on the far end. Every time I went down there I put on my skates and shoveled as I skated, pushing the shovel in front of me and making a wider and wider skating area, freeing my skates as I went along, freeing myself to skate a wider swath unencumbered. I was shoveling the rink when I heard a car driving up the point. I stopped to listen. Without Brandy I was keenly aware of every noise, knowing that I no longer had a second pair of ears to be on the alert.

The car pulled up and the engine was turned off. Someone got out and was coming down to the lake toward me. It wasn't Dale. I recognized that it was Seymour when he finally called out, "Hallooooo down there . . . " in his funny vaudevillian delivery.

"Hello Seymour! Merry Christmas! Is my mom here?"

My heart leapt at the thought that maybe they were back for good.

"No, no. I don't want to get you all excited. No, I'm afraid it's just me stopping in."

I unlaced my skates and slipped on my boots. I could take the snowy steps I'd carved out to get up the bank in a few bounds now. I was soon up on the snow-covered lawn with him.

"You've still got the skating going. I'm impressed."

"Yeah. It's fun. I don't have that much to do. I don't have very many hours at work and school is so easy. Except calculus which I'll probably flunk!"

"I'm only here to stop by and check in on you, Sidney. I promised your mother I would."

"Oh yeah, well that's okay. I mean I'm fine. You don't have to do anything. I mean I'm doing just fine."

"I know. I knew you would be. You're a strong person. You have a lot of determination and energy. You will go places in life with that."

"Well, I hope so. We'll see I guess. Not really going places right now!"

We talked for a minute about how Mom was doing, what was happening in Chicago, what he was doing driving around on Christmas Day.

"I'm renting a place up here now. I'm not sure what your mother's plans will be and honestly I'm staying open to several scenarios. But I care about your family and I want to be supportive in any way I can."

I didn't have anything to say to that. I didn't really know what my mom thought of her new relationship with Seymour, so I didn't want to weigh in.

"Come up to the house. I have something for you. A Christmas present. I talked to your mother about it and she thought you might like this."

I followed him. I couldn't imagine what a man like Seymour would ever get somebody like me for a Christmas present.

But there they were on the porch leaning up against the kitchen door. Skis. Cross-country skis. Made of wood with metal bindings, brown leather boots with special toe fittings clipped to the bindings. Red poles with white leather hand grips too.

"Oh my gosh Seymour. These are fantastic!"

"That's a promising reaction."

"Oh wow, are you kidding? These are great!"

"Well, do you think you can use them? Try on the boots. Do you think you can figure out the technique? Maybe some of the other kids up here know how."

"Yeah, for sure. A lot of the kids at school know how to ski cross-country."

"Well, here's a book to go with it. Between the book and some practice, you should be up and skiing in no time. You're a natural athlete, the way you improved in your skating so quickly."

He handed me a wrapped book from a bookstore in Virginia.

"Haha, well I have plenty of time. School's out this whole week and part of next."

"I want to get on the road before nightfall. I'm driving down to be with your mother and hopefully we will celebrate New Year's Eve together. Here's some extra cash in case you need anything. Is your new friend still coming around?"

"Dale, yeah he is. We'll probably be playing a show with his band on New Year's Eve. I'm really excited about that. I get to sing some of my own songs and harmonies with the brothers."

"Well, it sounds like you're on the road to stardom. Good for you."

I took the money he handed me, didn't count it, just stuffed it into my coat pocket. The sun fell fast now and the sky was bright pink out over the ice.

Seymour gave me an awkward hug, "Merry Christmas, kid. I have a lot of faith in you. You're really something."

"Thanks Seymour. I feel the same way about you . . . " I said, not wanting to miss an opportunity for a good joke. He winked and straightened his dark fake-fur hat, the kind that old guys wore in the '50s.

"I assume you don't need me to reload your gun."

"No. I haven't touched it, I swear."

"Well, don't hesitate if the need arises. At your age, we could probably get you out on self-defense no matter whom you decide to shoot. Take care of yourself Sidney. I know your mother wants to come back up as soon as she gets your great-aunt's affairs settled."

"Yeah, I know."

"Okay, good luck."

"Same to you Seymour."

I watched him walk up the darkening path. The car engine started right away and he headed back to civilization. I didn't care that I wasn't going with him. I had no desire to be back in Chicago. That place was just shame and bad memories for me. At least this life was fresh and new and all mine.

I loaded my arms with wood and went inside to tend the fire. Christmas night. I had the wood stove stoked to the gills. The flames were flickering right up to the little glass window and throwing shadows around the room. I sat cross-legged on the wool carpet, guitar on my lap, staring at the chimney stones.

I thought about how often I'd heard my mother say, "If you look at the stones you can see the faces of Indian spirits."

I laughed out loud as I remembered one of the first funny things Seymour did up here. My mother was knitting in the early fall when they first came up together. She had been telling Seymour about seeing faces in the stones.

As she sat knitting, she looked up at the stones and gasped. Seymour, who had his head buried in the local newspaper, lowered his paper and looked at my mother. Then he looked at me. His eyes were smiling. My mother looked shocked.

"Mom, what?" I said, looking at Seymour like I wanted to get in on the joke if there was one, "Mom. Why are you gasping like that?"

"Well, it's just . . . well, it's just that the spirits' faces are more distinct tonight than I've ever seen them. I can see them really clearly. It's like they're all laughing. Look! Look at them. Come over to where I'm sitting. Here, do you see that? Look at that stone over there! Oh, oh my goodness!"

I looked at the fireplace. Sure enough, the spirits' faces were shining forth like never before. It was crazy, really scary-looking, like the masks of Comedy and Tragedy laughing and screaming and crying all at once. Almost every stone had come to life.

"Oh my God! They were never like this before," I agreed.

Mom and I stared. I looked at Seymour, but he hid again behind his newspaper. My mother got up out of her chair and went to the fireplace. She peered at the stones and then rubbed her finger on one of the faces. She looked at her finger, "Seymour?"

She rubbed another stone, "Seymour! What have you done?"

Seymour said nothing from behind his newspaper.

"You did this, didn't you!"

The newspaper lowered and Seymour was smiling. The trick had worked. When we weren't around, he had taken a burned stick from the fire and rubbed charcoal on the rocks' indentations, where earlier, there had only been the suggestion of faces. It was brilliant. Really funny. I liked Seymour.

I sat on the rug with my guitar. The spirits' faces on the old stone fireplace were smiling down at me. The red letters spelling out my grandmother's slogan "Life Is Too Short To Be Little" were blazing a reminder for me. The truth was that I wouldn't want to be anywhere else. I tried to write a song about it.

It's fine here now when the air is cold and the snow is white and silent.

I'm happy knowing that all I need is what I got at present.

Cuz the winters in Chicago are a hell I can't withstand,

and if you looked out my window at this view you'd understand.

I been living in the city much too long to be naïve.

The attraction of this peacefulness has convinced
me I should leave.

I'm living life the way we started out so long ago,

and although I like Chicago, I just can't call it
home.

I came a'wondering whether I could take the ice
and snow

but the icicles that decorate my windows make me
know

there ain't nothing like a winter's night when
you're safe and warm in bed

and it sure ain't like Chicago where I went to sleep
in dread.

I been living in the city much too long to be naïve.

The attraction of this peacefulness has convinced
me I should leave.

I'm living life the way we started out so long ago,

and although I like Chicago I just can't call it home.

I strummed it and worked it out on paper too. I sang
it with a bluegrass feel. I played it through many times. I
sang it loud and it felt great. I decided to play it for Dale
the next time I saw him. I went to bed feeling good about
myself and my life so far just as it was.

The holiday break was two weeks long and I still
had another seven days to go before I could return to
town on the school bus and be a part of civilization, so
over the next few days, I read the book about cross-country skiing and went out for short excursions.

I saw that there were two very different ways to ski. One was to be relatively safe and calm and just ski out on the lake, mostly following the snowmobile trails that gave a fairly easy and smooth path to follow, no uphill, no downhill, and really, no turns. This was the easiest.

Much more challenging was to follow paths made by either animals or snowmobiles in the interior of the peninsula. The center of the point was uninhabited and had a deep indendation that people called a crater from a meteor hit, even though I wasn't sure anyone could verify that. It was as deep as the tallest trees that grew up from its bottom so the sides were not manageable for me on skis. Around the periphery, there were trails with high lookouts and dark wooded knolls that criss-crossed all down to the very end of the point. In this interior area there were hairpin turns and sudden drops. The snowmobilers made the trails for me and I followed them. If the drop-off was too steep, I took off my skis and waded down through the snow rather than risk smashing into a tree like a skier in a cartoon with his legs and arms flailing and face planted squarely in the middle.

Dale came out to see me during the week. I was on the road on my skis, returning from following a new path that some snowmobiler had made over Christmas.

"Hey! Look at you! Skis, huh? When did this happen?"

I laughed and was glad I could surprise him. I pulled off my leather mittens, put them between my knees and lifted the earflaps on my trapper hat so I could hear him better and wouldn't sweat too much. Once I stopped moving on the skis, I'd always find that I was way too bundled up.

"Yeah I got them for Christmas from my mom's friend, Seymour. He came by on Christmas Day."

"I want to get some too. You want to go into town with me, pick out some skis and then get some dinner?"

"Yeah! I'd love to. I'm starving! Seriously! All I have left at the cabin is pancakes and I'm getting so sick of them."

I skied down to the porch and popped off my skis.

I stood them up on the porch and ran in to take a look at myself in the mirror and change my shoes.

"Okay, I can go in just a second. I think I should pee first before we drive all the way back. Don't you have to, too?"

"Nope. I'm like a Russian racehorse."

"What the hell is that supposed to mean? Maybe I don't want to know."

"Oh, you do want to know. Yes, you do."

"Dale. Geez."

"Don't you geez me little lady. Get up in that car before I pull you back into that cabin and tear all your clothes off of you."

"Dale! What's the matter with you! You've gone mad!"

"One of these days you're going to find out what madness lurks behind this mild-mannered demeanor of mine. And then you'll be sorry."

He chased me up to his car. I screamed and jumped into my seat just before he grabbed me and I slammed the door. I could use the bathroom at the store once we got to town.

We drove happily with him telling me about Christmas festivities with his family. We went to the sporting goods store in the mall and picked out skis on sale.

It didn't take much time at all because there was still a good selection, as though the store had been hoping everyone for fifty miles around had planned to buy all their relatives cross-country skis for Christmas. I sort of felt sorry for the guy working because the store wasn't very busy even though it looked festive. I wasn't sure how many people were going to buy skis now that the holiday shopping was over, but at least we did.

On our way back out to the car Dale asked where I wanted to eat. As we ran down the usual eight or so places to pick from, I heard a little yelping noise. I stopped. We were out in the middle of the snow-covered mall parking lot. Even though it had been recently plowed, there was snow piled high in all the corners and around all the light posts. I heard the yelp again. We looked all around for an animal, maybe in one of the parked cars.

"It would be pretty bad to leave a dog locked in your car at this temperature," Dale said.

The temperature was maybe ten degrees Fahrenheit at around four in the afternoon.

"What's that box?" I said and we headed toward a box that was half-covered with snow, backed up against a light pole in the center of the parking lot. A cardboard box with the lid folded over itself to keep it shut. No markings, just tan cardboard. We went near and heard the yelping get louder.

"Oh my God, Dale."

I ran to the box.

"Be careful Sid. You don't know what's in there. You don't want to get bitten."

I opened it a crack and peeked in, and as I did a little black wet nose came through to greet me. I gasped and pulled the lid open a bit wider. Another nose, a brownish one this time. I pulled the cardboard back until the box opened up and there were two chubby puppies. They were pretty big, not newborns.

Dale shouted out, "What the heck, Sid?" and started laughing. He grabbed one and lifted it up to his face and the puppy licked him all over. I picked up the other one and wrapped my coat over him as he licked my hand like crazy.

"Guess we just got ourselves some puppies," Dale laughed.

I looked all around. I almost felt like someone must be watching. I couldn't believe they'd just get abandoned like this. Dale grabbed the box and looked it over carefully.

"No note, no markings. And they weren't out here long 'cause there's no poop in the box."

We looked all around and there was no one to be seen, not even a car parked near ours.

"Okay, well I've been missing having a dog ever since poor Brandy died. Do you think these guys could be outdoor dogs? I wouldn't be able to keep them inside while I'm at school. It's too long for puppies. And my mom would probably get mad."

"I think they're part husky or something. Maybe part German shepherd. This one's got a thick coat."

"This one's coat is more like a beagle or a Lab or something. They're related, right? I mean they have to be from the same litter right? They don't look that much alike but they're the same exact size."

"Yeah, they're both girls too huh? Yep. They're sisters. Oh, poor little girls. Up here some people don't like girl dogs as much. The rest of the litter probably got sold or given away and these two were left over and they were getting too old to sell. These are some pretty big puppies. And healthy-looking. They were probably eating too much too. We'd better stop and buy a big bag of dog food."

"Do you think they've had shots and everything?"

"Knowing folks around here, probably not, Sid. That'll run ya quite a bit to take two puppies in for all that stuff."

"Well, I'll just keep them outside on my porch and they can come in when I'm home and they can sleep in the cabin with me at night."

"Yeah, they say if you want a dog to be an outdoor dog up here you can't have them inside because it screws up their ability to make a thick enough coat of fur. Then their body doesn't know what to think. If you're going to keep them out, they have to be out all the time I think."

"Oh geez. I don't know."

Dale paid for a huge bag of dog food. We bought two collars and two leashes. We put the collars on and they didn't seem to mind them.

"What are you going to name them?"

"I was thinking, since they're girls, we could call them Ribbon and Bow."

"Which one's which?"

I had the puppies on my lap in the car. They wouldn't stop licking my hands and face. I held one puppy's face and took a good look at her. She was scruffy and had a thick coat, colors like a calico cat. Her face was big and her nose was tannish brown and big like a bear's nose. She had intelligent eyes and I knew that she was grateful and relieved. I loved her already. "This one's Bow. She's the leader. She's the smart one."

The other one was just not as great all around. Her fur was shorter and flat like a beagle. She was mostly white with black and brown spots. Her shiny black nose was a bit pointed. Her eyes were close together and darted around to the sides, not willing to return my gaze. She seemed fretful and restless. I didn't think she was as smart, maybe just not as empathetic with humans. "And this one is Ribbon."

As soon as we arrived at the cabin I got out Brandy's old dishes and filled them with water and the new food. The pups fell in gulping and sloshing immediately. They both seemed healthy enough and pretty happy-go-lucky.

Dale suggested we line one of the wardrobe boxes left over from when our stuff came from Chicago. We gathered supplies and got to work out on the porch. We had the kitchen and the porch lights on and the wood stove in the living room stoked to the gills so we could warm up whenever we came inside. Dale helped me use the staple gun and attach an old blanket to all four sides of the box's interior. The thin wood stays along the corners made the blanket staple easily. We used another big old comforter and set the box under the kitchen porch roof, up against the house, with its back to the wind off the lake. We stapled some of the plastic sheeting that Seymour had given me all around the outside.

"This thing is snug as a bug in a rug for these guys."

"Do you think they'll run away?"

"Well, if they do, then good riddance. They'd have to be awfully stupid and ungrateful to run off this time of year. They're not going to find a sweeter deal any place else."

"Do you think this is a bad idea, Dale?"

"Idea! It wasn't your idea and it wasn't mine. It must have been God's idea. And if it was God's idea, then it's most likely got some kind of wisdom behind it. If you ask me, God knew you needed some companionship out here, and he gave it to you. No sense looking the gift horse in the mouth as they say."

"Oh okay, whatever that expression means."

"Right. Exactly."

Dale was smiling at me with his twinkling eyes. "Of course I've been offering my companionship too."

"Yes I get that."

"How'd you like a little companionship right now, Missy?"

"Is that what you're calling it now?"

The puppies had eaten everything in the bowl and drank all the water. I filled both again and we went inside.

"You think they'll know to get in the box? How am I going to know if they're warm enough?"

"I think the thing is to not let them in the house 'cause if you do, it'll be all over and they won't be happy out there. You're gonna have to stick to your guns."

Dale and I got cozy on the rug in front of the wood stove. It gave off so much heat it made your cheeks hot. Dale was playful and romantic and tapped into everything that I found arousing, and I knew he wouldn't push too far. I also knew he wasn't a super cool sex machine kind of guy. On some level I wanted to meet some-one like that some day. But right now what Dale offered in my life was gentle and kind and perfect.

We made out on the rug by the fire until midnight and then he went home.

As he was leaving, he checked the puppies and they were wrapped up together under the quilt. The dishes were empty again so they had full stomachs and I had a full heart.

Soon school started and I fed the little rough-and-tumble sisters before leaving, when I got home, and then again before bed. They got bigger and funnier and more affectionate every day. Bow knew everything. Ribbon did what Bow did. I talked to Bow. Ribbon watched me talk to Bow. If I talked to Ribbon she'd look over at Bow to see what Bow was doing or to say, "I have no idea what you're trying to say. Just talk to my sister."

I would look at Ribbon, trying to connect with her, bending down and taking one of her paws in my hand, and Bow would bust in between and stick her paw up instead. And Ribbon would happily let this happen and grab onto Bow's tail with her mouth and growl while I talked to Bow. So, that was the arrangement.

Bow learned tricks and commands. And she obeyed. I let Ribbon be a goof-off because whatever Bow did, she'd do anyway so I could control them easily enough. But really, I could already sense that control was an illusion when it came to the two of them or anything else in this strange foreign land.

REAL WINTER

I thought I
was managing
winter in the Great
North, but in January I
discovered that in fact winter was just being easy on me. In January, the seriousness
of the place hit full force. Things happened
like a one-two punch in a prize fight, me
against Old Man Winter in the ring,
losing terribly, backed into a corner
by the reigning champ.

My mom and Seymour had started up the furnace at Thanksgiving and
they advised me to keep it set low, just to
keep the place from freezing if by some unlucky
chance I let the stove die. The furnace was fueled by
an oil tank under the house. It had been filled for the
winter and was to last until spring. You did have to let the
wood stove die every once in a while to clean the ashes. I'd
let the fire die one whole day when I was to be at school.
When I got back, I was to shovel the still-warm ashes
into the tin bucket by the fireplace, empty it behind the

woodpile, and rebuild a fire from scratch. The furnace was employed and kept at fifty degrees all the time. The theory was that the furnace would keep the base of the house warm too so that the pipes wouldn't freeze once the real cold set in. Even with the wood stove and the furnace and all my efforts, I was losing the battle.

First I noticed the toilet wouldn't flush. The night temperature had hit a dramatic new low and when I got up in the morning to use the bathroom, I saw that the toilet acted like it was plugged but I had only peed. Later that first day it did flush through. The next morning it didn't flush and that afternoon it still refused to empty.

I talked to people at school and apparently the septic system was now frozen and if I flushed, the water had nowhere to go. The only thing to do was stop flushing and wait until spring. Wait until spring. To ever use the toilet again. This was mid January. I got out an old tin pan that my grandmother had used to scrub the floors and it became my chamber pot. The place behind the woodpile where Brandy used to poop became my place to poop too.

I put a roll of toilet paper out there on a stick in the back of the woodpile and I'd just do what I had to. Everything froze solid pretty much the minute you did it. Then every few days I'd go out with the shovel and scoop the whole mess up and throw it deeper into the woods. The puppies did whatever I did so sometimes we'd all be out there together pooping. I would laugh so hard I'd almost fall over into the snow, looking at the two of them squatting because I was squatting. If they didn't have anything else to distract them they'd come bounding over and start trying to lick my face and jump on me and I'd have to yell at them to leave me alone.

I found out the hard way that the bathroom sink and the tub were all connected to the same septic system. One night I got out of the tub and let the hot water out and it didn't budge. The water was still there the next morning. Same with the bathroom sink. The water just wouldn't drain.

I only had the kitchen sink after that. The hot-water heater still worked. I found that if I left the hot water trickling all night and left the lower cupboard doors open to get heat to the kitchen pipes, then the kitchen sink wouldn't freeze. The one time it did, Dale showed me how to plug in a hair dryer and blow hot air on the pipes until they thawed.

Dale helped me get a block heater installed in the old red truck and we ran a big orange extension cord out the kitchen door, chipping a wedge of wood out so the door would still shut. I could plug in the truck and keep the engine from freezing up. I didn't drive very often at this point, mostly only to work at the resort which was down to the odd Friday or Saturday night if they had many reservations for the dining room.

Now that it had been bone-chillingly cold, I had been driving down to the bus stop in the mornings and waiting for the bus. I could leave the heat blasting and the headlights on. Corey the bus driver had cautioned me that leaving the truck out without the block heater plugged in, even during the day, might be risky. He said, "I'd hate to see you not be able to start that thing one of these days when we get back out here."

The thing about getting back out there in the afternoon was that I was one of the last to be dropped off and by four in the afternoon it was dark again. So I left the truck plugged in under the carport every morning. I stoked the wood stove. I checked the furnace setting. I left the puppies to fend for themselves. I headed out each morning at six on foot, walking as fast as possible or jogging through new snow. I wished I could ski down to the bus, but I would have to switch out of my cross-country ski boots to my hiking boots, which I didn't want to deal with.

Now that it was truly cold, I prayed while I waited for the bus to come. I stood alone in the dark, my small flashlight making a dim wisp of light through the impenetrable northern woods. These mornings my grandfather's thermometer hit a new low each day. Twenty below, twenty-five below. The numbers were surreal. Cold was a bottomless pit. Cold was what hell was described to be; something simultaneously interminable, inescapable, intolerable.

The woods were so still, especially when it was dark. I half expected some cadaver to rise up out of the wilderness, to march toward me through the thin spaces between the trees. Only the dead could survive this. This cold was not for the living.

My eyeballs would get so cold I'd have to close my eyes and just listen for the wheezing engine. I would pray, "Please God let the bus make it. Please God let the bus get here."

I'd usually hear the music over the engine these cold mornings. Corey the bus driver was in his glory it seemed, in the battle against Old Man Winter. I'd hear the rock music blasting. Then I'd hear the roar of the old engine. Then I'd see the blazing headlights. Then I'd feel the heat as the folding doors of the bus would rattle open, and I'd step up into the last safe haven of civilization between me and death. I'd pause and self-consciously pull the ice chunks off my eyelashes, throwing them down to the bus floor to melt. Damn you, Winter. Damn you, frozen North Country.

Corey's music would be so loud that I wouldn't be able to talk to him but he'd yell, "Good Morning Sidney, glad you could join us!" over one of his favorite eight-track tapes blasting through his rigged up surround-sound that went front to back of the old school bus. The music enveloped your head whether you liked it or not. Often Corey's morning party was Meat Loaf's epic album that always distilled down to "I Can See Paradise by the Dashboard Light" with most of the kids on the bus singing along. Once I knew the words and found myself singing along too, I knew I had fully assimilated. I sat with the girls I loved. We hooked our arms together for extra warmth and sang at the tops of our lungs all the way to town as the sun came up over the pines and the white frosted icy pavement threatened to throw our clubhouse off the road at every wild turn on Corey's treacherous route.

At school everyone acted like they wanted the cold to let up. "Everybody's got a bad case of cabin fever," the principal could be heard commenting in the halls. The cold made people not care about much of anything besides survival. There was a whimsical girl who sat in front of me in our English class. She was tiny like a fairy and the kids teased her about smoking too much "reefer" as they called it. I noticed that by the end of January, she wore her sweatshirt with the hood up all day every day. If the teacher yelled at her to take her hood down, I would see, sitting just inches behind her, that the back of her hair was a fried mass of short tangled frizz that in no way resembled the shoulder length smooth brown tresses she had in front. I was not going to comment on this, ever, but the other kids never missed an opportunity to find something novel to enliven the day's passing.

"What the hell is with your hair Melissa?" one bold young gentleman launched.

"Shut up. I didn't want to take down my hood. Just shut up."

"What'd you do, set your hair on fire with your bong?"

More scholars turned around in their seats, more chortles.

"No, God, leave me alone. Just mind your own business. You're all a bunch of ugly pigs anyway. Look at your hair, Bobby."

"Oh ouch, yeah I spent so much time getting my hair right before school this morning."

"Come on, Melissa," one of the sweeter girls joined in, "Tell us. It does really look weird. It's like it's fried off. What happened?"

"I don't know."

"You must know."

"No, I don't know. All I know is I've been napping on the radiator at home and I think the radiator is melting it."

Masses of guffawing. "The radiator is melting it! You think the radiator is melting it? You think so? You think so, huh?"

A big brazen girl named Lila from the lake whose parents owned one of the bars on the main highway

stepped in. She was kind-hearted and smart but was il-
literate for all practical purposes. She was always putting her arm around me and saying, "Sidney's my secret
weapon, aren't ya Sid? She's gonna make sure I graduate
and all's I gotta do is sit next to her on the bus every day
between now and graduation. Right, Sid?"

I would say "Yep. You got it. We're doing this."

She was fun to help and to be with and I enjoyed
teaching her grammar and easy math and doing most of
her writing for her. She was affectionate and grateful and
I loved her.

She stepped up about Melissa's hair. "Hey, Meliss.
Don't let these A-holes get you down. I happen to be an
ace number one hair stylist. I plan to go to beauty school
in The Cities once I break out of this dump. Somebody
get us some scissors!"

Scissors appeared and the styling began in English
class; the unwanted hair fell onto my desk and I gingerly
brushed it into a pile and threw handfuls into the waste-
basket at the front of the room.

The English teacher slash gym teacher had long
since given up on everything: the class, her career, life
in general probably. She was silently grading our quiz-
zes on Shakespeare's biography, an essay in our lousy
textbook which was only a page and a half in length
and barely had one single interesting fact about the life
and times of Shakespeare. It had been required reading
for the past three nights in a row. Lila finished the haircut. I liked it. It was a huge improvement and seemed
fresh and mod and no longer did little Melissa look like
some crazy dreamer girl living her own little glass me-
nagerie.

"Hey Lila," I asked, "If I cut mine this weekend, will you fix it up if it needs fixing on Monday?"

"Of course Sidney. I keep telling you I'm gonna be your personal assistant. Whatever you want girl, I'm with you. You're gonna be somebody some day."

That night I ran home from the bus stop, freezing all the way, and was greeted by the big playful puppies. I was excited to chop off my hair. I'd been thinking about it for a while. I hadn't had it cut in such a long time, it was sort of shoulder length but it got caught in the drain in the kitchen sink and I couldn't keep it nice wearing my fur hat almost constantly. I even wore my fur hat to bed these days. I thought it would be better to have short hair again. Plus it would go with my tomboy wardrobe. The puppies wrestled on the kitchen porch, fighting over the new water and food I put down for them. I stood at Grandpa's big shaving mirror with the black kitchen scissors in my hand. I figured super short was the way to go, the shorter the better. I chopped each section about two inches from my scalp. I kept going until there was nothing left to cut. The bangs were jagged and the hair around the ears was jagged. Success!

With the holidays over, playing music became a new focus. I practiced for the talent show, the band concert, and the school musical. I played music with Dale too. One weekend I performed in back to back shows with Dale and his brother and their band. I loved those gigs. People really liked when Dale and I sang a couple songs as a duet, and said that we really had something special and that we should go on the road. We agreed to keep playing as many shows as we could. The band split their money with me and I went home with cash in my pocket, which was great too.

The winter cold was relentless throughout January, but some days were beautiful—bright and sunny, which made up for a lot. I practiced for the talent show that was coming up. I was going to perform my new song and play the guitar. The kids in choir heard me sing it for tryouts and everybody liked it. Some of the girls asked me to sing their songs in harmony with them too. I was happy to have so many performances to look forward to.

Dale kept asking me what I wanted to do for my birthday and Valentine's Day—my birthday was the day before Valentine's Day. I told him I didn't care, it was still a long way off, and whatever he wanted to do would be great. He was good at planning fun dates.

The resort didn't need my help in the restaurant at this point. They were managing with just the owners and the cook. The only money I had coming in was what I was getting from playing with Dale's band, which wasn't much. In the midst of all the whirlwind of music and fun, an unforeseen accident gave me a new job. Jeannie, the young woman I liked so much who ran the cabin cleaning in summer, had apparently been in a snowmobile accident.

Her husband, Danny, called me one evening asking if I could start coming over three days a week after school to help out with their little boys and help with cleaning the house and cooking. I was happy to have a new source of income and I liked them all very much. Danny offered to pick me up and bring me there and back. We agreed I'd start right away.

The first time Danny came to get me, I thought he'd be arriving later, so when I heard tires on the gravel I jumped. There wasn't much for food in the cabin, mostly because I rode the school bus every day and didn't have a chance to go to the grocery store when I was in town. I didn't have much money, so I was just getting by on what I had. That day I had come home from school hungry and decided to make pancakes because I had the kind of mix that only needed water. I had a stick of butter in the fridge and a big glass bottle of Aunt Jemima syrup. I made myself a tall stack of steaming hot pancakes and I sat down at the table to eat them, thinking Danny wouldn't be there for another fifteen or twenty minutes. When I heard the tires on gravel, I had just spread butter between the layers of pancakes, and was getting myself a fork. As I heard the truck door slam, and Danny's shoes on the porch floor, I suddenly felt embarrassed. The stack of pancakes, not exactly a health- or weight-conscious option, was huge! I didn't want Danny to think I'd forgotten or wasn't ready because I really wanted the job. So as his footsteps grew louder and he was about to knock on the kitchen door, I dashed to the kitchen cupboard and stashed the whole plate of pancakes with the fork still on the plate, into the cupboard where the other dishes were stacked, and shut the door.

I pulled myself together, and as I opened the door to greet Danny I had a fleeting sense that the smell of pancakes was very strong especially to someone just walking in.

"Danny, hi! Thanks for picking me up. This is so great. I'm really excited to see Jeannie and the boys. Here's my coat, let's go." But even talking fast wouldn't save me. Danny was talking too, but looking around curiously.

"Yeah hey Sidney, great to see you. Is everything okay? Are you ready to go? Are you sure you got everything shut off in the kitchen before you go? Don't want to burn the place down, haha . . . what's that smoke there? Hang on, I think we better check things before we go."

"No, I checked everything. Let's head out."

"No, wait a minute, it's like there's smoke coming from the cupboard over there. What could that be?"

I turned and saw that my hidden pancakes were steaming so much in the cold air of the corner cupboard that it looked like something was smoldering. Before I could do anything, Danny crossed the room and opened the cupboard. He stood for a minute staring at my stack of pancakes.

"Hey, did I interrupt your dinner? I figured you could eat at our place with the boys. Geez that's quite a stack you got cooked up there."

"Yeah well, I don't know . . . " My face was burning with embarrassment.

"What, were you planning to have a big pancake party tomorrow or something? Getting a head start on making some kind of big pancake thing like the Boy Scouts do it? Haha, boy that's quite a stack of pancakes."

"Yeah. Haha. Okay well, let's just go okay?"

Danny took one more look at me, then at the pancakes.

"At least let's put some kind of tin foil or something over 'em."

I got out the tin foil and covered the pancakes and

left the covered plate on top of the stove this time. Danny seemed satisfied and we headed out the door.

Once we were in his truck, heading to their house, Danny forgot about the pancakes and started talking about the accident and how their lives had changed. I could hear the sorrow in his voice, "I wanted to wait to talk to you in person, Sidney. This has been pretty tough on all of us. Jeannie's had a rough go of it."

"Oh, I'm so sorry. She's such a cool person."

"Well, she's changed a lot. I want you to be ready for it. See, when we had the accident, we got thrown and we were riding together and I was unconscious. What I didn't know was that Jeannie's chin strap on her helmet got lodged in a funny way and while we were both out of it, she lost oxygen to her brain for a while. We got picked up by the Johnsons who thank God were out for a ride, and they got us to the Virginia hospital. We thought it was all going to be okay, but then Jeannie didn't really know who I was when she woke up . . ."

Danny trailed off and turned his face away, looking out his side window.

I was silent.

"So tonight, when we get there, it's like we're all just kind of starting from scratch. She won't know you, and hopefully if anybody can win her over you can, she always loved you and you've got a good way with people. The boys have been kind of crushed by the change . . ."

He stared out the window again and we were getting close to his driveway when he said, "So we'll just get you situated. You can see Jeannie and then I'm gonna get her bundled up and take her out for a burger. We'll just get out of the house for a while and you just do what you can. Make the kids pizza. Watch a movie with 'em. If you see anything that doesn't seem right, it probably isn't. Just straighten anything that needs straightening. Jeannie has a real hard time knowing where things go . . . "

We walked up to the front porch and he opened their kitchen door.

"It just kind of is what it is these days," he finished, and then "Hey boys! Where's Mommy? Look who I have here! You remember Sidney?"

The boys started jumping around, they were both wearing footie pajamas that looked clean. Their faces were cheerful. I took off my coat as they tugged at my knees. The bigger boy was about three and a half and they were only a little over a year apart. Their hands were a little grubby and their noses needed wiping so I turned to the kitchen to see what I could find. I had never been in their place before. But it must have changed a lot recently. I was stunned to see yellow Post-It notes taped to almost every surface. Some notes just indicated the name of the object. STOVE. Others had directions, BURNER HOT. On the refrigerator was a summertime photograph of their little family smiling. Under the photo all four of their names were written out on four separate yellow notes.

Jeannie came out of the back bedroom looking as beautiful as ever but more docile and tired. Her eyes showed no recognition when she saw me. The boys ran and clung to her legs and she patted their heads but made no show of real affection. When she spoke it was slow and deliberate with a bit of a slur.

"Hello. I hope the house isn't too messy. My husband says you're going to babysit the boys. Thank you. We don't get out much these days. This is nice."

I could see that Danny was worried about what I thought, but I didn't care, I still liked Jeannie a lot. "I'll do as much as I can! Have a fun time and stay out as late as you want. I don't have school tomorrow so I can stay up late."

To me Danny said, "Okay, so far so good. Have a good time with the boys. If Jeannie feels like it, we might stay out and go hear the band at the roadhouse."

"Yeah, fine by me. Have a good time."

"Thank you so much, Sidney. Once the boys go to bed, feel free to check out the record collection, they won't care as long as it's not too loud. And see what you can do with the kitchen and stuff. I promise I will make this worth your time. I really appreciate it."

They left and I launched into wrestling with the two boys like I wrestled with the puppies. Then we read through a few of their picture books they had on a low shelf of a small bookcase.

I took a few minutes to put a frozen pizza in the oven, and cut up an apple sitting in a bowl. I looked in the refrigerator and decided I'd try to organize that and throw some stuff away. I went to the sink and determined that some serious dishwashing and sink-scrubbing was in order too. Once the kids went to bed, I'd get on it.

The boys and I ate pizza and apple slices. We watched an old Disney movie. I played their parents' Carole King *Tapestry* album and we danced to "I Feel the Earth Move. "

Finally the boys rubbed their eyes with their chubby little fists. We went to the bathroom, which I saw was another frontier for cleaning and organizing. First we washed their little faces with a warm washcloth. Then we brushed their teeth with their cartoon-character tooth-brushes.

We bundled up the boys in their little room in the full-size bed they shared and I read to them. They had a strange quiet life in the winter, but come summer they'd be allowed to roam the resort with its beautiful beach and endless wooded paths. Their mom was changed but not ruined, and maybe she'd get better with time. And their dad was a good guy. They had everything they needed. I kissed them on the forehead.

I spent the rest of the evening cleaning, scrubbing, and organizing with Carole King making it all worth-while in the background.

Jeannie came through the door, her husband close behind, around midnight. She was happy, if still sort of dazed. Danny took a look around the tiny house and was noticeably pleased, "Wow Sid. You're the white tornado! This place looks great. Jeannie hon, what do you think?"

"I used to be able to do all this but I just can't do that much now. You have a lot of energy."

"Ha, yeah I guess I do. Well, I'm glad you guys feel good about it. I can really use the money right now, so I'd be happy to come back as often as you want."

I got my coat, put on my hat, made sure I had my mittens. I said goodnight to Jeannie who was rummaging around in the refrigerator. I hoped I hadn't moved stuff around too much for her.

Danny took me home in their big four-wheel drive four-door. I hadn't been in a family car in a long time. There were car seats in the back. Danny seemed kind of drunk and he took the opportunity to give me some un-solicited advice on the drive.

"Sidney, if there's one thing I'd say to a pretty young girl like you is take good care of yourself. Me and Jean-nie, you know, we may never be the same again, I mean as a couple. You can't drink and drive. You can't do stu-pid shit. You gotta think first. You can really fuck shit up for yourself. And so many of the pretty girls, they get out of high school and they just start having kids and letting themselves go. Your life doesn't have to be over once you graduate."

I had never considered that anyone would think their life was over when high school ended. I had always thought that you didn't start living until you got out of your terrible purgatory of a mandatory high school ed-ucation. In Chicago I felt like everybody was just wait-ing to graduate and get started with their lives and their dreams. I thought the same was true in this tiny commu-nity, but maybe I was wrong.

Danny was still talking, "See like Jeannie and me, we were the homecoming king and queen. Everybody looked at us as the stars. We were on top of the world. We got married right after graduation. I got the mining job. Then Jeannie had little Cade and then we got this opportunity to help manage the resort. We had Mikey. We weren't expecting nothing but blue skies and sun-shine. Clear sailing. Straight through. Now the accident. Bam."

He was pulling into my driveway and my dogs were running up to the truck.

"You got yourself these crazy dogs huh? They just puppies?"

"Yeah, they're ridiculous but I love 'em. They must have been off running around when you came before. They're outdoor dogs. Well, thanks again and I'll do this as often as you guys need me. I really had fun with the boys."

"Yeah, great. We'll do this a few times a week I think, okay? Listen Sidney, so I'm just saying to ya. It's important to get out and do what you can with your life and not just settle down right away. And you know, you're very attractive. You're real pretty, you know. You gotta watch your figure. You gotta stay in shape. Don't start eating too much. Take it easy on the pancakes." He smiled a knowing smile and I nodded politely, "Don't get fat. It's easy to get fat up here. I've seen the girls at the high school. Most of them is way over what they should be. Don't let that happen to you, I'm just saying it for your own good. I care about you. You got a lot of potential."

"Thanks Danny. I really appreciate that. Yeah, I gotta be careful. Definitely. Okay, good night."

I was shutting the passenger door and he said, "Yeah, I mean I hope I'm not saying too much, I mean I'm just trying to watch out for you."

I ran down through the bitter cold to the cabin. The fire was almost out so I stoked it up. I took the dogs for a little jog around the drive. They followed me, nipping at my heels as I ran. I grabbed as much wood as I could carry and brought it in for the wood box. I went back out and peed in the snow with the pups. They were big now, eye-to-eye with me if I was squatting down. They licked my face while I maneuvered the toilet paper.

I said goodnight and they burrowed deep into the comforter in their box. Luckily they had each other. Luckily I had them. I went inside and looked at myself in the full-length mirror behind the bathroom door. Hmmm. Maybe I would have to get serious about what I was eating. I ate whatever I could get my hands on for the most part in an effort to conserve on cash. At school the only things I liked were the doughnuts that the town kids brought in small white paper bags from the bakery on Main Street. Somebody was always trying to get me to eat a doughnut and I usually said yes. At lunch the small cafeteria served meager rations but great french fries in red and white paper baskets. So a doughnut for breakfast, fries for lunch. When I got home to the cabin I usually only had pancake mix, which I'd stir up with one egg and some water. I had a big bottle of maple syrup and there was butter in the refrigerator. If Dale came to get me, which he did a couple times a week, then I had a real dinner.

At first I was doing so much skating and skiing that it didn't catch up with me, but when the real winter set in, I became homebound. The skating rink had finally given way to the wreckage of Old Man Winter. The ice heaved and distorted the shoreline so drastically with its constant expansion and contraction that the ice that had been the rink was now forced five feet in the air in a great arching curve like a wave frozen high up in a picture of Hawaii, ready to crash to the rocky shore. I guessed the giant ice wave would only get more exaggerated until the big thaw in the spring. At night I could hear the ice groan and crack in the most eerie and ominous ways. The shoreline was transformed daily by the shifting of the ice.

The ski trails froze harder than I could ever have imagined. The snow changed into hard packed white styrofoam. My skis had nothing to grip, nothing to kick up. The world froze over and I felt claustrophobic in the whiteness as if I had been marooned on a glacier. My dash down to the bus at six a.m. and back again at four was becoming my only exercise which wasn't enough compared to what I was used to.

To beat the threat of getting fat, on Saturdays I wore my denim shorts and old bandana halter-top, and started dancing to whatever music I could tune in to on the radio. I danced in front of the living room picture window so I could see my reflection and be reminded of the bulge that was threatening to form around my hips. If I danced long enough I'd get really hot and sweaty even in the chilly cabin.

Dancing in front of the picture window is how I first discovered what my dogs were up to out in the yard. A big fat snowy white and grey jackrabbit suddenly darted out from the brush and was running in clear view at one end of the snow-covered yard. The snow was so frozen that the rabbit was running along on top, his feet staying on the surface of what was probably three feet of snow beneath him. From the corner of my eye I caught Bow jumping off the kitchen porch out onto the snow, breaking through the hard crust and scrambling after the rabbit, her feet sometimes staying on top, sometimes breaking through. I was fascinated as she ran fast enough to get near the rabbit and then out of nowhere Ribbon came flying, lighter on her feet, faster than her sister. Ribbon quickly gained on the rabbit and Bow, and as Bow worked to keep the rabbit running straight by flanking the rabbit's left side, Ribbon caught up on the rabbit's right and then in one expert quick move Ribbon turned in on the rabbit's path and caught it in her mouth. Within seconds as I watched with my mouth open, the rabbit was dead. The two dogs dragged and tore at the rabbit the rest of the day until they had gnawed all the bones clean. This scenario became commonplace.

The dogs took to a spot on the road where the sun shone against the back cabin wall. They enjoyed this location because they could watch for someone coming down the road, and be on the lookout for deer crossing on the paths across the road in the interior. When I got home from school or pulled in with Dale, they would almost always be gnawing on bones in front of the cabin. The carcasses of dead animals were starting to multiply. They killed a young deer at one point and the longer bones lying about really made the scene in front of the cabin look gruesome.

FEBRUARY

I sat in chemistry class looking out the window at the white football field to the south of the school. The kids in this class were a year younger, mostly juniors, and there were twin sisters in the grade below me whom I admired a lot for their brains and beauty and fearless individuality. Today was my birthday. It was also the day before Valentine's Day, and there were all sorts of silly rituals going on in the school to celebrate. Most of the pretty girls were getting anonymous Valentines asking "guess who" delivered by freshmen girls who were being given a lot of time off during school hours to go around interrupting any semblance of learning to deliver these random messages. The twins asked me about Dale.

"Yeah, he's from Virginia," I answered nonchalantly.

Both girls' eyes got big. "That's so huge. You're dating an older boy and he's already graduated? From

Virginia? That's so cool."

I thought about Dale and I knew it wasn't that cool, but if they thought it was cool that was great.

"Have you done it with him?"

That was always the next question out of these kids' mouths and they were a year younger than me. In a school where the size of each graduating class was under twenty, there was at least one if not two pregnant girls in each grade.

"I haven't done it with anybody."

"You're a virgin?!"

Both twins leaned in and stared at me.

"Isn't anyone a virgin in this school?"

"Probably not," they answered simultaneously.

"Well it's my birthday and I'm eighteen now so maybe it's time. Dale's always talking about going all the way. Maybe I should just get it over with."

"I would."

"I would too."

No hesitation. From either one of them.

"Yeah, well after a while it's just like something to get over with. And Dale is the nicest guy in the world. I mean, I'm not that crazy about him, he isn't exactly a rocket scientist, but he is sweet."

One twin offered, "I've seen him, I think he's gorgeous."

The other added, "And he sings and plays guitar."

"Okay well I guess you guys made up my mind for me. Thanks, girls."

After school I went home and got ready. Dale was driving out to pick me up for a birthday dinner date. I wore my white cotton blouse with the high lace collar, which looked really cute with my extra short hair. I wore my tan leather Frye boots under the denim maxi skirt that I had recently bought. I wondered if I might have to wear my mom's long shearling coat like I did at Christmas, but I didn't want to because it looked so obviously expensive and like something an older woman would wear.

Dale was dressed up in a black wool turtleneck sweater and grey wool work pants that we had recently bought for him. He looked handsome and sophisticated, and showed up with a big box with a red bow. The card was full of handwritten sentiments about how wonderful our relationship was. I opened the box and was thrilled to find the rabbit fur jacket I had tried on so many times when we were at the mall in Virginia. The tan jacket was very warm and matched my leather boots. It looked perfect with my long denim skirt. I put it on and we headed out for dinner.

He took me to a really beautiful lodge on the far end of the lake that I had never even heard of. The restaurant served duck with wild rice and walleye with mashed potatoes. They had fresh broccoli which I couldn't get enough of so we asked for a second order. They brought us a huge piece of chocolate cake at the end with a candy heart and a candle on top.

Dale sang "Happy Birthday" to me and I cried, "Dale, seriously, without you, my life would suck so bad right now. You've made this winter so much fun for me."

"Good, because I feel the same way about you Sidney my dear."

On the way back to the cabin, Dale held my hand tight and asked, "Well? Is tonight the night of all nights? Did you make up your mind? I brought the party favors if you know what I mean."

"I don't know, I mean, I guess. I figure, what have I got to lose, ha ha."

"I mean, it's a bigger deal for girls I realize, but I feel like you've given the whole virginity thing a respectable run Sid."

"Oh brother."

"I'm glad I'm not your brother, but I'm sure your brother would think it was time to join the twentieth century. I lost mine a long time ago. I've been looking for it ever since."

"Dale, those jokes aren't funny."

"You're just saying that."

"No really. Not funny, Dale."

We got to the cabin and we played with the dogs. We went in and Dale brought in as much wood as he could possibly carry and filled the wood stove and the box. I had made up my mind that I was going through with it. I decided we should get into an actual bed and my tiny pink bed was not going to work so I suggested we go into the room my grandparents, my parents, and most recently my mom and Seymour had slept in. I didn't like to think of all those people, but I couldn't get them out of my mind. Dale was eager and competent. He knew exactly what he was going to do and there was no hesitation. He wasn't self-conscious and he kept saying how beautiful I was and how lucky he was, which definitely helped. Everything worked and it was over pretty quickly. I felt sort of shook up and got up to go to the kitchen. There was a bit of blood, which I wanted to clean up to make sure we didn't mess up the sheets. Dale had used a condom, which he was fairly experienced with. He said it worked right and didn't break.

I stood in the kitchen after peeing in the pan and dumping it down the sink. I put my hands over my face and cried. This was all too weird and too hard. I was alone with no parents. A guy who worked in an iron ore mine and was never going to college just had sex with me. Where the hell was this all leading? I was never going to college the way things looked now. There was no money, no father, barely a mother. What were Dale and I going to do, get married like the town kids? I would be a miner's wife in Virginia, Minnesota? Or could we play music and make a living? Could we get famous like Dolly Parton or Willie Nelson?

Dale came in showing off his beautiful bare chest and his white wool long underwear bottoms. He looked gorgeous just like the girls had said.

"How's the most beautiful girl in the world feeling now? Was that okay? Are you okay? What'd you think? How'd I do?"

"You were great. Thanks, Dale."

"Happy birthday, Sidney. I love you." He'd never said that before but I knew he did love me.

"I love you too, Dale." He stayed the whole night with his arms around me and I shut my brain off. I was happy and warm and grateful.

The next morning was Valentine's Day. I walked into the main hall off the school bus and some kid said, "The principal's looking for you."

The principal was never looking for me. I walked down to the office and stuck my head in at the door.

"Hi Mr. Harlan, the kids said you wanted to see me?"

"Sidney! Sidney, my dear girl. Come in and take a load off."

He was in a good mood so I sat down in one of the wooden chairs, leaned it back on two legs and put my feet up on his desk, red laced hiking boots inches from his stacks of papers.

I smiled my biggest smile. He smiled back.

"You're a great kid but get your feet off my desk."

I laughed. "Sorry."

"Listen Sidney, I've been thinking about your situation."

"Good, at least somebody is."

"You're an excellent student. You have almost straight As with us."

"Except calculus."

"Except calculus, where I'm happy to say we are kicking your city-slicker butt."

"Very funny. And true."

"I heard that song you wrote for the talent show. And I've read a few of the papers you've written. You're a real talent in the creative writing area I believe."

"Thank you."

"The point is you need to go to college."

"I don't think that's a possibility at this point."

"Why not?"

"My dad's not going to pay for me to go to college now and my mom doesn't have any money."

"There are other ways to skin a cat, if you don't mind the expression."

"I think I do mind."

I was getting uncomfortable. I was thinking of making money by getting Dale to quit his job and go on the road with me. Maybe we could get famous.

I hadn't discussed it with Dale and I didn't know if I

even liked Dale enough to do that with him.

"Sidney, what I'm getting at is I have taken the liberty of contacting an old schoolmate of mine from up here on the Range. He and I went to the University together, first Duluth, then in The Cities. He is the head of the English department of a very fine liberal arts college in St. Paul. I told him about you and he is willing to meet with you."

"I really appreciate this. I'm not sure how I'd get there or what he could do for me when I don't have any money. I mean, I have like thirty dollars right now."

"I am prepared to buy you a bus ticket to St. Paul from our needy student fund. We can use that money any way we see fit to help students who can't afford something that is crucial to their academic advancement. I believe this would be good use of the money."

"And then what? What if he likes me? I can't pay for college. No way."

"I talked to him at length and he feels that his school, because it's small and privately run, has many financial opportunities for someone like yourself. He thinks you could maybe get a complete financial aid package. Sidney. This is your chance. Will you go? I can buy you a ticket and you can go down this Friday for the day."

"Okay."

I smiled. He smiled. I had no idea what I was getting myself into. I had never been to St. Paul. I had never gone to a college interview.

When I returned to the cabin that evening I called my mother and told her that I was taking a bus to St. Paul.

"Sidney, I don't like it that this man is paying for my daughter to get on a bus to somewhere I've never heard of to meet with some man we've never met and don't know anything about. I think this is terrible. Sending a girl alone on a bus to an unknown city."

"Mom, Mr. Harlan the principal is a really great guy. He's totally trustworthy. If he says this might work I have to at least try. It's the only chance I can see of going to college. Mom, I'm going."

I told Dale the next time he stopped over. He shook his head in bewilderment. "You are really something. How does this stuff happen to you? You just have the craziest luck. Puppies in a box, bus tickets to colleges. You're always full of surprises. Well, I for one sure am proud of you. Your mom's just an old worry-wart. And she's probably jealous 'cause all the cool stuff happens to you."

On Thursday night Dale stayed over and got up at four in the morning to drive me to the bus station. He wouldn't be late for work because the bus was leaving early. The dogs had food and water and the furnace got turned up a little since the stove would go cold before my return. Dale wished me luck and promised to be there when the bus got back that night around nine o'clock. The plan was that I'd have several hours between eleven in the morning and four in the afternoon to do the interview. The principal had told his friend I'd be stopping in at the school to meet with him sometime in the middle of the day Friday.

I took the bus and slept most of the way. When we pulled sleepily into the St. Paul bus station I felt the whole arrangement was kind of crazy. I was wearing my red long underwear. I looked out at the urban setting and thought, "Oh my God I've been up in the woods too long. I look like some kind of mountain man."

I had my ripped jeans, my hiking boots, my down vest and my down coat. My trapper's hat. My chopper's mitts. My do-it-yourself haircut. Well, at least I looked the part for the story I was about to tell. I had about twenty dollars on me and the papers for my return ticket to Virginia. I had my Illinois driver's license. I had a cherry-tinted lip balm. That was about it.

I started walking, asking people if they knew where the college was. I got pointed up a huge hill, past the St. Paul Cathedral. I walked along a stately long boulevard called Summit Avenue. Eventually, after maybe three miles of walking, I arrived at the college. I asked where the English department was. Some students pointed to an old red stone building. I walked in. The weather in St. Paul at the end of February was balmy compared to where I was living, four hours straight north. I unzipped my coat and my vest. I checked out the students as I made my way through the halls. None of them were dressed the way I was. I felt like I had gone out sledding and everybody else was studying and working. I realized I would have to completely rethink my way of dressing, my way of living, if I were to be accepted. Going to this nice college would be as big a culture shock as going through the transition of living up in the cabin had been. I found the office door with Dr. Blake, the head of the department's name on it, and I knocked.

I heard a cultured voice, "Yes. Feel free to open the door." This guy didn't sound like he was from the Iron Range at all. I opened the door and there sat a distinguished older gentleman wearing a bow tie and a tweed jacket. Books everywhere, papers everywhere.

"Hello Sir, my name is Sidney Duncan and Mr.

Harlan is the principal of my school in Northern Minnesota and I understand he's a friend of . . . "

"Sidney! You made it! Come in, I've been looking forward to this!"

We liked each other right away. He told me about his childhood in the North Country. I told him about my situation and about Mr. Harlan's school.

We spent nearly an hour in conversation and then Blake got serious, "Listen now, Sidney. You're not going to learn a damn thing from that English teacher up there between now and the end of school. Some of these students come from very serious preparatory schools. They will have a big advantage over you. I think you can do this. I think you're bright enough and confident enough to do anything. But you must do your own supplemental reading at this point, and writing too. Let's give you a real book to read. You can take these with you and bring them back next fall. I want you to write a few pages about each one as you finish it. Just your impressions and musings. You return it all to me when you arrive in the fall, all right?"

He turned to his bookshelf. I was shocked that he would trust me with his own books. I was shocked that he was talking as if this whole college thing was in the bag.

"Let's see. What would be most amusing in your situation is to read about small towns and public education from the masters. *Main Street* Sinclair Lewis is a must. He knew exactly what you are going through. *Bleak House* Charles Dickens, the finest essay on the terrors of the poor, the narrow minded, the oppressive cultural void. You should read both."

He held the books out to me. I took them. Paperbacks, very worn. I flipped the pages and saw many handwritten notes in the margins. I would start reading on the bus, I promised.

"All right, very good. We need to walk across campus now and visit the financial aid office. You'll have to tell them what you told me. They may ask some very serious questions. It'll all be to help them determine your eligibility for financial awards. I'm excited for them to meet you."

We crossed the campus. Dr. Blake, who was tall and lanky, surprised me by moving at a much faster pace than I was used to. I almost ran to keep up with his long brisk strides. When we left his office he had added only a beautiful hand-knitted wool scarf, wrapped several times around his neck, trailing behind him as he walked, and I was proud and also mortified to be crossing the formidable campus alongside this impressive figure. We arrived at the financial aid office and I was out of breath but he was not. We burst in to an old wood-paneled room with several women sitting at large wooden desks. My chaperone greeted them and asked after a man who came out from a back office. He was obviously the head of the financial aid department.

Dr. Blake seemed to be enjoying this. With a big grin he said, "Ladies and Gentlemen, it's my pleasure to introduce to you Miss Sidney Duncan."

Everyone nodded and said hello. He put his arm around my shoulders and declared, "Sidney's an excellent student and I believe she deserves to be here in the fall."

The man whom Dr. Blake referred to as the bursar crossed the room and offered to shake my hand.

"Sidney, hello. We'll need to have you come in and tell us more about your circumstances. Is that all right?"

"Yes, sure. Thank you for the opportunity."

"Oh well, this is what we love to do is help students achieve their dreams." At this point Dr. Blake added, "Sidney has quite a story. Very remarkable, really. Wait 'til you hear this."

We all sat down and I was grateful that Dr. Blake stayed with me. I saw my situation at the cabin very differently as I narrated it. I saw how shocked they were that I was there alone. I saw how cold they thought it was up there. I saw how isolated and crude they thought the townspeople were in a place like that. I saw how sad they thought it was that I didn't know where my dad was. I wanted to break down and cry, but I wanted them to respect me and think I was handling it all well, so I fought the tears and told it all like I didn't care. I told it like an adventure story. I enjoyed their attention and I tried to make them laugh with my retelling of some of the trials and tribulations of my life.

When I was finished and the questions had all been answered, they were all looking at me with such poignant empathetic faces that I thought I really might cry. Dr. Blake stood with me to say goodbye. He put his arm tightly around my shoulders again.

They shook my hand and I heard, "Don't worry dear, you'll be here in the fall" and "Don't worry, we're getting you out of there."

I was given many forms to fill out and mail back as soon as possible. They filled a college canvas book bag with the books Dr. Blake had given me. I was so excited to be carrying that bag.

The bursar said, "Don't hesitate to call us Sidney, if you need any help with the paperwork."

I walked in silence beside Dr. Blake as we left the building.

"Sidney, I have to get to my next lecture now. Will you be able to find your way?"

"Yes, for sure. I know exactly."

"All right. You did a great job in there. I think it's all going to work out fine. They seemed confident, as am I, that this would be a great opportunity for you and a good fit for you academically. I will see you in September, my dear girl. Take care and give my regards to our Mr. Harlan."

"Yes I will. Thank you again. Okay, goodbye."

"See you in September." I kept saying those words as I walked across the city in fading late winter light. I again passed the beautiful cathedral on the hill. I picked my way down the steep slope past the capitol building on my way back to the bus station in the center of the city.

I read the beginning of *Main Street* as I waited in the warm bus station. I chuckled to myself as Sinclair Lewis began his tale of a small town in Minnesota in the early nineteen hundreds. I could see why Dr. Blake thought this would be a good book for me. These small towns had hardly changed in the past seventy years.

Back at the cabin, I saw everything differently. The depleted woodpile didn't scare me any more. The trickle of water at the kitchen sink, the mounting pile of frozen excrement and toilet paper behind the woodpile, the oil tank for the furnace running low, all of this was someone else's problem. I would be going to college in a much warmer place next winter. I'd be saved. I worried about my dogs. Dale had said he'd probably be able to take them, but we were pretty sure his mother wouldn't be thrilled. The dogs' habit of killing animals and dragging their carcasses back to the front yard wouldn't go over so well anywhere else. I wasn't sure if they could be tamed at this point. They had become wild. They loved me and I loved them but I wasn't sure if they could adapt to any other life. They had thick coats of fur like sled dogs, that you could sink your fingers into. I didn't think they could be happy in a house now.

At school, word of my successful interview got around. There were a handful of college-bound kids and I had miraculously joined their elite circle. Mr. Harlan beamed when he told me that Dr. Blake had called to thank him for sending me his way. Mr. Harlan offered to help me go over the whole packet of application forms to be sure I was doing everything right. We thought he might have to cover the application fees out of his student fund but when we called the financial aid director he found out they would be waiving the fees. They also told Mr. Harlan that they had dug up an endowment from an alumnus from Northern Minnesota who wanted to give money to a student who was willing to be an English major and pursue a license to teach high school English. He asked me about that.

"I was planning on being an English major anyway and if I get the education certification then I could teach if I can't do my music."

Mr. Harlan liked this.

"To leave there after four years with an actual license to teach in the state of Minnesota would be very practical.

You could always fall back on that then the rest of your life."

"Tell them yes," I said, and my course was set.

One morning in the first week of March, I stood waiting for the clanking old bus and Corey the party guy bus driver to come barreling down the road. Snow was piled high above my head all around me in the turn-around. The temperatures had let up a bit and it was maybe only ten below that morning, with a high planned for well above zero. The faint light of day was becoming more evident each morning as I stood at six-thirty waiting for the bus. When the bus doors swung open and the welcome blast of hot air hit me in the face, I saw Corey's eyes brightly fixed on me.

"Hi?" I said in inquiry.

"Sidney. How ya doing this morning? I have something I want to tell you. Can you stay up here for a minute."

"Yeah, sure. What's going on?"

I stood at the front of the bus and he didn't step on the gas and peel out like he usually did.

"My wife and I had our first baby last night."

"Congratulations."

At six-thirty in the morning I didn't have a lot of enthusiasm for this.

"Yeah, thank you."

He looked like he was going to start crying. I decided I better listen more carefully.

"Yeah, so . . . well, see . . . I've been telling my wife about you all winter. And I haven't said this to you, but I feel like I want to now. When I first was picking you up in the mornings, and I mean I had heard stories about you being down there on your own and all, and just kept thinking this city girl ain't gonna make it. I'm sorry, but that's what I thought."

"Thanks. Thanks a lot."

"Okay, well, just let me finish. So winter came and when it got real cold I'd be driving down here in the morning and it'd be pitch black, not a soul for miles, and I'd say, she won't be there. There's no way she's gonna be standing there waiting for this bus. And lo and behold there you'd be. Every day. I couldn't believe it."

I felt the warmth of what he was saying. I felt for this one moment that time stood still. I stopped caring that he was holding up the other kids, holding up the drive to school, to talk to me. I listened.

"So I kept telling my wife all this while she's been pregnant, and I just want you to know that when our baby was born early this morning, it's a beautiful baby girl, just perfect in every way, and we decided to name her after you."

I stood with my eyes meeting his, "And I just hope she turns out to be as fine a young person as you are, Sidney."

I said nothing but I smiled. I nodded my head and we looked at each other with tears in our eyes. Corey revved the bus engine then and I turned and made my way to a seat near the back. All the kids were dozing or listening to the music. Corey turned the music back up to its usual raging volume. The bus bumped along on its well-worn path. I looked at the ramshackle houses and shacks and cabins we passed, and kept my eyes on my favorite sign as we went by, "Why Live In God's Country Without God?"

PRESTON'S VISIT

Preston surprised me with a phone call in March saying he want-
ed to come up and stay with me over spring break. I had the week off from my school too. I picked him up in the old red truck on a snowy late afternoon in late March and we made the drive out to the cabin. My big brother looked thinner, smaller somehow, than he had at the end of the summer. He had lost his suntan and looked pale and tired. I no-
ticed that his thin hands, which had always seemed elegant, were strangely fragile now, and stained on the fingertips, a dark tobacco brown, which I knew meant he was smoking a lot of hand-
rolled cigarettes. He was wearing his same black wool be-
ret pulled down over one eyebrow, the same black pea coat he was wearing when he left for school over a huge fish-
erman-knit cream-colored sweater which had been our dad's. The cuffs were soiled and pulled down, almost

covering his hands. He had a plaid wool scarf wrapped several times around his neck and up to his ears. He appeared world-weary, and was quiet. I wasn't sure what to say. I was frightened by his appearance and worried about him staying with me for the week. I kept wondering what he was going to want to do and how we were going to pay for food.

As we drove, Preston stared out the window and I saw the endless frozen landscape of unbroken treeline through his eyes. I felt like I was driving him out into the middle of nowhere. My colorful life of music and school and fun disappeared and it was just trees and snow forever.

As we approached the cabin though, Preston seemed to light up with anticipation. He suddenly became animated, talking too fast for me to answer.

"Oh my God, Sid. I can't believe you've been up here all this time. How cold did it get? What did Grandpa's thermometer do? Oh my God, it completely bottomed out? No fucking way. Holy shit. Fucking insane. This is crazy. It's crazier than I thought it would be. Look at you, you've fucking adapted, in that fur hat. You're like some woods woman."

I could see his mind jumping all over, trying to catch up with all that had happened since the summer.

"When was the last time you saw old Mom? Seymour? You've seen Seymour too? What's he like now that he's fucking our mom? When did you last hear from Dad? Poor Dad, God Sid, I feel so bad for him. I feel so fucking terrible for the guy. Damn. God damn. He tried so hard, Sid. He loved Mom so much. He really did. I think Mom is a bad person. I think she pushed Dad too hard to make money so she could come up here every summer while he was toiling away. Then when the money got tight she jumped ship with his old best friend."

I listened, not sure what to think. I stared out at the snow, keeping my eyes on the yellow line.

Soon we were on our road down the point and Preston was peering out his side window watching for the cabin lights. As soon as I turned into the drive Preston hopped in his seat with excitement.

"The snow is so high! What? I can't fucking believe this! Who plows this? I cannot believe this place. Oh my God Sid, this has been so insane for you, I can see it man. Fucking intense."

Suddenly my brother fell silent and I knew he had laid his eyes for the first time on my two half-wild dogs and their yard of bones. They were both sprawled out like great lions on their smoothed area of packed-down white snow smeared with the red bloodstains from their kill.

I smiled as my brother stared in silence.

Finally he spoke in a slow solemn way, "Sister Sid. Those are your dogs you told me about, but you didn't tell me they got a hold of Mom and ate her."

We both laughed a long time and then we got out and I introduced my brother to Ribbon and Bow.

A day or two into his visit, I told Preston we were going to need to buy more food but I didn't have much money. He said he had some and that we should drive to the big grocery store in Virginia. I protested that we could go to the small store in the tiny town where my school was but he insisted on us going to the big store.

We drove to town the next morning and pulled up in front of the grocery store. Preston said, "Okay, you get whatever you can pay for, whatever you would normally get, and I'll go around and get some more stuff okay? I'll take care of my stuff myself."

I got a small cart and walked through buying my usual basics.

Preston disappeared down the aisle toward the butcher at the back of the store.

I paid for my things and wondered where Preston was. I waited by the front door.

Suddenly Preston appeared. "Let's get out of here. This place doesn't have very good meats. I'm not spending my money on this."

He grabbed me by the arm and we headed out to the car. I got in the driver's side and Preston said, "Let's go!"

We pulled out of our spot and headed toward home.

"Preston, what was that all about? You didn't get anything?"

I looked over at him and he grinned a big stained-teeth grin at me.

He opened his pea coat and showed me the cellophane packages of ground beef and pork chops all stuffed into a tear in the lining.

"This is what I'm eating the rest of the week. You can have some too little sis."

The next few days Preston and I sat in the main room, with him drinking coffee, me, nothing much, mostly water, maybe orange juice. Preston finished all the coffee in the kitchen cupboard and when we bought him a big can of Folgers, he made coffee all day and night and stayed up scribbling in a notebook, saying he was writing a story about the cabin, about Grandpa.

Dale took us out for a steak dinner one night. Preston loved that. He ate everything in sight. Dale asked the waitress if we could have more bread. "Better bring more bread before this guy eats the basket."

At the end of the week I drove Preston to the Greyhound station. It felt good, like we had a solid mutual understanding of the current state of things for us both. I would go to college and work hard to get good grades. He would graduate soon and try to get a job at a small newspaper so he could work on articles while writing the great American novel in his spare time. I couldn't say I was sorry to see my brother leave though. He was unpredictable in his emotions and impulsive in his actions. I felt like he was a drain when I was trying to be careful. He was too reckless for me.

THE END IN SIGHT

n May, on a Saturday morning, I looked out my picture window at the still frozen lake. Much of the snow had melted in several big thaws but the ice was holding on, grey and dull with old snowmobile tracks criss-crossing the length of the bay in all directions. The sky was bright blue and the temperature was probably going to be in the fifties. I had spring fever. I was thinking of the kids I knew in Chicago, how they'd be getting ready for graduation. How girls would be wearing new spring outfits to school every day. I wondered what was in style this year, I felt so out of touch with city-kid fashion. I decided to try to tune in to a Chicago radio station I could sometimes pick up when it was clear like this. The station that I used to listen to at night, that I used to cry myself to sleep by, was called WLS. I went to the radio on top of the old refrigerator in the kitchen and fished around on the dial. WLS came through faintly.

I smiled as a familiar DJ's voice came on.

"The high in Chicago on this beautiful spring day? We're hitting eighty, folks! Eighty degrees for a high today all across the metro area. Summer's finally coming on strong!"

Eighty degrees? Here I was trapped in this ridiculous never-ending winter. Ice on the lake still! A high just pushing out of the forties and I had been thinking it was a goddamn heat wave. I ran to my bedroom and found my bikini from last summer. I pulled off my stupid long underwear and threw it in the kitchen garbage. I prayed my bikini still fit.

I got the strings tied and I went out to the living room where I could still hear WLS rocking out with a great song by The Lovin' Spoonful, "Summer in the City."

I looked at myself in the mirror. I sucked in my stomach. I turned sideways. Okay, this life had not been easy on me. I definitely was going to have to pull it together if I was going back to the real world. I danced to WLS for the rest of the morning in my bikini by the wood stove and then got dressed and jogged up and down the road with my two wild dog companions barking and rough-housing as they chased me.

The end of school was in sight and I had to look great for everything coming up. I was asked to sing my current favorite song for the graduation ceremony. I had bought the sound track to a new musical called *The Wiz*, which was a soul-music version of the story of *The Wizard of Oz*. I loved the song "Home."

The kids at school heard me sing it once and they said it gave them chills. It seemed like the perfect words for my situation so I could belt them out with conviction. But now with the school year ending, the other seniors said it was the perfect song for them too because so many of them would be leaving home for the first time when they turned eighteen and graduated. The choir teacher said I could sing it at the graduation ceremony and he would accompany me on piano. We had to order the sheet music in Virginia. I was really looking forward to the graduation. Mom said she'd be coming up to see me. Preston told Mom not to come to his college graduation because he didn't want to be part of it anyway, so she was coming to mine.

I wasn't sure when she was expected, so when Seymour and my mother came rolling into the driveway that afternoon, I was caught off-guard and came running from the cabin. My dogs went crazy, barking and jumping all over, trying to see the new visitors. They were always friendly. They weren't mean at all and they listened pretty well if I told them not to jump. But as Mom got out of the car, they were all over her, in her lap, and got muddy wet paw prints all over her trench coat. She was mad immediately. As soon as she got out of the car, she got a good look at the melting burial ground the dogs had been working on all winter filled with wild animal bones, fur pelts, and skulls like some kind of Death Valley from the Wild West.

My mother's keen eye didn't miss a thing. She stood surveying the property, *her* property, and I followed her gaze as she stared up at the carport ceiling. I hadn't noticed, and there wouldn't have been an easy way for me to do anything about it, but dear old Brandy's body was thawing out and one of his big paws had come loose from the wrappings and was hanging down from the rafters. My mother uttered, "Good Lord," and turned to face the cabin.

She stormed down the path and the next thing she saw was the backside of the woodpile where the dogs and I had been pooping and peeing all winter. Now that everything was thawing out, the layers of toilet paper and excrement were visible where once I had covered them with snow. It looked bad. I was embarrassed, but I had survived and now it was finally over.

Within hours of their arrival, Seymour and my mom had assessed the entire situation. They sat me down and said that my puppies were an unsolvable problem. My mother did not waver. They were a threat to the wildlife. With summer folks coming back to the lake, they could not be allowed to run wild and terrorize everyone. They weren't vaccinated or neutered. I was leaving for college. They were a burden and a liability. On the last official day of school, while I was gone during the day, my mother and Seymour drove them to the vet and had them put down.

With the puppies gone, my mother and Seymour whipped the place into shape. I was heartsick, but I helped them with everything. I went out with a shovel and dug into the thawing earth deep enough to remove all the winter's mess I had made and bury it way back further in the woods. I cleaned all the wild carnage that my beautiful puppies had strewn across the front of the cabin.

The spring rains came and the dirty snow gave way to the sweet grasses and wild flowers I remembered.

Brandy was buried in the yard with Dale and Seymour's help and we planted a great clump of wild daisies over his grave and rolled a big boulder for a headstone. We stood in a circle over his grave and I sang the Doxology like we used to in church choir long ago, in what felt like another lifetime, "Praise God from whom all blessings flow . . . "

Graduation Day came and I sang the song. The motley group of fifteen graduates all stood on risers in the old gymnasium and we received our diplomas. We stood together dressed in uncomfortable clothes, full of relief over what we had endured and achieved and in anticipation of what life held in store. I had lost so much but life was full of new possibilities.

JOE POLLOCK

COURTNEY YASMINEH is a rock musician and singer-songwriter with a classic rock chick's frankness, irony, and guts. She has several albums and thousands of road-gig miles to her credit. *Renegade* is her latest record. *A Girl Called Sidney* is her first novel.

GIBSON HOUSE connects literary fiction with curious and discerning readers. We publish novels by musicians and other artists with a strong connection to music.

GibsonHousePress.com
facebook.com/GibsonHousePress
Twitter: @GibsonPress

READING GROUP GUIDE

If you are reading this novel with a book group, here are some questions to start the discussion.

1. The book title is "A Girl Called Sidney" and at that time in America (1960s–70s), the name Sidney was mostly used for a man's name. What is the significance for Sidney to carry a name that was usually assigned to males only?

2. What relevance does the subtitle, "The Coldest Place," have? How many meanings can that title take on for Sidney? Who utters those words in the story?

3. By the end of the story, Sidney is eighteen years old. At that point, does she understand or know her parents? As we read, are we able to glean a realistic view of either parent through Sidney's telling of the story?

4. Is Preston, Sidney's brother, a character to love or revile? As a reader, would you say that you and Sidney share the same feeling about him?

5. Are there moments in the story, for Sidney or for
    her mother, where being female is a drawback? In
    1970s white suburban America, these two women
    were making difficult choices. What strikes you as
    different from how they could operate as women
    today?

6. Could a story like this take place in today's America?
    How have things changed or not changed in almost
    fifty years, especially with respect to families in
    crisis, teen emancipa

7. How does Sidney fe
    Chicago? How does
    do these places com

8. Music is a strong thr
    would Sidney's life l

9. What is your reactio
    betrayed in this story
    more subtle, betraya

10. Does Sidney come o
    does she hurt? Who
    changed the course
    had conducted herself differently? What should she
    have done?

FOR AN EDITABLE DOWNLOAD OF THIS GUIDE, VISIT
GIBSONHOUSEPRESS.COM/READING-GROUP-GUIDES